"Thank you! Thank you!" Meggie, on her hands and knees, struggled against coils of rope.

"Are you hurt?" Hawken asked. He, too, was on his knees, tugging at the bindings, before it occurred to him that he had turned his back on an armed man.

Meggie did not reply, and when he jerked the rope free, she clung to him, burying her face in the folds of his hunting shirt. Hawken spread his hands on her back, cautious lest his movement be perceived as an embrace.

"Don't leave me alone," she whispered.

"Of course not."

"He'll come back. With the others." Her fingers dug through leather, painfully compressing muscles against his shoulder blades.

"I'll be here." She nodded dumbly, rubbing her face into the laces of his shirt. The buckskin tightened faintly on his ribs and shock waves ricocheted off his heart.

Dear Reader,

If you've never read a Harlequin Historical, you're in for a treat. We offer compelling, richly developed stories that let you escape to the past—by some of the best writers in the field!

Since her debut in March 1996 with *The Pearl Stallion,* author Rae Muir has sold five more romances, including her RITA Award finalist *All But the Queen of Hearts.* Her authentic, innovative writing style has earned her several 5 star reviews, as well as a reputation as "an author to watch." This month's *Hawken's Wife* is the third book in THE WEDDING TRAIL series—romances of the young women from a sewing circle in Indiana. Here, a beautiful tomboy falls head over heels in love with an amnesiac mountain man.

Be sure to look for *A Rose at Midnight* by the talented Jacqueline Navin. In this passionate Regency, a powerful earl who thinks he's dying must find a wife to have his child. *For Love of Anna* by multipublished author Sharon Harlow is a heartwarming Western about a handsome cowboy "outlaw" who finds shelter—and love—at the ranch of a young widow.

Rounding out the month is *The Highlander's Maiden* by Elizabeth Mayne. In this tension-filled Medieval tale, a handsome Scottish mapmaker wins the heart of a fearless female mountain guide from an enemy clan. Don't miss it!

Whatever your tastes in reading, you'll be sure to find a romantic journey back to the past between the covers of a Harlequin Historical® novel.

Sincerely,
Tracy Farrell, Senior Editor

Please address questions and book requests to:
Harlequin Reader Service
U.S.: 3010 Walden Ave., P.O. Box 1325, Buffalo, NY 14269
Canadian: P.O. Box 609, Fort Erie, Ont. L2A 5X3

HAWKEN'S
WIFE
RAE MUIR
THE WEDDING TRAIL

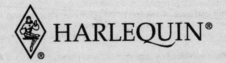

HARLEQUIN®

TORONTO • NEW YORK • LONDON
AMSTERDAM • PARIS • SYDNEY • HAMBURG
STOCKHOLM • ATHENS • TOKYO • MILAN • MADRID
PRAGUE • WARSAW • BUDAPEST • AUCKLAND

ISBN 0-373-29050-0

HAWKEN'S WIFE

This edition published by arrangement with Harlequin Books S.A.

® and TM are trademarks of the publisher. Trademarks indicated with ® are registered in the United States Patent and Trademark Office, the Canadian Trade Marks Office and in other countries.

Printed in U.S.A.

Books by Rae Muir

Harlequin Historicals

The Pearl Stallion #308
The Trail to Temptation #345
All But the Queen of Hearts #369
The Lieutenant's Lady #383
Twice a Bride #414
Hawken's Wife #450

RAE MUIR

lives in a cabin in California's High Sierra, a mile from an abandoned gold mine. She is, by training, an historian, but finds it difficult to fit into the academic mold, since her imagination inevitably inserts fictional characters into actual events. She's been a newspaper reporter, has written and edited educational materials, researched eighteenth-century Scottish history, run a fossil business and raised three children in her spare time.

She loves the Sierra Nevada, Hawaii, Oxford and San Francisco. Her favorite mode of travel is by car, and she stops at every historical marker.

To the staff of the Bishop Branch of
the Inyo County Library

Chapter One

The horse paced deliberately through the sky, upside down. The fringe on the rider's coat and the horse's tail ignored the law of gravity and rose like tendrils of smoke.

Hawken closed his eyes and counted to ten. He opened his eyes. The apparition was, if anything, a bit more distinct.

"Les. Monty," he called.

Two heads poked out of the brush, eyes straining, scanning the horizon. The men edged out of the thicket that surrounded the spring.

"Do you see anything?" Hawken asked, pointing at the sky.

Les crossed himself. "Mary and Jesus protect us!"

Monty shoved his hat to the back of his head and squinted. "Someone coming," he said.

"Devil, likely," Les said, coiled to spring for shelter.

"Seen something like that once on the Mississippi," Monty continued. "A steamboat, paddling right toward us through the sky. Somehow the air turns into a mirror...see! There's a wagon coming."

Sure enough, the front half of a covered wagon rolled

into view. The wheels pointed upward and the hooves of
the oxen trod empty sky.

"Emigrants," Monty said. "Heading for Oregon or
California. You'll be seeing them on the road soon." He
nodded to the ridge above them, where the trail ran. Les
appealed to another battery of saints.

A new ghost galloped past the wagon. The horse's feet
lifted puffs of sky dust, the rider's broad-brimmed hat
magically clung to the reversed head, and a billowing
lightness floated upward on the horse's flanks.

"Devil, for sure," breathed Les. "He's snatched some
poor doomed soul!"

Hawken took his eyes off the vision long enough to
see his hired hands backing into the brush.

"Best we disappear," Monty muttered, "till the boss
finds out if Missouri slave catchers ride with these
folks."

The spectral horses vanished, leaving one wagon and
part of another, while hoofbeats heralded the arrival of
the actual beasts. The rider bearing the ghostly burden
slowed, twisted to study the horizon, not a difficult movement because she rode bareback.

She! A woman, by God! The billowing pouf was her
skirt, hiked up because she had her legs on either side of
the horse. Hawken scrambled to his feet, eyeing this feminine phenomenon with greater interest than he had the
airy parade. He had never seen a white woman ride
astride.

"Howdy," Hawken called, and lifted his hat no higher
than courtesy dictated. Doeskin leggings covered her legs
but did not conceal their length and shapeliness.

"Our scouts, Mr. Godfroy and Mr. Sampson, said
we'd noon at this spring," she said, removing her hat
and peering first at the brush-filled gully, then at Hawken,

snaring him in the deepest blue eyes he had ever seen. "We didn't expect to find anyone here."

He shifted his gaze to the ridge. Disconcerting, to be stared down by a woman. "Sampson and Godfroy?" he said, trying for haughtiness to disarm her breezy confidence. Tendrils of hair escaped the confinement of her braids and edged her forehead. My God! He was staring again.

"I've been waiting two days, but didn't expect you for a week," he said gruffly, eyes fixed on a spiral curl in the center of her forehead. "The name's Hawken." He removed his hat. "From Independence." Freckles drifted across her nose and cheekbones, like gold seen through a thin film of water. A faint rustle in the thicket recalled Les and Monty. "Where're you people from?"

"All from Indiana, except Mr. Reid, who's English." The intensity of the prairie sky must exaggerate the color of her eyes.

"Any got slaves with you?" he asked, too harshly.

"No. You were waiting for us?" she asked. Her pointed chin lengthened with the quizzical expression, and turned her round face into a heart. The murmur of the stream behind him seemed to grow louder. He looked down to escape her eyes and found himself turning his hat in his hands like a timid bumpkin.

Why doesn't she gallop back to the wagons? he thought angrily. Why doesn't she let Godfroy and Sampson know I'm here? Relieve him from blue sparks that pulled like a magnet, no matter how he concentrated on affairs of greater importance. No matter where he looked.

He slammed his hat on his head, disgusted with himself. He'd ignore her and she'd leave. His business lay with Sampson and Godfroy, not a girl too old to be forking a horse.

"You were waiting for us?" she asked insistently. "How did you know we'd be along?" Bound again by blue pools and a smile without a hint of contrivance. A completely natural, happy girl…a young woman. But not a truly feminine woman, for she showed no speck of shyness at being alone with a stranger.

"I met Godfroy and Sampson on the trail last summer," he said, to fill the silence and justify taking a step toward her. She did not object that he stood two feet from her boot, only made a little noise, neither agreement nor disagreement. A sound to show she was listening. "They were eastbound from California, said they'd lead a party west this year. I'd like to join them." She leaned over, seemingly absorbed by his explanation. He should be flattered by her close attention, but from the way she moved, he knew she did not wear a corset.

Astride a horse, not properly clothed, alone on the prairie—

"Hawken!"

Hawken swallowed his sigh of relief. A gray Indian pony lunged down the slope, tail and mane flying. The rider slid off before the horse came to a complete halt. No mistaking the broad face of the French-Indian trapper.

"Godfroy!" The trapper threw his arms about Hawken and pounded his back. Hawken tried to show a similar enthusiasm—hadn't Godfroy saved him from making a fool of himself?—but the embrace pinioned his arms.

"We thought to see you in St. Joe," Godfroy exclaimed.

"I supplied in Independence. I'm heading for Bear River." Hawken tilted his head in the direction of his wagons, since Godfroy still held his arms. The waggle brought his eyes within range of the blue ones, and he was doubly trapped. "Like to join you," he said, and heard his own breathlessness, only partly the result of Godfroy's extended bear hug.

"Supplies for trappers?" Godfroy asked, eyeing the wagons doubtfully.

"For emigrants. There's no trappers in the Rockies worth mentioning these days. They've all gone to hunting buffalo or stealing horses. Or guiding wagon trains. I plan to set up a trading post in Bear River Valley."

Godfroy released him and swung toward the woman, showing no embarrassment at her dress and behavior. "Meggie, meet the wagons and turn them off the road." She nodded, twisted her head just enough to give Hawken a private grin, like they shared a secret, and a chill wrapped his ankles.

She put her hat on and retreated by backing her pony up the slope. A fine bit of riding, although showing off in a most unladylike fashion. His hand was, for some reason, in front of his face. Good grief! He'd almost saluted her in appreciation of the feat. He bent his fingers and pretended his forehead needed scratching.

"Who is she?" he asked.

"Meggie MacIntyre. Jim Mac's daughter."

"Jim Mac? A trapper?"

"No, a farmer from Pikeston, Indiana. Him, his brother Ira MacIntyre, his son Pete, Ira's three boys—"

"Whole clan?"

"—Ira's daughter Tildy, who's married to our captain, Matt Hull. Guess you could say it's a clan. Got the old lady along, too. Jim Mac and Ira's mama, Mrs. Mac-Intyre, but everybody calls her Granny."

Good, Hawken thought with relief. Surrounded by a big family, the blue-eyed charmer would be suitably chaperoned in the presence of a single man.... But then

why did she ride ahead of the party, and dress so out-
landishly? So...flexibly?

"I've heard the Pawnee might be out," he said
weakly. "I'd rather travel with a group."

"You alone?" Godfroy examined the wagons more
closely.

"Got two hired men to drive the oxen." Godfroy's
eyes flickered and silently asked to meet the men.
"Blacks, who took French leave of their owners a month
or six weeks ago, judging from the healing of the whip
tracks on their backs. No slave catchers with your
party?"

Godfroy laughed. "These Hoosiers don't give a damn
about slaves. The Englishman—he drives Captain Hull's
wagon—he's an abolitionist."

"Good. That'll relieve their minds." Hawken had another question—a personal question—that he wished
could be asked and answered so directly. *Would anyone
in the party recognize him?* He shrugged away his anxiety. Time would settle the matter. For three years he'd
had no success, even though he had displayed himself to
emigrants on the trail and in Independence.

"Only to Bear River Valley?" Godfroy asked. "We
could use three strong men all the way to California."

"Bear River's far enough," Hawken said. "Just where
emigrants wish they'd packed an extra sack of flour, or
want to trade worn oxen for fresh."

"A good place," Godfroy agreed. "We're seeing
tracks on the road. How many parties ahead of us?"

"Just one. Eighteen wagons, bound for Oregon. They
camped a mile or two west of here last night."

The first wagon swung off the road under Meggie's
guidance, stopping a hundred feet above the spring. A
gaggle of boys herded loose stock toward the rivulet that

flowed from the other side of the thicket. A good-looking party. Sturdy wagons, tough, well-fed oxen, neither too young nor too old.

An unexpected barnyard cackle, and Hawken twisted so fast his backbone creaked. Speckled hens fluttered and pressed against the bars of a cage hanging from the tailgate of a wagon. Not a good sign, hauling chickens. It hinted at other useless things under the canvas covers, weight that would tire the oxen.

The women dragged wood from slings and set about building dinner fires. They had not yet accepted the necessity of burning buffalo chips. Meggie, off her pony, talked to a tall young woman. She looked over her shoulder, not the unconscious glance of an instant, but two or three seconds, and her roving eye found him. Large beads of sweat chose that exact moment to slither down his backbone. Had her look been wary? Or suggestive? *Lord preserve me from a bold woman accompanied by a brother and father,* he prayed.

She removed her straw hat and spun it beneath the wagon. Beautiful hair, just enough red in the brown to hint at a wild spirit. Her long braids looped against the back of her neck, but the score of escaped tresses made a halo, one too red for a saint, he thought with trepidation.

"Sampson'll be along directly," Godfroy said. "He's out with the hunter, looking for game. Here's Captain Hull."

Captain Hull had a military bearing, all six feet and two or three inches of him. His inscrutable gray eyes lodged deep beneath level brows, and seemed to take in the situation with one glance. Not a man to toy with, Hawken judged, and the man he must impress to become a member of the party. A son-in-law to the MacIntyre

clan, so related to Meggie in some fashion. He tipped his
hat to the captain and made a point of meeting Hull's
eyes without wavering. Very difficult, because beyond
the captain's shoulder Meggie stood, arms akimbo, bla-
tantly staring. Auburn hair, cobalt-glass eyes, a pouty upper lip that seemed made for kisses. Almost irresistible.
He *would* resist, as he had resisted respectable women
for the past three years. He noted an internal tremor and
dismissed it. Only two months, maybe two and a half,
between here and Bear River.

Hawken concentrated on the bridge of Hull's nose, and
made a determined effort to end every statement with
"sir," even though the captain could not be many years
past twenty.

"His name's Hawken," Meggie whispered to Faith,
turning her back on the man so no one guessed that she
talked about him. "He's carrying goods to set up a trading post on Bear River."

"He wears buckskins," Faith said, disapproval in the
set of her mouth and the narrowing of her eyes. "Mr.
Sampson says the only men who wear buckskins this
close to the settlements are those who can't afford store-
bought clothes. Mr. Hawken's poor."

"He invested his money in stock for his trading post,
not fancy clothes," Meggie said strongly, but a sliver of
doubt lodged in her vague calculations.

"How do you know he had trade goods in those wagons?" Faith asked. "He could tell you anything."

"Why would he lie to Mr. Godfroy? They met on the
trail last year, and greeted each other like old friends."

"Meggie, do you think I'm so dense that I don't see
what you're up to?" Faith asked. She tilted her head,
forcing Meggie to look up because Faith was taller.

"Here's the wild man you've dreamed of. I suppose he even looks a little like Captain Frémont—"

"No, I've seen a picture of Captain Frémont, and he wears a beard. Mr. Hawken has a fine chin, don't you think? A shame to cover it with a beard."

"You're setting your cap for Mr. Hawken."

Meggie scuffed her toe in the dirt, taken aback by Faith's quick grasp of her intentions. "Granny told my fortune last winter," she said.

"She said you'd marry a poor mountain man?" Faith sniffed, dismissing fortune-telling as nonsense.

"Granny said I'd marry a storekeeper, and I said I'd die rather than marry a man trapped behind a counter in town. Don't you see, Faith? I didn't know there were storekeepers who lived in the middle of the wilderness. Men who wouldn't care that their wives rode out alone or—"

"He probably has an Indian wife in Bear River Valley. Like Mr. Sampson."

Meggie risked a peek over her shoulder. Two dark-skinned men stepped out of the thicket at Hawken's call. Fugitives, slaves who ran for refuge in Indian country. Good for them! Good for Hawken, who risked helping runaways. She pulled a kerchief from her belt and wiped the back of her neck. A little breeze had come up and her skin felt damp and quivery. Curiously, the leaves in the thicket hung motionless.

"He must be very strong and confident," she whispered to Faith. The back of her neck quivered again. She touched it with her fingers and found it dry.

"Strong, confident and poor," Faith said sarcastically.

"Granny's fortune was right," Meggie said, seized by an inexplicable need to defend Hawken. "I'll marry a storekeeper, but one like Mr. Hawken, who'll trade on the California trail. Bear River Valley's a pretty place.''

"You've never been there!" Faith exclaimed.

Meggie pulled herself erect to close the distance between Faith's eyes and hers. "Frémont says Bear River Valley is one of the beauty spots of the Rockies. Look! Captain Hull's taking Mr. Hawken to your wagons.''

"Captain Hull's bound to take Mr. Hawken to all the wagons,'' Faith said wearily, "to introduce him, so the men can decide if they want him along.''

"We'll wander over and help with the cooking. It's not fair to leave it all to Louisa,'' Meggie said.

"Louisa and I do it turn and turn about. Today I'm washing up.''

"You like having a stepmother,'' Meggie said, steering Faith off the topic of Hawken. "Someone to help care for your brothers and your father.'' Faith had been in despair when her father married a woman younger than she, but now seemed reconciled to the situation.

"Louisa and I are determined to get along, that Pa should not be upset,'' Faith said. With Faith distracted, Meggie took two steps toward the Tole wagons. And Hawken. "The only disagreeable thing about Louisa—'' Faith continued sadly, "she expects me to visit you.''

"So you'll be around my brother,'' Meggie said. Several days ago she guessed Louisa Tole was plotting a match between Faith and Pete.

"Every day she says what a fine man Pete MacIntyre is, and how prosperous he'll be in a new country, making wagons and carriages. If you remember—'' she waggled a finger "—I said from the beginning that a stepmother would try to marry me off. But I'll not be hounded into marriage.'' She skidded to a stop, but Meggie had succeeded in getting them within ten feet of Mr. Tole and Hawken.

"Pete shows no interest in taking a wife," Meggie said smoothly, laying a hand on Faith's arm to keep her where she was. "You're safe. The only other single men along, well, Godfroy's too old for you."

"My father wasn't too old for Louisa," Faith whispered, a foot reaching backward, as if preparing a retreat. "I don't want to marry anyone."

"Then there's Mr. Reid," Meggie said hastily, to keep the conversation going. "Although I don't suppose you'd want to live in England. I understand it's wet and foggy."

"In California I'll start a school and make my own living," Faith said. "I can't for the life of me see why all my friends paw at the ground like bumptious colts the moment a single man swings into view. First Tildy marries Matt Hull, only four months after he comes home from the army, and Rachel lets her father talk her into marrying Will Hunter when they'd known each other two weeks. And now you, eyes big as a bug's, ogling the first mountain man we meet. When we get to California you'll all be so busy setting up housekeeping, our sewing circle will never meet again."

"If I marry Mr. Hawken I won't go to California," Meggie reminded her. "I'll stay at the trading post."

"Your father won't allow any such thing. Besides, you're a fool to marry. It's nothing but slavery for a woman," Faith said in a voice so intense she did not seem to notice that Meggie steered her closer to the fire. "You don't understand, because you've always had Granny and your mother to do the work, but I know, taking care of Pa and four boys since I was fourteen. With Mr. Hawken you'd live in a log shanty and be burdened with a baby every year, nothing to make life easier, a cookstove or plaster walls—''

''I'd give up cookstoves and plaster for a man who'll let me ride my pony and explore the country.''

''You can't keep galloping about after you're married, no matter where you live. A woman who rides loses her babies. All men want sons and Mr. Hawken will tell you to stay off John Charles just as fast as a city fellow.''

Hawken spoke to Faith's father, Mr. Tole, but his eyes flickered and Meggie knew he'd spotted her. Dark eyes, with long, thick lashes that cast shadows on his cheeks. A vain woman would give years of her life for lashes like his. His broad chin and straight nose lent a suggestion of command to his profile. The breeze danced at the back of her neck again. Meggie edged around the fire to see Hawken head-on. The laces of his hunting tunic hung loose, he wore no shirt, and she could just make out a hint of dark chest hair. The angle of his collarbone threw a shadow across the depression at the base of his throat.

A flood of shivers, from neck to feet, and muscles low in her abdomen echoed the quick clutch of nerves that came when she rode John Charles very hard.

''Come with me,'' Faith snapped, and now Meggie found herself being dragged along against her will, to the rear of the wagon where Louisa had spread her cooking gear.

''You don't have to help,'' Louisa said as Faith picked up a spoon and a bag of rice. ''You might fetch water, though. There's not enough for washing up.''

Fetching water meant disappearing into the thicket around the spring, and losing track of Hawken. ''Mrs. Burdette's milking the cow that wandered off this morning,'' Meggie said with happy inspiration. ''Faith and I thought perhaps...well, Mrs. Burdette already filled her churn this morning. We could ask for a pint." What a great excuse to stay near Hawken and snoop!

"Milk would be nice," Louisa agreed. "The eggs I brought won't last in this heat. We could have milk and egg flapjacks for supper. Or would your father prefer an omelette, Faith?" Louisa still pumped Faith about Mr. Tole's likes and dislikes, lest she distress her new husband. Meggie resolved she would not be so fawning when she got a husband of her own. "Mrs. Burdette forgot to bring nutmeg. Tell her I'll trade for milk."

Mrs. Burdette cuddled against the flanks of a brown cow. While Faith negotiated the trade of nutmeg for milk, Meggie pretended to pull burrs out of the cow's tail. Mr. Hawken was slender. Too slender. He needed a woman's care to fatten him. Not too much fattening, Meggie decided when he squatted beside Tole. The buckskins tightened across the front of his legs. He moved precisely, every part of him properly placed, like a cat. A big cat. A panther.

He mopped the back of his neck with a bandanna. The breeze must cause him shivers, too, flowing across his damp skin. His long hands moved with economy, never wasting effort. A reflection of his internal confidence. Confident enough to help runaway slaves. Confident enough to ignore the sneer of "squaw man" and take an Indian wife? Perhaps Godfroy or Sampson would know.

"Come along, Meggie." Faith held a small tin pitcher in both hands. "Your braids are down. I'll pin them up."

Meggie waggled her head and the prickly end of a braid scraped across her neck. Maybe that's what had caused the quivers and shivers. "My hair's a great bother. I think I'll cut it all off."

Faith stumbled and nearly dropped the milk. "Margaret MacIntyre! You wouldn't do such a thing. A woman's hair is her glory, and yours, almost red—''

    "I hate it." She had not liked her hair in Indiana, and she found it an even greater nuisance traveling. She lifted the weight of the braids. Definitely better. She would cut it. She would speak to her mother. No, Granny first. If she got Granny on her side, Ma was more likely to listen to reason.

Chapter Two

Les and Monty stood behind Hawken, out of sight, but he felt their tension. On exhibit before all these people, they must relive the horror of the auction block, where they'd been forced to display their muscles for their owner's profit. They trusted him to keep his promise. He'd take them far beyond the frontier. But they would not trust these strangers until they showed a lack of interest in rewards for runaway slaves.

The men of the wagon train clustered about Godfroy and Sampson, talking in low voices. Hawken made careful note of every glance in his direction. None carried a sign of recognition. He searched his emotions, found himself both happy and sad. Certainly it would settle his mind to know his real name and where he came from. But finding out now would bring another disruption. He would be duty bound to search for his family, not set up a trading post.

Captain Hull counted yeas and nays on his fingers as the emigrants cast their votes. Only one head shook in a negative, and when the man saw he stood alone he nodded, too. Hawken breathed easier. Hull touched his hat

in a salute. The group broke up, men heading off singly
and in pairs to eat their dinners.

"You're in," Hull said in a low voice, "if all three of
you agree to stand night watches, every fourth night,
along with the rest of us."

"We're accustomed," Hawken interrupted. "Watches
have been a burden with just three. Every fourth night is
no more than a stargazing party."

A smile softened Hull's gray eyes and put crow's feet
at the corners. "If you have questions, I'll be over there."
He pointed to a wagon that had drawn Hawken's attention the moment it pulled off the road, one with side steps
and a door like a stagecoach. It carried no canvas on this
balmy spring day, but bundles of weeds dangling from
the hickory bows obscured the interior.

"That's my wagon, or rather Granny MacIntyre's
wagon. My wife, Matilda, is her granddaughter, and we
travel with her. The wagon looks like a gypsy herb shop,
but Granny assures me she'll pack the stuff away as it
dries, and she'll gather fewer plants as the spring
passes."

A buxom young woman tended a fire near the odd
wagon, obviously Mrs. Hull, and a grandmotherly lady
turned the meat in the skillet. Her figure had thickened
with age but she did not stoop.

"The man unhitching my oxen, his name's Reid. Two
English hunters traveled with us out of St. Joe, but one
turned back, taking all the gear and the servants. Reid
decided to come on for the adventure."

Hull pointed to the three wagons behind his own, including the one with the chickens. Someone had lifted
the door of the coop and the chickens pecked in the grass.
Meggie and an older women tended a small fire built
prairie-fashion in a trench. "James MacIntyre, everybody

calls him Jim Mac, his son Pete, who built most of our wagons. Meggie's his daughter. She's eighteen, and has her chickens, cat and pony along. The pony's named John Charles—'' he appealed to the sky for aid and understanding ''—in honor of Captain Frémont.''

"I met Meggie first of all," Hawken said. He raised his voice slightly on the final syllables to hint a question, but got no reaction from Hull. "Should she be riding out ahead like that?"

"I spoke to her father, he told her to stay with the lead scout. She does, sometimes. Next two wagons—"

"Don't the chickens run off?"

"She clips their wings and hobbles them, like a horse. Next wagon, my father-in-law Ira MacIntyre and his three boys, Josh, Lewis and Eddie." The clan, just as Godfroy had described. Hawken had seen parties like this before, dominated by one family. They often broke up because the outsiders resented being eternally outvoted by the kin. But, Hawken admitted to himself, the MacIntyre men had shown good sense, not electing one of themselves as captain. They had given that post to a son-in-law.

"The three wagons with gray tops, they belong to Abnet Tole."

"I talked to him about repairs on my wagons," Hawken said.

"His wife and daughter are at the fire. The plump one's Mrs. Tole."

The tall blonde, the woman he had seen with Meggie, was Tole's daughter. Tole had taken a young second wife. An unexpected ripple surged in Hawken's loins. He tensed to control himself, gritted his teeth against the aimless lust. As the threat faded he wriggled his head and shoulders to work out the stiffness, and accidently, from the corner of his eye, saw Meggie lift a hatchet from pegs on the side of a wagon.

"Tole's the best blacksmith I know," Hull said. "If anyone can help you, it's Tole."

"Good to have a blacksmith along," Hawken said. "A splice of iron here and there will get my wagons to Bear River." Meggie wandered into his field of vision, carrying the hatchet.

"Burdette...Marshall..." Hull rattled off names as he pointed to wagons farther down the line. Hawken filed them for future reference. Meggie disappeared into the thicket.

"Here come Sampson and Hunter. No fresh meat. Game's been scarce. I'll introduce you to Godfroy's daughter, Rachel, who's married to Will Hunter. We hired him to hunt for the party."

A hunter named Hunter, Hawken thought, and frowned so he did not grin. He was not the only man traveling under an assumed name. He studied the strung-out wagons—fifteen—and felt both disappointment and relief. No name sounded familiar. No face had caused a quiver in the drapery separating him from his past. No man wrinkled his brow and said, "You remind me of a fellow from my hometown."

He would head west to Bear River Valley, build a new life and forget there had ever been another. He hoped from now on the curtain between past and present thickened, became a solid wall cutting off any chance of ever knowing.

Monty and Les scrambled out of the gully, interrupting his reverie. They stared over their shoulders wide-eyed, as if chased by a panther, but no animal sprang in pursuit.

"Woman!" Monty gasped. Hawken laughed, recalling Meggie's wood gathering expedition. Monty and Les wanted no encounter with a lone white woman, and the risk of being charged with molestation. For a black man a trial would be considered superfluous. Simply two wagon tongues lifted to form a gallows, and a rope.

Meggie thrashed her way into the open, burdened with thin sticks. A final grasping branch pulled one of her braids free of its pins and it bounced between her shoulder blades in the steady rhythm of her strides. Her braids looked fuzzy, rather like a wooly worm, and like a wooly worm they tempted a man to reach out a finger and touch.

No man would call her beautiful. Then again no man would call her ordinary. Unique as a sunset, elemental as wildfire.

"By the way," Hull said, and Hawken was embarrassed that he started, as if awakened from sleep. "You related to the Hawken who makes rifles?"

"No." He had been asked the question so many times the answer came automatically. So automatically that even as he answered, he could consider how he was to avoid Meggie MacIntyre for the next two months.

He should ask Tole how much he'd charge for the repairs to his wagons. But there came Meggie to Tole's fire, tripping over to help the blonde—Tole's daughter—wash dishes. She moved the basin so she faced his camp, showing more interest than a woman should.

Tole put down his tin cup and spoke to the biggest of his four boys. The two of them headed downhill. Hawken hailed them before they reached the spring.

"I don't charge members of the party," Tole said in answer to his question. "Wouldn't be fair, for one of these days I'll look to you for help." Hawken stammered his thanks, but Tole dismissed it with a wave. "Godfroy says we'll stop over a day when we reach the Platte River. Kit and I'll look at your wagons then."

"Some of the men want to shoe their oxen," Kit said. "That's where we're bound now, to look their feet. Want that we should do yours?" The eldest of Tole's sons, so like his father one would think he had sprung full-grown from his head, as Zeus had birthed Athena.

The ground heaved beneath Hawken's feet, he put a hand out to catch himself in case he toppled over. Sky and earth disappeared as the curtain billowed, the instant of vertigo passed, leaving a scrap of memory.

"I forgot to tell Monty and Les to drive in the oxen," he said, an excuse to abandon the blacksmith and his son. He plunged into the thicket, and stopped only when the bushes blocked his view of the wagons. He circled the spring, away from the rocks where he had seen a rattle-snake. He leaned on a sapling, closed his eyes and tried to empty his mind, shoving his thoughts into the pattern of that revealing moment. *Kit's like his father, as if he sprang full-grown....* Damn frustrating, the occasional fragments that pierced the curtain. Zeus. Athena. In his former life he had known Greek mythology. He whispered the names. In three years only a handful of memories had crept out. He suspected he had lived in town, for standing before a brick house in Independence, he'd had a vision of steps to a broad door with a polished brass handle. And with the scene, a warmth that must have originated in home and love.

One night in a tavern, a line from a temperance song had trailed through his soused mind, causing a momentary awkwardness. Last summer he had misspoken, called the Missouri River the Maumee. Had he come from Ohio? He had considered spending his summer's profits on a trip to Ohio, asking, "Who am I?" He had finally dismissed the trip as a search for a needle in multiple haystacks.

Now Zeus and Athena. Not the memory he desperately needed. Had there been a woman, specifically, a wife? Was he married? Without that knowledge, he had to avoid respectable women, for fear one might take his friendly demeanor for the preliminaries of courtship.

"Zeus. Athena," he whispered to the dusty leaves over his head. "Athena the daughter of Zeus." Did he have a daughter who grew up without him? He covered his face with his hands, pressed on his eyelids with his fingertips until streamers of light played through his eyeballs. Nothing.

"Boss?"

Hawken lifted his head slowly, so he had time to relax the emotion out of his face.

"Something wrong, boss?" Monty asked.

"No. Just the…the sun," he stammered.

"We got the oxen together. Should we yoke them?"

"Yes. But don't hitch them to the wagons. Let them graze until Captain Hull calls 'Chain up.'"

Les poked Monty, reminding him of some question he wanted asked. "These men." Monty waved toward the wagons. "Do they expect us to call them massa?"

Hawken wriggled his shoulders against the narrow trunk to work the tension from his back. Monty and Les had debated for two days about what they should call him, searching for a word reflecting their status as employees, not slaves. While debating they slid into saying "boss."

"Call the men 'sir' and the ladies 'ma'am,'" Hawken suggested. "None of these families have ever owned slaves."

"And that skinny gal with the braids, could you tell her to be more careful? She walked right where we was loafing. We don't want no woman trouble."

"She was gathering wood. I'll tell her." Now here came an instant awkwardness, just as he'd vowed to avoid Meggie at all costs. He *could* speak to her father and let *him* lecture his daughter on trail manners. Although from what he'd seen so far, her parents made no effort to tame her.

"Thanks," Monty said, walking away. Les stayed put.

"She's the devil," he said. "The one we saw carrying a soul to hell."

"She's no devil. You saw her skirt out behind."

"I know a devilish witch when I see one," Les said darkly. "She straddles that horse like a man, and she got a cat. I saw her pat it."

"What's her cat got to do with—"

"All witches got a tame critter they talk to. A bird, or a cat," Les said, glowering that he should encounter disbelief. "She talks to the horse *and* the chickens *and* that cat." His breath hissed at a movement in the underbrush.

Hawken stirred uneasily, recalling the big rattler, dodged when a tabby cat sprang from the grass and landed in a drift of leaves. It came up with a furry, gray thing wriggling in its jaws. A female with a litter, Hawken saw from the protruding nipples. The cat's tail flicked, and she trotted up the slope.

"Chain up!" Captain Hull cried. Les turned sourly to join Monty and the teams.

"You'll fall in at the rear," Captain Hull said when Hawken emerged from the thicket. "Right behind Jim Mac, who's the end today."

Right behind Meggie, who sat on a tailgate covered with cats. Kittens, rather. They climbed the back of her dress, one swung from her looped braids and brought the whole arrangement tumbling. Two plaits now to bounce on her back. One kitten scrambled over her shoulder, teetered on the slight bulk of her breasts, uttering faint meows of distress. The tabby jumped lightly into the wagon, still carrying her victim. She switched her tail, the kittens abandoned their games and crowded around their mother as she disappeared under the wagon cover.

"Damn cats," Hull said, and Hawken saw that the captain, too, had watched the performance. "If I'd known sooner she'd have left the cat at home, but it hid until we were days on the road, and by then it had a litter."

"Don't the dogs chase it?" Hawken asked.

"Kit's dog, the black-and-white one, remembers Tabby from back home and walks out of his way to avoid her. The yellow dog—" he pointed to a medium-sized dog with a coat of tawny gold "—lunged at the cat once. Tabby jumped on his back, hung on, drawing blood, until the dog dropped."

The yellow dog had a broad head and wide stance. "Who owns the yellow one?" Hawken asked.

"No one. It joined us in St. Joe and the boys toss biscuits its way now and then."

Monty and Les led the teams to their places and hooked the chains. "Move out behind the other wagons, but ahead of the loose stock," Hawken told them.

The clatter of a pot tossed in at the last minute, the shouts of the drivers, the rattle of chains drawing tight, the creak of wheels and the tinkle of cooking gear settling into position. The black-and-white dog trotted off with Kit Tole. The yellow dog stood his ground ten feet away.

"Ho!" Monty and Les yelled simultaneously. The dog stepped back. Monty had waited until Jim Mac's wagons were well down the road. A good driver, with sense enough not to tramp along in the dust of another. Hawken walked at the oxen's pace, examining the running gear and the wheels. The iron tires had not loosened. That would come as they traveled up the Platte River and across the desert.

Meggie rode beside her father's wagons, her skirt lifting slightly with the movement of the pony. The blossom of fabric concealed the curve of her hips and upper legs. The warmth of the sun seeped into Hawken's veins and sank into his belly. He tugged his hat lower and jogged around the wagon to the shady side, which cut off both the sun and his view of Meggie. The yellow dog circled warily, hanging ten feet behind. Hawken pretended not to notice. The dog inched forward, and after a mile trotted at his heel. My first new friend, Hawken thought wryly. The dog did not care that he had no past, or call him a coward for his forgetfulness. The dog would ignore his reputation, a reputation that made it awkward—almost impossible—to return to Missouri.

"Granny," Meggie said, poking her head through the thicket of herbs hanging from the bows.

"Come in," Granny said.

Meggie climbed up the wheel and over the side of the wagon, rather than bothering to walk to the door. A prickly pod tugged at her hair and she had to balance on the edge of the wagon bed to untangle it.

"You're all wet," Tildy said.

"Just my hair. I washed it in the creek. At the end of a hot day it smells like a pigpen."

"Here," Granny said, handing her a pair of shears. "Cut these stems into pieces as long as your little finger."

Meggie tested the edge of the shears. A touch of the whetstone and they would be ready for cutting hair.

"Granny," she said, after clipping the first bundle of stalks, "my hair's a big bother."

"Curly hair never wants to stay up," Tildy said. "Rachel has the same problem, little wisps sneaking out."

"I braid it," Meggie said, "and by midmorning I look like a porcupine, hair sticking out all over. Then it scratches my neck and my ears, and I sweat—"

"I suppose you want to hear how my ma whacked off all my hair the summer we moved from Ohio," Granny said with mock resignation. She laughed, and Meggie knew her subtle approach had been wasted on Granny.

"I want to cut off my hair," Meggie said. "It'll grow out after we get to...California." No sense letting her family know she planned to stop with Hawken. Come to think of it, if she stayed on the Bear River she could keep her hair short forever. Wild mountain men did not care how women wore their hair.

"Ma had to cut my hair because it got gummed with sap when I slept with my head on a root," Granny said. "So sticky no comb would go through it." Meggie regretted the treeless, sapless vistas of the plains.

"You needn't cut it," Tildy said. "I'll help you keep it up. Just come by my wagon every noon. Maybe if I pinned the braids on top of your head—"

Meggie tossed her head so her hair flopped over one shoulder. "It won't work. See, it's all jaggedy."

"Your hair's like mine, thick and wiry," Granny said. "The only good thing about growing old is that part of your hair falls out and the load's more manageable."

"Please, Granny. Talk to Ma."

"After we finish with the herbs. Matt's antsy about stretching the cover on the wagon, for he says we'll face thunderstorms along the Platte River. He's like a mother hen with no shelter, eyeing those clouds to the west."

Sure enough, a line of clouds barred the setting sun. Meggie went back to work, but her eyes wandered frequently and anxiously toward the sunset. Soon it would be too dark.

"Now, you two stay at your work and I'll go talk to Eliza," Granny said. She put on a bonnet, opened her door and stepped out as if the wagon were not wide-open to the world.

"I suppose," Tildy said cautiously, "that your hair *would* grow back, and probably healthier for the trimming."

"That's my idea," Meggie said. It was not her idea at all. She wanted to chop the whole mass off. Men were so lucky, wearing their hair as long or short as they pleased.

The wagon shifted under Granny's weight on the steps. She hung her bonnet on a hook and took her seat on the cot. "Eliza agrees it won't hurt to trim your hair," she said. "Just so it's left long enough to pin up in the back, where your sunbonnet will cover the ends."

"I hate sunbonnets. They're like wearing blinders," Meggie said, but cut off her protest when Granny lifted a warning finger.

"Eliza says there's length enough to make a hairpiece, a bun, from what we cut off, and when you want to appear proper, it will disguise—"

"Good," Meggie said. She could not imagine any event in the next three or four months requiring an elegant hair arrangement. Granny tested the blade of the shears with her finger. "I'll have Pete bring up a better edge on these. You go to your mother, let her consider what's best."

"I hadn't realized how bad things were," her mother said, lifting the mass of hair off Meggie's shoulders. "Your hair's all straggly, I suppose from being outdoors so much. Here, sit on this." Her mother flipped over the empty water pail. "What do you think, Tildy?" she called. "Here come Faith and Rachel. Maybe they've had some experience. Don't turn around, Meggie."

Meggie sat very still while all the women congregated behind her, remarking on the condition of her hair, jerking at it with combs and brushes.

"Sharp as I can get 'em on short notice," Pete said behind her.

Meggie felt the first tentative snip and wondered who wielded the shears.

"It could be a trifle shorter, I think," Granny said.

"But too short..." Her mother's voice trailed off uncertainly. So Ma was doing the cutting. It would not be short enough. From the corner of her eye Meggie saw Tildy and Faith holding a towel to catch the tresses.

"Don't tangle them," Louisa warned. "What thick hair! I think there'll be enough to make side curls, too."

Meggie turned her head to object to side curls. "Don't move. I'm not done," her mother said. Hair tickled her neck. Someone combed it back, and the shears clicked in short bursts. The tickle turned to an itch.

"What do you think?" Ma asked. She must have directed the question to no one in particular, because a host of voices answered.

"Go to the creek and dunk your head in all the way," Granny said. "That takes out all the little clippings so they don't fall down your neck."

Meggie stood up and ran the comb through her hair. It ended at her shoulders. Ma laid the shears on the vacated bucket. "Turn around slowly," she said. "I guess it's even." She gathered the trimmings from the towel and twisted them into a hank. Meggie edged her hand to the bucket, lifted the shears carefully so they made not

the slightest rattle, and slid them into the top of her boot
as she turned to the creek.

She took a deep breath and plunged her head under
the chilly water, came up sputtering, shaking like a dog.
She combed her hair from a rough central part, the wet
mass clinging to her cheeks. She started there, whacking
at random, front to back, until her exploring fingers could
find no tress longer than three or four inches. She would
go directly to her bed and her mother would not see the
damage until morning. Ma would raise a ruckus, but
mornings were so busy she'd have little time to be angry.
And protests were futile, for hair cut off could not be
restored. No fake bun, no side curls with her hair this
short. She leaned over the water, ruffled her fingers
through the mop to get rid of any stray trimmings. It was
already nearly dry. She patted the cushion of curls with
both hands.... On the other bank of the lazy stream a
man leaned against a spindly tree. Dusk hid his face, but
the relaxed angle of his legs suggested he had been
watching her for some time.

He shoved at the tree to bring himself erect, and loped
into the shadows. The grace of a large cat. Hawken.

Meggie grabbed the shears and ran. No slow revelation
possible now. Hawken had seen her chop off her hair and
he would spread the word. No harm done, she decided,
as she fought through the brush. A scolding, whether tonight or tomorrow morning, would pass very quickly.
And Hawken's reaction would determine whether she
flirted with him or not. She'd have nothing to do with a
man who equated short hair with doubtful morals. How
convenient short hair was! She was through the trees
without snagging a braid.

She considered the sequence of her flirtation. She
would find excuses to ride near Hawken's wagons. Next

time Ma got out the reflecting oven she would make a pie of dried apples and offer him a piece. Maybe Captain Hull would let her figure the daily distances, thus demonstrating her talent for arithmetic, which would be handy in a trading post. And some night she'd show him how she could start a fire with a single match, even with flint and steel. He'd already seen her perform on John Charles. Since his wagons came behind her father's, it would be easy to strike up a conversation.

She stopped in confusion. Her fantasies had distracted her, and let her feet carry her almost into the light of the campfire.

"Margaret MacIntyre, what have you done to your hair?" Pa asked firmly, although the sigh that followed rather weakened his question.

"Margaret!" her mother cried, and Meggie resigned herself to a few bad minutes before she was allowed to go to bed. And think of all the ways she would flirt with Hawken.

What a strange girl-woman, Hawken thought. The hubbub she had caused with her whacked-off hair dissipated faster than he had thought possible. Her family had disappeared into bedrolls and tents after only a few cross words and a mild scolding. Riding astride and ahead of the wagons, going without a corset, cropping her hair until almost nothing remained. In Independence these were signs of a loose woman. But Meggie's family and friends gathered about her, as if protecting her from her own foolishness.

He tossed in his blankets. The unaccustomed noise of people and cattle kept him from dropping off. And the creek, a faint swish of moving water, carrying strands of auburn hair downstream.

Chapter Three

The sand hills had a sort of barren beauty, but after a few miles Meggie found her thoughts shifting from the landscape to Hawken. The man was terribly shy. She had delayed mounting John Charles this morning, so she ended up beside his wagons. She had complimented him on his fit teams, but in response he'd shrugged his shoulders and turned back to help drive the loose stock. The dirtiest place on the trail, and she had no inclination to join him.

The distant view shimmered in waves of heat, distorting the landscape. Hills rose into mountains and valleys on the right, and left filled with sparkling lakes. Twice Meggie thought she saw trees in the distance, and pushed John Charles into a trot to reach the shade. Both times she pulled up before a few straggly bushes. Feathered Indians stood in conclave on a hill that floated in the sky. She tapped John Charles with her heels. Mirage chasing was more exciting than riding beside a taciturn man who couldn't even accept a compliment gracefully.

The Indians metamorphosed into tasseled grass growing atop a narrow ridge. Meggie squinted her eyes, searching for the next puzzle. Black spots wavered far away, egg-shapes that gradually elongated into sausages. Taller, taller, until they resembled the giants in fairy stories. Six giants, grouped around a mass big as a house, and that mass flowed from square to oval, and sometimes divided in half, one part floating above the other.

Last year an emigrant had tossed out a crate or trunk, she decided. Something square. It split into three parts, the center offset from the top and bottom. The house reassembled itself and the giants gained legs. Someone or something moved toward her. She looked nervously over her shoulder. Sampson rode a quarter mile behind, and the dust of the wagons hovered farther back yet, on a sweeping curve where the trail passed from one ridge to another.

The ghostly bulk resolved itself into a square, although the edges crinkled like a flag in the breeze. Dust roiled, cutting off part of the vision. Not a box and low bushes, but definitely men riding east, toward her. The faint breeze gained strength, and now carried the sickening smell of rotting flesh. A dead animal lay to windward.

The giants coalesced into horses and riders, the house a heavily loaded wagon. No, a cart. Two carts, piled high. Thin mules strained for footing in the drifts that blocked the road, and sand lifted with the turn of the wheels so they appeared solid. The odor of death thickened, gagging and hideous. Meggie could make out the colors and patterns of the horses, but the riders remained black statues. Greasy buckskins, mahogany skin, filthy, smoke-encrusted hair. The mountain men reined in, the mule skinners cursed the animals to a stop. They stared, their eyes bulging, white hemispheres in dark masks, reminding Meggie of a hungry beggar her father had once brought into the kitchen just as her mother put dinner on the table.

"Howdy," said one of the men. He shifted the long rifle that balanced on the pommel of his saddle; the barrel foreshortened as it swung in her direction.

"A party bound for California," Meggie tried to say, but to speak meant breathing, and breathing...she pointed over her shoulder, riveted by the vile reality that had materialized from this mirage. She wished she had stayed with Sampson, like her father had told her. The man with the rifle eased his horse forward. Meggie pulled on the reins and John Charles stepped back to maintain the space between them. If she had stayed with the wagons, she might be helping Granny cut and grind her herbs.

"A buffalo robe for you," the man said thickly. He wanted to give her a buffalo robe? Instead of moving toward the cart, he lifted his long buckskin tunic and plucked at the cloth beneath, dragging it from its restraining thong. In that instant Meggie realized what he meant to show. Himself.

She jerked the reins, kicked her pony violently, and nearly collided with Sampson.

"Two robes!" the man shouted. "Two robes to lie with me."

"Get behind me," Sampson ordered, sliding his pistol from his belt. Meggie lifted her foot to kick John Charles into a gallop, away from this death-carrying crowd. "Stay here," Sampson warned. "They might cut you off."

The wagons were closer, but the mirage made it hard to judge distance. Wagon covers moved without wheels to support them, the front oxen seemed to labor several feet off the ground, while those behind waded in sand to their bellies.

"We'll trade robes for flour," said a new voice behind her.

"Buffalo robes are too heavy," Sampson said. "I make my people travel light." Sampson jerked a thumb over his shoulder.

Meggie stole a glance down the road and relaxed a bit when she saw the front wagon come together, the oxen safely founded on the road, the cover shivering as it jolted in the ruts.

Sampson guided his horse off the road and Meggie hid from the hunter by moving at his pace. A curt order, a signal to the mule skinners, who yelled at the teams. The mules strained, the carts creaked, and the stench flowed over her like a liquid. John Charles trembled, his skin working as if he shook off flies. Meggie's stomach heaved. She could not stay here.

"Go!" she whispered frantically, bending low over the pony's mane. John Charles bounded, all four feet off the ground, headed down the trail as if on wings, almost ran straight into Mr. Marshall, who fought bucking and bellowing oxen. He cracked his long whip and grabbed at the yoke, struggling to hold them on the trail.

"Those men carrying something dead?" he yelled at Meggie.

"Buffalo hides. It's awful." Marshall's oxen raised their heads for one more sniff, then plunged into heavy sand at the side of the road, Marshall cursing after them.

"What's going on?" Captain Hull asked. He was on foot, and the gritty dust of the sand hills had turned him light tan, from hat to boots. Meggie stammered a few words about buffalo hunters, but did not mention the odor, for it crowded behind her.

"Ride back to your kin," he ordered. "Tell them to get off the trail at the most likely spot and hold the oxen till the hunters get by. I've seen animals panic from the smell and run for miles. Put rags soaked in vinegar over their noses if there's time. A few rifles and pistols in the open would not be amiss.''

Meggie shouted the instructions to Uncle Ira as she trotted by. Her mother and Granny were walking, so Meggie slid off John Charles. Granny nodded with instant understanding, fortunately, for Mr. Reid stood stock-still, nose in the air with disdain, his whole face wrinkled in disgust. Ma ran back to warn Pa.

"Tell Hawken and Godfroy," Pa said to Meggie. "And Kit, so he can herd the stock away from the trail."

Hawken's wagon trailed several lengths behind to avoid the dust. Her father had cautioned her about getting too close to Hawken's drivers, so she guided John Charles off the road and shouted her message. They scrambled to the foremost yokes. No need to speak to Mr. Godfroy, who had had experience with buffalo hunters.

A man with a raking stride came out of the dust cloud. Hawken, so filthy she could not make out his face. The yellow dog loped at his side. "Buffalo hunters," Meggie gasped. He nodded curtly, stared at the ground, either a complete idiot or in deep thought. She waited a few seconds.

"I'll stop the herd," he said rapidly, pointing to the oxen-shaped wraiths in the dust. "Ride back and tell Kit. There's a gully downhill that will serve as a refuge." He whistled, the dog lifted his head and Hawken turned away.

Kit, to Meggie's distress, demanded a full explanation of what was going on, for the odor of death had not reached him. She pointed into the dust. "Mr. Hawken's in front of the herd. Hear him shout?"

"You ride to the bottom of the gully and keep the animals from turning back to the last water," Kit said.

She guided John Charles downhill and found a tiny spring at the bottom of the gully, and a patch of thin grass, no more than a quarter of an acre, but sufficient to interest the herd. She also found Hawken, holding a pistol. "Dismount and get behind the horse," he said.

Meggie hesitated. Kit and the boys would stay at the top, leaving her alone with Hawken.

"These rascals will try to grab fresh horses if they're like other buffalo hunters I've met," Hawken said mildly.

She slid off John Charles and clung to his mane. Now that she thought about it, the hunter's horses were little more than skin and bones. How could she fight them if they came for the pony? An eddy of wind thinned the dust, exposing the line of wagons, and beyond them the carts, laden with stacks of hides taller than the wagon covers.

Quite unexpectedly the foul cavalcade loomed on the left. She had forgotten the curve in the road. Hawken stood with legs spread, his pistol in plain sight, his head turning at the pace of the hunters. The yellow dog's growl rumbled in his throat. Hawken's torso twisted, causing the leather of his tunic to pull across his back, and it emphasized the shape of him, from wide shoulders to narrow hips. The buffalo hunter had narrow hips. Meggie lifted her eyes.

Two of the hunters were stopped, eyeing the herd. Hawken lowered the pistol and held it in both hands. A wild laugh flung on a gust of wind, along with the scent of decay. Meggie only noticed she was digging her fingers into John Charles's neck when the pony tossed his head. The hunters trotted after their companions. In less than a minute the erratic atmosphere flung them into ragged specters.

Kit and the boys piled down the hill to get the herd

back on the road, but Hawken remained rooted, his eyes on the wavering black specks. The folds in the buckskin changed with the tension of his muscles, the tunic now loose, but the leggings taut on the back of his thighs. He slipped the pistol in his belt, and the leather shirt creased diagonally from waist to shoulders. His grim mouth twitched, producing a faint, momentary smile.

"Safe now?" she asked. He came around John Charles, bent before her, his fingers intertwined. At first she did not understand the gesture.

"Boost you up?" he said.

She did not need his help, but rejecting it would cause an awkwardness. She slipped her moccasined toe in the cradle of his fingers, laid her hand on his shoulder, and smiled her thanks. John Charles tossed his head, sniffing. Meggie imitated him, and smelled a faint but distinct odor of buffalo hunter. She patted the pony's neck to reassure him and urged him into a trot, and breathed a prayer of thanks when she rode into the dust and camaraderie of the wagons.

Mr. Reid hovered over the front yoke, talking softly to the oxen, perhaps telling them—and himself—that the buffalo hunters had gone for good. Granny stood a few feet off the trail, plucking leaves from a stunted bush.

"Mr. Reid's becoming quite handy with the oxen," Meggie said to Granny. She needed to talk, to banish the vision of the buffalo hunter.

"Mr. Reid tells me that gentlemen in England spend a great deal of time with their horses," Granny said. "He knows animals."

"Strange how things happen on the plains. Mr. Hawken hires two runaway slaves to drive his teams, and your driver's an English aristocrat."

"Not strange at all," Granny said. "Practical men do

what's necessary to reach their dream. Les and Monty want freedom. Mr. Reid wants adventure and hasn't the money to do it like a gentleman."

"There are some things I wouldn't do to reach my dream, no matter how much I wanted it," Meggie said, shuddering. Granny set out after her wagon, giving Meggie a sidelong glance that asked for elaboration.

"Say I wanted to live in the Rocky Mountains," Meggie said, looking at the sky and flipping her hand to show the hypothetical nature of her statement. "I wouldn't marry a buffalo hunter to do it."

Granny wrinkled her nose and laughed. "Take a strong woman to stand that."

"I don't think any woman could stand it. I almost got sick. The oxen shied and Mr. Hawken's dog growled."

"Mr. Hawken's dog?"

"That yellow stray. He's taken up with Mr. Hawken."

"Good. Your cousins have been wasting food, tossing biscuits to the cur when they thought Ira wasn't looking. But why should you even think of marrying a buffalo hunter?"

"I wasn't thinking any such thing," Meggie said, aware that her denial was a little too fierce. After a year in the mountains, would Hawken look like a buffalo hunter? Worse, smell like one?

"It's dangerous for a woman to marry, expecting her husband to furnish what she dreams of?" Granny asked.

"Women should do what men do, set out on their own," Meggie said. Hawken could have bought clothes in Independence, but he chose to wear buckskins. Lovely buckskins, golden in their newness. She had not realized what time and exposure did to buckskins.

I'd make him take a bath. And I'd wash his clothes.

She and Hawken would bathe in the river. The wind

toyed with the short hairs dangling on her neck, brought a shiver, and a stirring of her heart. A warm dawn, dipping into sunlit water, him undressed...not so shocking to see a man's paleness if he exposed himself completely, from neck to ankles. Those broad shoulders, narrow hips...and she...she would be naked, too.

But summer did not last forever. Her imagination clouded the sky and dropped the temperature until snow fell. She froze the idyll to a winter's morn. A pot of melting snow hung over an open fire, a struggle to get water enough for coffee and cooking, let alone laundry and bathing. Hawken could not build the entire trading post before winter, perhaps no more than a stockade and a cabin. The cabin would serve for everything, store, warehouse, living quarters. At her order mountain men crowded the shack, shouting for warmth and whiskey. Her stomach heaved.

"Whoa," Mr. Reid called. The wagon directly ahead had come to a halt, a few hats careened above the dust, followed by cheers.

"What is it?" called Granny.

"The Platte River Valley," Hawken said, unexpectedly nearby. He lifted his hand as he passed, the dog at his heels and his two drivers close behind. A streak of charcoal blackened one legging, and circles of sweat stained the underarms of his hunting shirt. By the time they reached Bear River, Hawken's buckskins would resemble those of the hunters. Sad, because as he walked the leather pulled taut on his calves, and moved with his muscles.

Hawken stood aside to let Monty and Les gawk at the Platte Valley. The river spread wide on a vast plain; the afternoon sun reflected on ripples and cast elongated shadows, a golden tablet marked with Oriental inscriptions. The rising heat played tricks, lifting the timbered islands so they appeared to float on the water. Emeralds strung on gold, Hawken thought, although he could not recall ever having seen an emerald. Was that a memory from his past? He closed his eyes a moment to observe the curtain, and found it motionless.

"Sure is wide!" Monty said. "Looks more like a lake."

"Why don't someone run a steamboat?" Les asked.

"Because the river's only three or four feet deep, less than that in a few weeks," Hawken explained. "Back to the wagons. Hull will order us out soon, to reach the river by sunset. I'm climbing that hill for a better view and will be along shortly."

The wagons moved slowly on the descent, still hampered by drifted sand. The dog remained at Hawken's heel and he did not order it away. A dog would not intrude on his musings. He did not need a better view, but he *could* use a quiet moment away from the crowd to organize his thoughts. Make plans. Blast Meggie MacIntyre!

Her teasing smile floated within the mirage. He massaged the shoulder where her hand had rested as she mounted. She had lifted her hat as she rode away. Her hands were long, with gracefully tapered fingers. There'd be no difficulty keeping his distance if she behaved like a normal woman. But she traipsed about like a gypsy.

Below, the wagons swung into their protective circle. He could camp separately. Hawken studied the valley, searching for a refuge. No trees, not even a willow on the riverbank. Not a good idea; a separate camp might give her the opportunity to corner him alone.

He snapped his fingers at the dog, who had stretched

out on the shady side of the hill. Where the sun caught his back, the fur and the river shone the same color.

"Platte," he said to the dog. "That's your name. Okay?" The dog sniffed at the wagon tracks and turned unerringly toward the river. "Platte," Hawken said, snapping his fingers as he said the word. The dog lifted its broad head and regarded him with thoughtful eyes, seemed to nod, then turned his attention to the trail.

Hawken loafed along the road, watching the strands of evening color reach for the zenith. No sense arriving before Monty and Les got a fire going and the coffeepot on. If he so much as picked up a pot they got huffy. In their experience, the boss cooked only if the underlings were inept. If he did more than fetch water, he insulted them.

I must do this more often, let the wagons roll ahead, and enjoy the solitude and silence of the prairie.

The dog huffed a warning. A man squatted in the road, studying a track leading to the river. Will Hunter, Godfroy's son-in-law, Hawken remembered, calling the name to the front of his mind.

"Buffalo?" Hunter asked, getting to his feet. New to the plains, but not ashamed to ask for advice, which was a good sign in any man.

"Buffalo, but not a herd. Old bulls, who travel alone. In a day or two we'll see buffalo enough to please everyone." Thin columns of smoke ascended from the camp and Hawken fancied he smelled boiling coffee.

"I left a prairie chicken at your camp," Hunter said. "You'd better hurry or your hired men will gobble everything but the neck and feet."

Hawken loped down the last hill, kicking up sand, his dry mouth pretending to drool in anticipation of roast prairie chicken. He sniffed, but caught no tantalizing aroma. Monty and Les leaned over the water bucket.

"This river's no river," Les said. "More a mud flat. Can't make coffee out of sand soup." He kicked at the bucket of opaque water.

"Sprinkle a handful of cornmeal on the top," Hawken said. "It sinks and carries the sand to the bottom, and leaves clean water behind."

"You'd best tell the MacIntyre ladies," Monty said, pointing to wagons on the opposite side of the circle. "You shoulda heard the squawks when they dipped their pail."

Hawken cautiously searched for Meggie, discovered her with the horses, grooming John Charles. Safe to walk to the MacIntyre's fire. But someone had already introduced them to the cornmeal trick, for their coffeepot steamed.

"Ho!" Tole yelled at him. "Hull says we'll lay over tomorrow, so we'll work on your wagons."

Lay over. He'd forgotten. On the trail he could escape her by helping with the stock. But when they loafed in camp? He'd help Tole, he concluded. No lady would hang about a blacksmith's fire.

Chapter Four

Meggie folded the first batch of laundry. Nothing more she could do until the clothes on the line dried. She dug through the load in her wagon, found her workbag under a sack of flour, smashed flat. She'd straighten her wagon after she put the clothes away.

Faith, Tildy and Rachel had spread a blanket in the shade and were miles ahead of her in their patchwork. She hesitated at the sight of John Charles nibbling grass. If she rode downstream, she might find the junction of the army trail. But Captain Hull had stressed that the animals must rest. She resolutely turned her face to the sewing circle.

Mr. Tole had set up a portable forge, and Hawken had pushed his wagons out of the circle, close to the fire. The clang of Tole's hammer echoed like a bell. Hawken held a wheel steady, bent nearly double. The streak of black on his left legging had been joined by one on the right.

"Hello," Tildy called. "We feared we'd lost you to blacksmithing." Meggie glared at Faith, accusing her of spreading gossip about her interest in Hawken. Faith kept her eyes on her Jacob's Ladder block.

"Blacksmithing is hot and dirty," Meggie said loftily.

She sat down cross-legged and dug in her bag for the Wild Geese Flying pattern she had traced in St. Joe. The corners of the cardboard templates had crumpled.

"Granny says you don't want to marry a buffalo hunter," Tildy said. Granny had gossiped, too. Meggie considered throwing the cardboard at Tildy, then decided a witty answer would serve better. But nothing witty came to mind.

"Weren't the buffalo hunters awful!" Rachel said. "Imagine living in such filth. It's unbelievable, but Father claims those we met are cleaner than most. Usually, he says, their horses are worn out by spring and they ride on top of the hides."

"Mr. Hawken feared they'd try to steal our horses," Meggie said, before it occurred to her that mentioning Hawken would lead to more teasing. "I suppose since they camp out all winter, it's too much to expect them to bathe and wash their clothes. I wonder how they *do* live?"

"Ask Father," Rachel said.

"Or Mr. Hawken," Tildy said with exaggerated innocence. She winked at Faith. *I'll never confide in Faith again,* Meggie thought. Or Granny.

"Mr. Hawken," Meggie said, lowering her voice and adding a weight of sarcasm, "is well on his way to looking like a buffalo hunter. Why should you—" she pointed the cardboard at Tildy "—think me interested? Just because you're married doesn't mean you have to match me—or Faith for that matter—with the first single man who comes around." Faith's eyebrows rose, a sign of agreement. Meggie nodded to her, enlisting an ally. The silence lasted longer than it should among old friends.

"What scraps are left in that bag?" Meggie asked.

Rachel shoved the muslin sack in her direction. "If you want red or blue, you're too late," she said. "Tildy took it all. And I picked out the pink and rose."

Meggie shrugged to show her indifference. "You two are married and must use specific colors to please your husbands." She felt a little wicked, disparaging marriage.

"It's quite rewarding to please a husband," Tildy said with the cadence of someone who feels insulted and tries not to show it. "Particularly one as kind and generous as Matt. Rachel, don't you find that's true?"

Rachel's dark lashes shaded her eyes, so Meggie could not tell if she agreed or disagreed. "Will doesn't ask...much of me," she said. *What he asks of her, she'll not talk about,* Meggie thought, *because Faith and I aren't married, and aren't supposed to know.* She dropped a roll of yellow calico as an excuse to lean over, just in case she blushed. She opened the scrap bag wide, pretending she had to put her face in to get a better view of its contents. A roll of white muslin confronted her, inches from her nose, so like that ghastly male organ...thank heavens, her friends didn't know the buffalo hunter had exposed himself.

"I guess I do try to please Will," Rachel said, "because he does everything to please me."

"You're both very fortunate," Faith said, with only a hint of bitterness. "One never knows until the ceremony's over and the paper signed." Rachel paled and Meggie guessed Rachel was thinking about her first abortive wedding, where no paper was signed, or license obtained, so it had to be done all over again. "Men," continued Faith, "are on their best behavior during courting, to tempt a woman, then..."

The conversation unsettled Meggie, half insults, half innuendo, not proper between old friends. She searched for a safe topic to end the tension. "How many Hull's Victory blocks have you finished, Tildy?"

"Ten." Tildy opened her workbag and spilled out the patchwork, spreading it one block at a time. Heads tilted and eyes narrowed, appraising how the completed top would look.

"Lovely," said Faith.

"Bright," said Rachel.

Not the sort of thing a housewife puts on the spare bed, Meggie almost said, then remembered in California even Tildy, whose father had been the richest man in Pikeston, would not have a spare bed. Lucky to have a bed at all on a new frontier, Granny said. What money they had must keep them for a year, until the first harvest.

Meggie had helped her father carve a hole in the corner stud of the wagon box, stow the small pouch of gold coins, and glue in a patch so cunning no one would notice. And Granny's money, hard to say where she hid it, if it existed.

"Well?" Tildy said, staring at Meggie. "What do you think of my Hull's Victory?"

"I was thinking...it would be so...appropriate on a boy's...I don't mean to imply that you're...in a family way, Tildy, but the bright colors—"

Tildy grinned at her discomfort. "You're right. A boy's bed. But there's no boy, or girl for that matter, on the way yet, so I've plenty of time to finish the quilt."

Meggie traced the largest triangle on the yellow calico. She would make her wild geese of yellow and green on a tan background, the colors of the Platte Valley.

"Tell Will thank you for the prairie chickens," Faith said to Rachel. "I buried them in the coals overnight and we ate them for breakfast. Such a pleasant meal when we stop for a day, no rush to wash the pots and yoke the oxen.''

"The birds were delicious," Tildy said. "Granny made herb stuffing with the biscuits left from dinner."

"Will expects to see buffalo any day now," Rachel said. "If he shoots one buffalo each day, we'll have all the fresh meat we can possibly eat."

Tildy stacked her blocks into a neat pile. "It will be a nice change from salt pork, although—"

"Buffalo! Buffalo!"

All heads came up at the wild shout. Meggie abandoned fabric, cardboard and pencil, a trifle guilty that the prospect of buffalo interested her more than patchwork. But her friends ignored their sewing, too, Tildy's blocks flying all helter-skelter. They leaped over the wagon tongue and almost collided with Granny.

"Buffalo?" Granny asked, her eyes more distracted than Meggie had ever seen them.

Men were dashing in all directions. Some pulled rifles from the wagons, others pawed through boxes for caps. But most headed in a disorganized footrace toward the horses.

"No!" Meggie cried. Someone would be sure to get a leg over John Charles. She hitched up her skirt and pounded along at the rear of the crowd.

"No! Stay away from those horses," Captain Hull bellowed beside her. "Fools," he muttered under his breath.

Last night Captain Hull had lectured everyone on the perils of running buffalo. And it exhausted the horses. The hired hunter would get sufficient meat. Men accused women of being emotional and senseless!

Horses galloped by, only one or two saddled. John Charles stood near the river, his back still empty. As she watched, hands wrapped over his dark mane and Tildy's brother Lewis leaped on his back.

"Stay off my pony!" she yelled, changing direction so fast her heel caught in the sand and nearly sent her flying. Lewis kicked John Charles and slapped his neck. Meggie whistled, loud and long. John Charles turned his head, confused by the mixed signals. Meggie whistled again, and John Charles spread his front legs and lowered his head.

"Buffalo!" Lewis screamed. "I'll kill a buffalo—"

"With what?" Meggie asked. She grabbed the pony's halter. "You don't have a gun. Plan to kick one to death?"

"Let loose, Meggie MacIntyre," Lewis yelled. "Girls don't run buffalo."

"Neither do you on my horse."

"You're not riding him today." Lewis unbuckled his belt, whipped it from around his waist and flipped it across the pony's rump. John Charles nickered in shock at this unfamiliar violence, tossed his head and jerked the halter from Meggie's hand. The belt landed once more and Lewis yelled in triumph, a yell that changed into a scream of terror, for John Charles stood on his front legs. He stretched his hind legs, bounced with all four feet off the ground, reached once more for the sky. The spinning bundle outlined against the blue was, Meggie knew, her cousin.

He's killed! Uncle Ira will shoot John Charles because he's killed Lewis.

John Charles wriggled his hindquarters to check that he'd relieved his back of the unwanted burden, then went back to nibbling grass.

"Lewis, Lewis!" Meggie ran to the boy, knelt beside him and rolled him over, prepared for blank eyes and a

death rattle. Lewis groaned, a wheezing groan. He tried
to take a breath, but the air seemed to stick in his mouth.

"What's going on here?" Uncle Ira ran toward her
awkwardly. "Was he on a horse?"

"John Charles," Meggie muttered.

"I told you boys to stay off the horses," Uncle Ira
said. He grabbed Lewis by the arm, jerked him up and
smacked his rear, all in one motion. Lewis took a sudden
breath, so deep his eyes bugged out.

Whack! Whack! Lewis screamed.

"That's enough for now," Uncle Ira said. "You'll get
the rest of your strokes with a switch along with Josh.
He went off on Rachel's mare. I'll let Will Hunter tan
his hide. Twenty-year-old muscles can put more power
behind a switch."

Lewis's tears dammed up in glistening pools above bits
of grass and dirt, then overflowed and flooded the corners
of his mouth. "Buffa...buffalo," he stammered.

"Buffalo be damned. If Josh ruins that mare I have to
pay for it."

Meggie turned her back on her anguished cousin, feeling in some way responsible for his pain. She whistled
softly to John Charles, and he came, nickering a question.
She scratched under his mane and behind his ears, looked
for swelling on his back, but Lewis's young arms lacked
the strength to raise welts.

"All that talk of leaving the hunting to Will Hunter
didn't survive the first buffalo herd," said a baritone
whisper. Hawken took off his hat and beat it against his
dirty leggings. "Tomorrow, you'll be the only one with
a fresh mount."

"Are you looking for a horse?" she asked, suspicious,
remembering he had none along.

"No, I've hunted buffalo and there are easier ways

than pounding beside them. Last year I saw a man go down. After the herd passed we found nothing left worth burying." His eyes darted from river to hills, never resting on her. "I came to help Captain Hull keep the men off the horses," he added lamely. "Not very successful, I guess. But no one got John Charles."

"Why should…?" The question she meant to ask slithered out of consciousness, leaving her feeling very foolish. He looked at his boots.

"I like to see you ride," he said shyly. "Not many women enjoy it as much as you do."

His long fingers caressed John Charles's rump, and through some magic the sensation transferred to her own back.

"Did the boy hurt him?"

"I don't think so." Why were they whispering?

John Charles stepped toward the exploring fingers, shoving Hawken in her direction. Meggie stepped back, but John Charles chose that moment to circle after a particularly succulent clump of grass, and block her way.

"Don't," she tried to say, but her tongue seemed paralyzed. The fingers of her left hand tangled in John Charles's mane. Hawken's arms flailed like a windmill to keep his balance, he clutched at her, and she felt the creases of buckskin on her arms, then his weight as he pinned her against the pony's side.

Meggie wrenched her hand free of the mane, ignoring John Charles's nicker of pain. She twisted to add power to her swing, heard the impact of her palm on Hawken's cheek as streaks of pain flashed to her elbow.

For an instant Hawken wavered before her, astonished, puzzled, and then he simply disappeared.…

Hawken knew he had fallen when his hands touched grass and he was eye to eye with Platte, who backed away, whimpering. Meggie leaned against John Charles, twisted in a way that defined her waist and bosom. Her wild eyes focused on thin air.

"I'm sorry," he said, but hardly any sound came out. Meggie looked down, and the wildness eased, turning to surprise. John Charles, who had been the cause of it all, grazed placidly.

Hawken took three breaths to reinflate his lungs. He moved experimentally to see what he'd broken. Both sides of his rump protested. He touched his cheek gingerly but could not feel a thing. Numb. It would turn purple in an hour and everyone would wonder who'd hit him.

Meggie scrambled onto the pony, awkward, not at all her usual graceful leap. The pony backed away and Hawken forgot his pain in admiring her skill, managing the animal without a saddle, reins or bit. Meggie scrubbed the back of her hand across the bodice of her dress, then down each arm, wherever he had touched her.

"Swine!" she snarled. Her breath came ragged, as if she had rolled with him in the grass and pushed her nerves to orgasmic tatters.

A bell tolled in his head, and a strange voice said, "Two full-grown swine...swine...swine." The tight rails of a pigsty before him. He heard the snuffling of grown pigs and the high squeals of piglets. Grab it! Hang on to the memory and follow it back, swine, Zeus, Athena, Maumee.

"Is that how you treat women? Act real shy until you get close, then throw yourself against them?" The vision from his past wavered under the force of her voice, then dissipated like smoke in a wind.

"I was there. I almost had it," he muttered. He rolled

over. Maybe if he did not see Meggie, the vision would return.

Reconstruct the memory.

The poles of the sty? Unpeeled saplings.

"You're ignoring me. You don't want to admit you shove women around and beat—"

"I don't do anything of the kind." Hopeless. The last wisp of memory faded.

"Then why did you try it?" she asked, her triumph accusing him of a thousand seductions.

"Your pony pushed me," he began, speaking toward the ground, "and I tripped over the dog. It was an accident." Meggie made a harsh sound, an audible sneer, and he gave up trying to explain.

God in Heaven, why couldn't—

God. It hadn't occurred to him before, but through everything he remembered God. Not specifics of worship, sect, or who had taught him, but faith of a sort survived the disaster.

"God, pigs, Athena, Zeus, Maumee," he said, only realizing he spoke aloud when the words hung in the air.

"That's no excuse," she said. "Are you crazy? I don't want a crazy man."

"Want?" He sat up. Might as well face her, since his memory had gone blank. His rear end ached where he had landed.

"Marrying a crazy man would be just plain...well, crazy! I had thought you might make an interesting husband. We could stay in Bear River Valley and I'd help with the store. I know arithmetic through long division and can do percents. Granny taught me what herbs to pick and how to make tea and poultices, so I can live well without a doctor. We could sell medicines to emigrants. And jam.'' A wrinkle across her eyes. "I suppose berries grow along the river.''

"You'd be of no use to me," he said softly. What unbearable fear and loathing, taking a wife with the chance of recollection hanging over his head.

"No use?'' she cried. "It's you who'd be of no use to me, a crazy man.'' She nodded to emphasize her opinion of his mental state.

"Maybe I am crazy," he said. "Maumee, Athena, Zeus, and now pigs. And God," he added. "God never left.''

"He wouldn't,'' she said. "God's that way.'' She turned the pony's head and picked her way across the sandy plain, toward the hills.

Hawken allowed himself one long moan after Meggie passed out of hearing. If she told her father, or Godfroy or Sampson, they'd pay no heed to his side of the story. He'd be kicked out of the party, be forced to camp here until another wagon train rolled out of the sand hills. He turned his head to the distant trail, half hoping to see wagons. A single horseman, with his rifle before him. A buffalo hunter? Why would a buffalo hunter ride west? Hawken got his feet under him, groaning in earnest because his rump hurt worse when he moved. Only one or two people around the wagons. Of course, everyone had rushed off to the buffalo.

"Monty! Les!'' Hawken yelled.

Les crawled from under a wagon. "Monty's gone to the buffalo,'' he said. He stared at Hawken, focusing on the brutalized cheek. "Told you that girl was a witch, but you'd pay no attention to old Les, would you?''

Hawken ignored the comment while he checked the loads in his pistol and rifle. He whistled for Platte, who hung back, not sure of his part in landing his master on the ground. Hawken handed the pistol to Les and pointed at the hunter.

"He's got no business here. Any other man about?" Hawken asked. Les shrugged. Hawken remembered Ira MacIntyre dragging his tearful son away from John Charles, but when he checked MacIntyre's wagons, found them abandoned. The women—and several of the men—had congregated on a slight rise between the camp and the dust cloud lifted by the buffalo. Meggie rode slowly in that direction.

Hawken considered borrowing a horse, the most efficient way to intercept the hunter, then remembered every horse except John Charles had been snatched. Les set out to position himself between the herd and the buffalo hunter, but the man was cutting off the trail, farther from the river. Sure enough, four or five oxen rested on the verge of a shallow gully. Hawken walked rapidly in that direction, lifting his rifle so the buffalo hunter, if he turned, would see his theft had been anticipated.

Hawken couldn't keep his eyes on the hunter while crossing a wet spot below a tiny spring. He gauged the leaps from hummock to hummock carefully, so he wouldn't be caught up to his knees in muck while six or eight oxen were driven away. But the hunter veered away from the cattle. Probably had noticed that a guard had been mounted. He'd give up and ride away.

The hunter urged his horse into an uneven trot. Hawken searched for cattle in that direction. Nothing but Meggie, astride John Charles, still as a statue on the brow of a sand hill.

Good God! Meggie! Hawken's mind cleared, every fold and gully before him preternaturally sharp. *Get away from the river,* he told himself, *a longer route but faster.* "Meggie, turn around," he said. No shout would carry

that distance. The buffalo hunter lifted a coiled rope. Unusual, but not unknown, for a mountain man to have
learned the Mexican skill with a riata. The loop uncoiled
against the sky, a living thing, a dreadful snake. Hawken
shouted, but Meggie turned only in the instant when the
rope settled about her. She jerked forward in startled reaction, then backward, off the pony and out of sight.

Chapter Five

"Fight! Fight!" Hawken muttered. Certainly Meggie would struggle against the hunter, delaying the moment when he threw her on his horse and trotted away. He dared not look up to see the progress of the kidnapping. A fall now would cost precious seconds.

A faint scream blended with distant thunder. Hawken noted idly that the buffalo herd had veered closer to camp. Platte dashed by, a snarling blur; Hawken wanted to call him back, but had no reserve of breath to whistle. The hunter would shoot the dog, of course, or slash its throat. Curses combined with shrieks that certainly came from Meggie. Hawken resolutely searched for a smooth path.

"Good dog! Good dog!" Meggie cried, surprisingly nearby. Hawken wasted two or three seconds making sense of what he saw. Platte clung to the buffalo hunter's right arm. The man staggered toward his horse, dragging the dog, his left arm stretched to grasp the rifle hanging from the saddle. Hawken raised his own rifle, but dog and man danced in the sights. He lunged the last few feet up the slope, his chest near to bursting, threw himself at the buffalo hunter just as the man touched the weapon.

No chance to aim and fire. Hawken swung his rifle like a club, the horse reared, and horse and hunter whirled away.

"Thank you! Thank you!" Meggie, on her hands and knees, struggled against coils of rope.

"Are you hurt?" he asked. He was on his knees, tugging at the bindings, before it occurred to him that he had turned his back on an armed man. "Are you hurt?"

Meggie did not reply, only stared openmouthed over his shoulder. He jerked the rope free.

"Run," he gasped, and spun to face the threat.

The horse bucked, wild-eyed, the hunter swung, a limp, doll-like figure, his wrist caught in the rifle sling. The horse threw himself to the ground, rolled, crushing the bedeviling weight. Hawken reached for Meggie sightlessly, drew her face into his chest as a shield against the horror.

I can cut the sling, Hawken thought, *the man may not be dead.* But Meggie squealed in his arms. Muffled against his hunting shirt, she sounded like a hurt kitten or a throat-cut rabbit. He got an arm about her and pulled her up. John Charles waited thirty feet away, eyes wide, mane erect, tail straight out, poised to flee.

"Whistle for your pony," Hawken said, then saw her hands covered her face. She moved her palms away from her mouth, tried to close her teeth and lips, but any whistle lost itself in gasping, shallow breaths.

"Get her out of here." Captain Hull stood over him, and half a dozen men staggered up the loose slope.

"Dead, ain't he," Les said, just as the buffalo hunter came back to life, his body arching in violent convulsions. The horse sprang in terror, another series of bucks and kicks, struggling to rid himself of the burden.

"Get Meggie out of here!" Hull roared. Hawken staggered toward John Charles, half carrying, half dragging her. He threw her over the pony, facedown. Now what? The wagons, but where were they? Platte barked expectantly. Hawken stepped blindly toward the sound. Platte danced before him, yapping, keeping him headed in the right direction.

Meggie pulled herself upright, both legs on one side of the pony, and clung to the mane. Women surrounded them, and Hawken dropped the bridle so he might be the one to help Meggie down. His numbed fingers bent stiffly about her waist. He stepped back the moment her feet touched the ground, but Meggie came with him, clinging to his shoulders, burying her face in the folds of his hunting shirt. He spread his hands on her back, cautious lest his movement be perceived as an embrace. She slammed against him.

"Don't leave me alone," she whispered.

"Of course not."

"He'll come back. With the others." Her fingers dug through the leather, painfully compressing muscles against his shoulder blades.

"I'll be here. Your grandmother should look at you, make sure you're not hurt." She nodded dumbly, rubbing her face into the laces of his shirt. The buckskin tightened faintly on his ribs and shock waves ricocheted off his heart.

"Go to your grandmother," he said, thrusting her away. "Granny," he called, and found her standing beside him. Hawken met the old woman's eyes, bleached by age, full of wisdom. Meggie was too frightened to comprehend his feelings, but her grandmother knew. Up the steps of Granny's wagon, her special friends, Rachel, Tildy and Faith, tagging behind. Hawken stepped after them to fulfill his pledge of protection, but a hand interfered.

"Here's your rifle," Pete said. "Thank you for being around. The rest of us rushed off like ninnies—"

"The first time I saw a buffalo I did exactly the same. It wasn't even a herd, but a lone bull, half a mile away. Of course he was long gone by the time I got in rifle range." He bit his tongue. He was babbling.

"Anyway, my family owes you—"

"The dog. That's who you owe." Platte calmly quenched his thirst at a bucket. "He's getting the taste of buffalo hunter out of his mouth. I wouldn't want to grip that man's arm in my teeth." Hawken laughed, heard it as a hysterical giggle and clenched his teeth.

"You came right behind the dog," Captain Hull said. "The brute meant to carry her off. But he's taken care of."

An unpleasant memory of the buffalo hunter obscured the prairie sky. "Is he dead?"

"I suppose. No one could get close enough to cut the sling. The horse bucked and jumped, then took off, trying to shake the body loose. Last time I saw him, just a glimpse, the...thing was still dragging."

Hawken shuddered.

"Yeah," Pete said, his voice unstable, "what a way to go. You look a bit green, you know. Granny has a bottle of brandy, for medicinal purposes...."

"She's tending Meggie," Hawken said. He heard a murmur of voices from the wagon, but no cry of pain. If Meggie ever cried out in pain. "I hope she's not hurt."

"She's hurt," Pete said flatly. Hawken stared at him, afraid to ask what injury Pete had seen that had escaped him. "Meggie's had the world by the tail since she took her first step. She always believed she could handle anything. For instance, when Uncle Ira insisted that Tildy marry a rich Yankee, everyone said behind his back that he was being unreasonable, but we just talked. Meggie got on her pony and rescued her.''

"So now she ran into something that got the best of her," Hawken said, half to himself.

"Exactly. She's finding out how bad men can be."

And I'm one of the bad ones, Hawken thought. He touched the side of his face. The numbness had worn off and it was probably turning black and blue.

"The bastard got a poke at you before you slammed him," Pete said sympathetically. "Ask Granny for a poultice."

"In a while." Hawken cradled his rifle and stepped to the rear of Granny's wagon. Platte shook water from his muzzle and slumped to the ground, drooling on his front paws. "I told your sister I'd stick around. In case the hunter comes back with his friends."

"That man's not coming back with anyone," Pete said roughly. "Here's Pa. You're in for another round of thanks. He just might have a bit of whiskey I don't know about. You look like you could use a slug."

Hawken refused the offer of whiskey until Meggie left the wagon, surrounded and supported by her friends. Meggie must have said something about his bruised face, for Granny laid a sweet-smelling damp cloth on his cheek.

Buffalo roasts were spitted over the fires and the flames sizzled from the dripping fat. Meggie looked around the sewing circle and noted that all the women seemed troubled, despite the prospect of fresh meat. Too bad the buffalo hunter had come and spoiled what should have been a memorable day. She lowered herself cautiously to the blanket, keeping the most tender spots off the ground.

"Matt is furious," Tildy said, poking her needle with great energy. "All the men agreed to abide by the rules before we left Missouri, and then they dash off at the first sight of buffalo. And my fool brothers—"

"I'm certain Josefa isn't permanently lame," Rachel said. "Will bandaged her ankle and Granny gave us a poultice. And—" lids hooded her dark eyes "—your father paddled Josh for riding off on her."

"Kit says all the horses are exhausted. No one can ride tomorrow if we're to keep up the proper pace," Faith said. "To arrive in California before the snow."

"And for nothing!" Tildy exclaimed. "Two buffalo killed, one by Will Hunter, the only man who should have been out there to begin with, and Mr. Hawken's driver, Monty, who just hung out by the river."

Meggie's spirits rose a trifle. Her friends were cranky because of the horses, not her encounter with the buffalo hunter. Perhaps they had forgotten the whole thing. She certainly would forget, as soon as…she glanced quickly, surreptitiously, under the wagon. Yes, Hawken's boots and the butt of his rifle, and the yellow dog, head on his front paws, eyes closed but his ears pricked.

"I'll get *my* patchwork," Meggie said.

Tildy jumped up and pressed her hands on Meggie's shoulders to keep her seated. "I'll get it."

"I can get my own workbag," Meggie muttered at Tildy's back.

Keeping busy would help her forget that moment when the buffalo hunter stood over her, when his hands looped the rope, touching her… Granny had helped her wash herself and her dress, to get rid of the lingering stink.

"The road by the river is smooth as a bricked street,"

Meggie said. "Tomorrow we could ride in my wagon and sew." Faith showed more surprise than a friend should. "Granny thinks, with the bruises on my...arms, I shouldn't ride John Charles for a day or two." The bruises that hurt most were on her rear end, where she landed when the buffalo hunter dragged her off the pony.

Tildy dropped the bag in her lap. Meggie spread out the incomplete Flying Geese block. If she could fly she would have escaped the brute without needing the dog and Hawken. She hated being rescued. A silly goose saved by a hawk.

"Mr. Hawken's worried," Tildy said, rethreading her needle. "He hangs around like a mother hen with one chick."

"Mr. Hawken and Pete have become friends," Meggie said. "Look, if I sew the flying geese around a square, they make a star." Her friends studied the new arrangement and made polite sounds, but none took the hint to change the topic of conversation. A shadow on the hillside suggested the buffalo hunter. Perhaps his horse hadn't killed him. The soft rasp of rope tightening? Only Faith pulling yarn from a skein. Geese in flocks, their long wedges darkening the sky. Hawks soaring alone, circling, spying out their prey, then diving, snatching doomed creatures in their talons.

I got rid of Hawken, Meggie reminded herself. *If I'd paid proper attention, John Charles could have outrun the buffalo hunter's bony horse.*

Hawken tugging frantically at the knots to free her. Hawken on the ground after she swung at him, shocked, babbling words that made no sense at all.

"Tildy," Meggie said, "when you and Matt...I mean Rachel's married, too, so I should ask her...do Matt and Will say foolish things when you're cuddling?"

"That's a very personal question," Faith said. "It hardly seems proper."

Rachel blushed, but Tildy's needle did not hesitate. "Matt can say very foolish things. Once he quoted some law book to show how much he loved me. Why, did that buffalo hunter say silly, loving things?" Tildy gasped and dropped her sewing, then laid a hand on Meggie's arm. "I'm sorry, Meggie. We took an oath we'd not mention that."

"It must have been dreadful," Faith said.

"It was dreadful," Meggie said. "I want to talk about it, at least a little. You see, the whole thing was my fault. I heard the horse coming and thought it was just one of the boys galloping out to see the buffalo. And then the rope fell over my head and the next thing I knew, he'd pulled me off John Charles." Stunned, as shocked as Hawken had been a few minutes earlier when she slapped him and knocked him down. "He smelled like death." She tried to match her seams, but could not bring the edges even.

"He yelled when the yellow dog grabbed his arm, and reached for his knife, but the sheath slanted the wrong way. So he went for the rifle, but Mr. Hawken got there first and clubbed him. I suppose Mr. Hawken was afraid to shoot, with his dog in the way."

"Mr. Hawken must have looked like a guardian angel," Rachel breathed.

A guardian angel? Angels went about in white robes and had fluffy little wings. Hawken had arrived more like a whirlwind, a fury of anger and vengeance.

"You're talking of angels, so you must be speaking of my wife." Will leaned around the wagon and smiled at Rachel. "The meat's nigh done. You asked me to warn you."

"Time I mixed the biscuits," Rachel said.

"We've run out of wood," Faith said, getting to her feet. "I must remind the boys to go out for buffalo chips."

"Who said foolish things to you?" Tildy demanded when they sat alone.

"Mr. Hawken."

"I doubt it's of any significance," Tildy said, making more twists in the thread than a knot demanded. "Women aren't the only ones who say strange things when they're frightened. Even Pete, he dashed about asking who had brandy to calm Mr. Hawken's nerves, but I suspect Pete needed the brandy just as much. It's an awful strain to see a man die, and to kill him—"

"Mr. Hawken didn't kill the buffalo hunter," Meggie said. "The horse did." Tildy shrugged, dismissing the correction as irrelevant. "The horse killed him while Mr. Hawken untied me and put me on John Charles."

Meggie put her hands to her face, afraid she might burst into tears. She longed to be back in Hawken's strong arms, feel him lifting her onto John Charles, leading her to safety.

She could ask him why he had done it, after she had been cruel to him, calling him crazy. They really did not know each other, and for a man to put himself into that kind of danger, in storybooks men did that kind of thing for love, and he couldn't love her, not the way Tildy and Matt loved each other, or Rachel and Will.

"I think supper's ready," Tildy said, drawing Meggie from the memory.

"First slice for Hawken," Pa was saying when she approached the fire. "Without him, we'd be chasing that buffalo hunter and Meggie clear back to the Big Blue River."

"First to Platte," Hawken said. He threw the chunk of meat to the dog. "He's the real hero." From the dip of his chin, he seemed as shy as he had been when he stood beside her and John Charles. At least he did not strut around, bragging how he'd dashed in to save her. He was honest, the dog had rescued her, and she admired him for that.

"Now, Mr. Hawken, you sit down," Ma said, bustling up with a plate heaped with bread still warm from the baking. Meggie recalled—had it only been a few hours ago?—digging through the load for the reflector oven. "Butter?" Ma asked cheerfully. "Mrs. Burdette churned today."

Hawken sank to the ground in his controlled way, cross-legged. Meggie squatted to be on his level.

"I haven't thanked you, Mr. Hawken," she said.

"No thanks needed," he muttered toward the plate of food. Meggie stared at her own serving, sure she could not swallow a bite. Meat, bread, a small piece of potato. The very last of the potatoes, the ones her mother had been hoarding for the Fourth of July dinner.

"I'm sure you would have ridden to the rescue of anyone attacked by that man," Ma said. "But since it was Meggie you'll have to bear with our gratitude."

Meggie wished she could sink into the ground. If she had not ridden ahead of the wagons, the buffalo hunter would never have come back looking for her. If she had stayed at the wagons, or with the other women, the buffalo hunter would have had no chance to attack her. It was her fault that Hawken had been exposed to danger, and if he had been hurt, or killed, everyone would have suffered for her stupidity.

She caught Hawken staring at her, worried, questioning. She owed this man her life, and hadn't the slightest

idea how to thank him. She put down her still-full plate
and stumbled away from the fire.

"Meggie, don't leave. I expect you to cut the pie,"
Ma called. It was not Ma's hand on her shoulder.

"Miss MacIntyre, if there's anything I can do," Hawken whispered, "it must be dreadful, that memory."

"It doesn't go away," she said. "I try to stop shaking,
but I just get settled and it all starts again. There's nothing you can do. Go back to your supper."

"You asked me to stay near, to protect you."

"I did?"

"When we got to camp I helped you off your pony
and you asked me not to leave, for fear the man would
return."

Meggie tried to recall the moment, but everything between finding herself on John Charles and Granny's
soothing touch was hazy. If she had asked Hawken to
stick around, she could not ask him to leave her alone,
or her family would accuse her of being fickle and ungrateful.

"I'm in your debt," she said. "If there's anything I
can do for you—"

"You can come to the fire and try to eat a little. You're
worrying your mother and father."

He took the fingers of her right hand in his, a gentle
touch, and she let him lead her back to the fire. She
managed to steady her hands long enough to cut the pie,
only a little burned on one side. She set aside the best
piece for Hawken. The best of everything for Hawken.
Except for his quick dash up the hill, the buffalo hunter
would have carried her off.

She would never in her whole life forget his words as
the rope cut into her arms.

*"I'll poke you first. Then my partners. You'll earn me
all the hides so I get to Independence rich."*

Meggie lay on top of her blankets, too frightened to
close her eyes. Pa had pitched the tent a long way outside
the wagon circle, and Pete had trudged off to take his
place in the first night watch. She had to stay alert, in
case someone untied the puckering string, or hands
closed on the tailgate. A horse neighed, startling her upright.

"Forget, forget, forget," she commanded. She
plumped her feather pillow, rearranged the blankets.
Think of something else. Her patchwork. How many flying geese in each strip for a full-sized quilt? Forty. Forty
hawks. No geese.

The buffalo hunter's fingers had curled like claws...
Don't think about the hunter. Think about Hawken
swinging his rifle. His lips had been pulled back, and his
eyes stretched wide, like a man trying to win a weight-
lifting contest. Then beside her, untying the ropes, his
eyes squinty, like a man focusing on the horizon, but
Hawken had been looking at her, peering deep, asking
questions with his eyes that she could not answer because
she did not understand.

Why had he risked his life to rescue her?

She crawled to the rear of the wagon and loosened the
puckering string so she could see the stars. Before she
could look up, she saw a shadow, someone walking toward the wagons...her wagon. She put her hand over her
mouth. She must not yell for help until absolutely certain,
or everyone would say she was like the boy who cried
wolf.

Pete leaned over the dying fire and poured a cup of
coffee.

"Hawken?" he asked. He faced her, as if Hawken were in her wagon. "Coffee?" The wagon stirred, a weight against the rear wheel, and Hawken moved in the starlight, his buckskin fringe creating an undulating silhouette.

"That fellow's not coming back and you know it," Pete said. "His horse stove him up, rolling on him."

"She asked me to stay. I didn't want her to wake and find no one on guard."

"I'll sleep under her wagon," Pete said.

"So will I," Hawken said.

"No need."

"Yes, there is. Meggie wouldn't have been out alone but for me."

"You?"

"I saw her run to her pony, to keep the boys from taking him after the buffalo. I followed—" he coughed "—followed Captain Hull, thought I might be of help, and the pony was skittish...I'm afraid it ended with my arms about her."

Pete sputtered into his coffee. He might as well have howled in disbelief. "My sister? You hugged my flat-chested little sister?" Meggie touched her breasts. She was not flat chested. Just...small.

"She let me know I'm to stay away from her."

"How?" Pete gurgled, caught with coffee in his mouth.

A long silence. "She slapped me."

"Sounds like Meggie."

"Please don't tell your folks. I want them to think well of me. I didn't mean...I mean it won't happen again."

"Don't suppose it will. Hugging Meggie must be like throwing your arms around the gatepost. It's just as well that Ma doesn't make her behave like a lady, because no man's interested in such a beanpole. Might as well let her have her fun where she can find it. She'll have to fill out a bit before any man asks her to roll in the blankets.''

Meggie crawled back to her bed, smoothed the pillow and lay down. She touched her arms where the rope had left bracelets of red and purple. If men didn't find her attractive, why had the buffalo hunter backtracked to capture her?

Because, she answered her own question with bitter truth, he hadn't seen a woman in months. Maybe a year. Any woman looked just fine to a buffalo hunter.

She would not only remember what had happened, she would welcome the memory and clasp it to her as an antidote to fright. The West was harsher than she had expected. She had peopled it with rough chevaliers, like the men who rode with Captain Frémont. It occurred to her that Frémont's men might not be as gallant as he portrayed them. Maybe they chased women with ropes and he just didn't write it down.

"I will not give up," she muttered. But, she had to accept the men of the West as they came, not as she had imagined them. No more riding ahead of the scout, no more talking to strangers.

The wagon bounced a trifle.

"Sorry," said Hawken's voice from beneath her. "Bumped the wheel."

"It's all right," she whispered.

He would stay, as he had promised. He might look like a buffalo hunter in his buckskins, but Hawken wouldn't hog-tie her and carry her off. She imagined him lifting himself onto the tailgate with his cat-like grace, sliding under the canvas.

Her weary mind found a strange equity in the idea.

Chapter Six

Rivulets of sweat ran down Hawken's forehead, into his eyes. He stepped to the side of the road, twisted his bandanna and knotted it around his head. He had to run to reclaim the place he had assigned himself, well ahead of his own wagons, within sight of Meggie and her grandmother.

He adjusted his stride to the patient trudge of the oxen, and regretted having hurried. Sweat tickled his ribs and soaked his hunting shirt. He lifted his arms, flapped them the way an overheated chicken flaps its wings and caught a faint whiff of buffalo hunter. The smell of sweat and greasy leather had never bothered him before. Last summer he had worn the same set of buckskins from the day he left Independence until he returned. Perhaps they'd find Indians camped at Ash Hollow or Fort Laramie, a band with women who could make him a fresh suit of clothes.

Hawken stepped out of the road to mop his forehead. The air seemed thick, almost the density of the river. The teams of his first wagon plodded by, alone. Monty had stopped, his goad propped against his legs as he took a hitch in his belt. Walking fifteen miles a day had trimmed

Monty's portly figure. In Independence only the largest trousers fit him, but now they gathered around his waist like an ill-fitting sack.

Trousers. He'd dressed Les and Monty from the stock acquired for the trading post. Why not clothe himself in the same way? No, he'd made do with buckskins before. He must not waste saleable merchandise. If he opened the bundles once, much easier to yield at the next temptation. A new bandanna, instead of washing the ones he owned.

The heat won't last forever, he told himself. In fact, those flat-bottomed clouds might hold rain. Or at least a cooling breeze. But Lord! it was hot, the air clinging, weighing heavier by the minute. The sun glared white, bleaching all color from its quarter of the sky. Were the clouds heavier in the west or was that wishful thinking? He sped up a trifle, to eventually catch Meggie and Granny.

"What do you think—?" he began. Meggie flinched and danced away, her face pale, then bright red. "Sorry, I should have called out."

"I'm just a bit nervy," she said. "I'll get over it."

"What do you think of those clouds? Are they heavier in the west? A rainstorm, maybe?"

"We can hope," Granny said.

"Hope what?" Captain Hull asked, looking like a gray ghost. He fished for a bandanna and mopped his brow, turning his face into a tapestry of gray, tan and moist black.

"Rain," Granny said.

Hull shook his head. "More likely just thunder and lightning. Sampson rode in, says we'll catch up with the Oregon party at noon. There's a spring of clear water above the river, plenty for all, but we'll stop a distance from it to fix our dinner. One of their men suffered an accident and there's to be a funeral. Hawken, tell your men to unhitch and cook as quietly as possible.''

Meggie closed her eyes and bit her lips, and Hawken wished for a miracle to relieve her of the bad memory.

"It was an unnecessary and stupid death,'' Hull continued, turning his hat in his hands. "He objected to his wife cooking with buffalo chips and set out to gather wood on the island.'' He pointed to the line of timber beyond half a mile of water. "For most of the distance the water's two feet deep, but a swift current runs near the middle. It swept him away. They found his body this morning.''

"I'll speak to Monty and Les,'' Hawken said. "But they'll probably stay out of sight with strangers about.''

He lagged to let Monty and Les catch up, explained the need for solemnity, then trotted back to resume his position. Meggie hurried to meet him, and he felt a little guilty that he had left her unattended.

"Granny asks you to join her—and Tildy and Captain Hull—for dinner. It's buffalo stew and flapjacks.''

The MacIntyre family's thanks would be complete only after he'd eaten with each division. "Tell Granny I'll be delighted. And warn her, the dog will tag along.'' Meggie fell in beside him, meeting his pace by adding a little hop every third step. He slowed down.

"Granny expects Platte. She saved a bone. She says he should have a whole roast to himself for his heroism.'' The next hop carried her ahead. She said nothing for the next thirty seconds as she adjusted her stride to his new pace.

"Granny meant to celebrate. She packed essence of lemon and was going to make lemonade. But now, with the misfortune of the Oregon people, it hardly seems suitable.''

''Buffalo stew and flapjacks will be celebration enough,'' Hawken said. ''Besides, Granny should save her lemon until we reach the Rockies. Lemonade's better with snow and ice, or with the water from Soda Springs.''

''Have you been to Soda Springs?'' Meggie asked eagerly. ''Does soda water truly bubble up from the ground? And beer?''

''Better soda water than you find in a restaurant. Beer Spring?'' He laughed, recalling last summer's argument among teamsters and mountain men. ''I don't think it tastes like beer, but when you've been in the Rockies for years—'' he shrugged ''—who's to say?''

''I can hardly wait. And Ice Slough? Does ice really last through the summer?''

''Almost as good as an icehouse.''

''Last night I decided…no buffalo hunter will spoil this trip for me.''

He noted the firm set of her mouth gave a jut to her chin, blunting the point of the heart. The determined expression in her eyes…he concentrated on the road before him. ''I was the first person in Pikeston to say I would follow Mr. Godfroy and Mr. Sampson to California. Besides, that hunter coming back, it was my fault. I acted like a wild woman. Even you thought…'' Her voice trailed off and she seemed to expect him to complete the sentence.

''I did not think!'' he exclaimed. A quick smile restored the suggestion of a heart, but also said she disbelieved his protest.

''I couldn't sleep last night until I made myself remember. Everything. But—'' she laughed ''—are you sure I asked you to stick by and protect me?''

"Just as we reached the wagons, I lifted you off John Charles." *Don't mention the embrace. Don't let your mind dwell on the weight of her body against yours.*

"I can't remember, but if you say so..." They walked five paces in silence. "I didn't thank you."

"I'm sure you did."

"Oh, I may have said 'thank you,' but there should be more than that." She narrowed her eyes against the brilliance of the sky, changing their color to black. "I'll think of something," she muttered, and her face bloomed so rosy beneath her tan that the freckles disappeared in the russet glow. She was still muttering when she dashed off to rejoin her grandmother.

Hawken slowed, startled by the hollow feeling in his chest. It came when she deserted him, as if she carried part of him away. He walked, he breathed, his heart beat, but still he felt empty.

Love? he thought with alarm. He had no idea what symptoms to watch out for, because he'd guarded against the emotion for three years. No danger, said a small voice. No danger that Meggie will fall in love with you. She's a brave woman. When she learns the truth about you she will dismiss you as a coward.

Far ahead a file of men climbed a sand hill, six of them bent under the weight of a narrow load. The funeral procession. This early in the journey emigrants took time for civilized rituals, duplicating as closely as possible what they'd do at home. The Oregonians succeeded rather well, except that the burial crew did not bother to hide their shovels. No women in the procession. They must be at the wagons comforting the widow. Poor woman, bereft of support.

Hull did not bother to direct the wagons off the road. "I believe we should send a deputation," the captain said, hooking a thumb over his shoulder. "I'll go as captain. Hawken—" he looked around to see who else stood nearby "—Jim Mac, come here. A few of us should attend the rites."

Hawken felt awkward in his buckskins. The Oregon men had trimmed their beards and changed their clothes. Two actually wore top hats. A man in a black clawhammer coat stood at the edge of the open grave, reading from a book. Hawken lingered at the rear of the crowd, far enough back that he could not quite make out the words, but he knew the cadence of the burial service and the rhythm of prayer. He bowed his head. Instead of praying, he puzzled why men packed silk hats for a five-month journey through wilderness. Inappropriate clothing hinted at wagons loaded with other nonsense. But then, he'd had the same suspicions when he saw Meggie's chickens, and they—

"Amen," said the speaker. Half a dozen men bent to the task of filling the grave. A man came forward with a short plank, suitably if crudely engraved.

"You're from the party that just rolled in?" one of the top-hatted men asked.

"We came to offer our condolences—" Hull began, but Top Hat cut him off.

"I'm Captain Moran. Cooper leaves a wife and two little boys, with no other family along. She's joining her kinfolks in Oregon." He lowered his voice. "Her family's prominent on the Coast. Gossip has it her father may be the first governor of the territory. But, you see, there's no suitable single man in our company to marry the widow. Just hired hands. I thought someone with you…she has a fine wagon, four yoke of oxen, and two milk cows, plus a saddle mule. And isn't bad looking."

Hawken shrank behind Hull and Jim Mac. "Are there bachelors of good family with you?"

"I'll mention it," Hull said, smoothing his beard in a gesture that Hawken had learned covered indecision.

"So there *are* potential husbands. How many?" Moran asked insistently. Hull shrugged instead of answering. "If you're willing, our parties can travel together for a spell. Until something's arranged. A lone woman can't yoke the oxen or hitch them, so she's a burden on everyone."

"Indeed," Hull said, still stroking his beard.

"The new husband will join us, of course, to Oregon, not California. Mrs. Cooper's family offers a great future."

Hull turned on his heel and plunged down the hill, ignoring the winding path marked by the funeral procession. Hawken and Jim Mac struggled to keep up with his long legs. He waited for them on the flat.

"Well, Hawken, here's your chance," Hull said. "An influential wife and a ready-made family."

"No. I'll let Pete MacIntyre have the prize."

"Pete's with me and his ma, heading for California," Jim Mac said roughly. "Godfroy's free to marry, although I doubt a political family would be thrilled by a son-in-law who's trapped in the Rockies for twenty years and can't read and write." He grinned.

"My two bullwhackers don't mention having wives," Hawken said, pleased that Jim Mac made light of the whole affair. "Even if they did, it wouldn't be legal, between slaves."

"Be serious," Hull snapped. "Captain Moran's offering us the opportunity to travel with eighteen wagons as far as Fort Hall. I counted twenty men and near-grown boys about that grave. We're sixteen men, and that counts Josh and Kit. Hawken, at least look at the woman. Mar-

ried to her you won't be stuck in a trading post with no
company from October to May. How old are you, anyway?''

"I wouldn't fit with a prominent family," Hawken said
to deflect the question of his age. "Let's put it to Pete."

"Pete's only twenty-two. Too young to carry the burden of children," Jim Mac said. "And his trade—wagons
and carriages—he's better off in California where
there're established settlements."

"Reid!" Hawken exclaimed. "He doesn't have money
and plays second fiddle to his brother in England."

"I doubt the daughter of a maybe-territorial governor
will impress the son of a lord, money or no," Hull said,
frowning. "And he probably needs his brother's permission to marry."

The odor of stew wafted from Granny's wagon. Hawken angled in that direction.

"Hawken!" Captain Hull barked his name, an order
from an officer to an underling. Hawken turned slowly,
slouching, to show Hull his military rank had no meaning
on the trail. Hull got the message, his face relaxed and
he sighed.

"Can I tell Captain Moran we'll all pitch in and help
Mrs. Cooper? That you and Pete…after all, your men do
all the driving and even cook for you, and Jim Mac can
manage without Pete occasionally."

Hawken turned the proposal over in his mind. If the
widow wasn't too clinging… "I'm going only as far as
Bear River," he reminded Hull.

"By that time permanent arrangements will have been
made," Hull said.

"How permanent arrangements?" Hawken chal-
lenged. "Pete or me? Godfroy? Reid may be your bullwhacker and take orders about the animals and the road,

but he'll laugh in your face if you propose he marry the woman. Or maybe Tole will give permission for Kit—''

''We're not alone on the trail,'' Hull said a bit weakly. ''Other parties will catch up, or we'll meet summer hunters at Fort Laramie.''

''I'm hungry,'' Hawken said. The odor of browning flapjacks and boiling coffee joined the smell of stew. He found Hull walking right beside him, resented his persistence, then remembered the meal was being served at Hull's fire. Granny, Hull and his wife, Reid—and there, turning the flapjacks, Meggie.

''So will you lend a hand?'' Hull asked in a low voice.

''Yes. Count me in if the Oregonians take their turns.''

The meat had stewed until it fell apart, the flapjacks were light as feathers, the coffee, made from spring water, left not the slightest trace of sand in the bottom of the cup. Hawken was on his second helping when Captain Moran approached, leading a woman. A young woman with cheeks scoured red from weeping, clad in a black dress that did not fit. So young she had not packed mourning clothes and had to borrow. Her hands twisted at her waist and the gold ring on the left winked in and out of the pale sunlight. Hawken lifted his face to the sky, uneasy at confronting such intense sorrow. High, wispy clouds. Forerunners of a storm for sure.

''Mrs. Lila Cooper,'' Captain Moran said. Hull handled the introductions. Mrs. Cooper looked at the ground. She does not want a husband, Hawken thought. At least not right now.

Hull proposed a rotation of men to help, pointing first at Reid and Hawken, then at Pete, far distant at his family's dinner fire. When Mrs. Cooper understood they promised assistance, not a wedding, her sobbing sigh of relief could have been heard on the other bank of the

Platte. Hawken turned back to find Meggie ladling another batch of hotcakes. She stared at him, then at Mrs. Cooper's retreating figure.

"Better tell Pete we've made arrangements," Hull said. "Relieve Jim Mac's mind."

Meggie's eyes flew open, she dropped the spoon in the bowl, scattering drops of batter into the fire. "Hawken, come with me, we'll talk to Pete and then you can warn your men they may be called on for extra duties."

Monty and Les lounged on the shady side of the wagon, slicing meat from the roast left from breakfast. "Any men in that party looking for us?" Monty asked.

"Sorry, forgot to ask," Hawken said. "I'll find out in a bit, when I hitch the widow's oxen. Hull and their captain agreed, we'll pitch in until she finds a husband."

"You thinking in that line, boss?" Les asked.

"No. I'm not a marrying man."

"Live on the Bear River," Les said, flipping another strip of half-raw buffalo into his mouth. "On the fat of the land, with fine Indian women to take care of us."

"Fine Indian women marry men who keep their tepee supplied," Hawken said. "Monty shot the buffalo, not you."

A shadow on the grass preceded Pete stepping around the wagon, his finger on his lips. He pointed toward the river.

"I'm not happy about this arrangement," Pete said the moment they had walked out of earshot. "That woman will start thinking up little chores to keep us around. I have enough to do, my family has three wagons, and anything that goes wrong with *any* wagon—now with the Oregonians, thirty-four—the yell goes up. 'Pete Mac-Intyre!'"

"Mrs. Cooper doesn't want a husband. She's overwhelmed with grief."

"Give her two or three weeks," Pete said with desperate cynicism. "Wait until we're in the mountains and the nights get cold. And the man who's tempted, he's trapped, for they've got a preacher along. He read the funeral."

"You'll be tempted?" Hawken asked.

Pete scrunched his mouth to one side. Hawken waited for a nod, but it did not come. "I'm going to California," Pete said. "Pikeston was about as exciting as a church ladies' ice-cream social. Step out of line with a gal, a father's at your back with a gun. I figure on sowing plenty of wild California oats before I settle down. But you're older, and spending your winters in Independence, you must have your belly full of dance halls and fancy women."

"I won't marry her." The moment had come to be honest. "I can't."

Pete whistled. "Running away from a woman?" he asked, awe lifting the last word. Hawken grabbed Pete's arm and steered him farther from the wagons, right down to the riverbank. A creek wandered from the spring and debouched in a tiny patch of clear water, whorls of crystal-blue blending into the Platte's tan.

"Have you ever heard of not remembering?"

"I've known many a fellow who can't remember how he got home at night, he was so soaked—"

"No, this has nothing to do with drink. I can't remember, nothing beyond about three years ago. One evening in May, 1845, I walked up to the barracks at Fort Leavenworth, a scarecrow, carrying a Hawken rifle. I didn't know my name or where I came from, and still don't. The soldiers called me Hawken—"

"Because of the gun," Pete said, his fingers rasping across the growth of beard on his chin.

"I worked for the army, driving a team, thinking in a few days or weeks my memory would come back. The sawbones at the fort said it would. But it didn't. Two summers I drove a wagon to the Rockies with supplies. I don't know how old I am, I don't know if I have a wife, I—"

Pete grabbed his arm. "You can't marry the widow because you may have a wife back in the states?"

"Yes." Hawken tried to dislodge Pete's grip, but fingers dug into his sleeve like a claw.

"Then what the hell were you doing smooching my sister?" Hawken dodged Pete's first swing but failed to see the second coming before it crunched on his left shoulder. Agonizing pains shot down his arm and into his chest. He staggered, but saw the double punch had left Pete's face exposed. Hawken's right found the scratchy jaw.

"Filthy bastard," Pete growled, coming with another right on the side of Hawken's head. Tumbling white stars blocked his vision, but he could track Pete by his snarl. "Whoring devil." Hawken pushed a fist toward the sound and felt satisfactory contact on a soft body, heard a whoosh of breath. He staggered backward, out of the reach of Pete's flailing arms; his heel caught nothing but thin air. He hit the water full-length, wondering that it should be solid as a granite ledge.

Hawken cleared mud from his eyes and crouched below the bank, using the tall grass as a shield. *Pete will be waiting to throw me back in.* Pete rocked back and forth on his hands and knees, moaning. Hawken spat sand out of his mouth and hoisted himself up the bank. Pete made a lunging crawl to trip him up, but Hawken side-stepped.

Pete hung his head, panting like a dog.

"If I were dishonest I'd marry the widow and go to Oregon. But one day I'd meet a man who knew me years ago."

"Why do you think...?" The words came on one exhalation, not long enough to complete the question.

"Why do I think I was married?" Pete nodded. "Because I like women." And haven't had one in a long time, Hawken added to himself. No need to reveal the full scope of the past three years. The gambling hall girls perched on his knee while he dealt the monte cards. Water ran down Hawken's legs, filling his boots. It streamed on his ribs and collected in his breechcloth. He ignored the discomfort, stood over Pete, waiting for him to recover his breath.

"I don't bother respectable women. No matter how anxious I get, your sister's safe, and so is Mrs. Cooper."

"I'm not marrying the widow," Pete choked.

"Neither am I. So that leaves Reid, very unlikely, or we all tend to her, polite as can be, but run like hell when she stands too close."

"Sorry I hit you, but you deserve it."

"Probably." The sodden leather dragged on his arms and legs, and the soaked breechcloth—this must be how a baby feels! He had stocked dozens of trousers and shirts, and packed them on top, safe from damp when they pulled through streams. No need to upset the whole load.

Hawken stripped in the space usually occupied by the cooking gear. He crawled forward, untied the parcels and selected without paying attention to size. The trousers proved to be a bit tight. He thought of finding others, then recalled Monty's decreasing bulk. By next week the pants would fit.

The shirt was too big so he let it hang free like a tunic, and cinched it about his waist with his wet belt. He must remember to dry and oil the knife, or it would rust, but right now he'd better talk to Hull. The captain should hear the truth from him—why he could not marry the widow—rather than from Pete's excited gossip.

Jim Mac's wagons lay between him and the captain, and he did not feel inclined to meet either Pete or Meggie. He swung wide to the left.

"Howdy," Jim Mac called. Hawken couldn't avoid turning in his direction. "Come here." Pete huddled between two wagons, one hand nursing his jaw. He looked hungover.

"Now," Jim Mac said, "you boys had a disagreement—Pete won't say over what—but you shake hands. There's not enough of us to give way to hard feelings, and from what Pete says, the fight ended in a draw."

Hawken decided it cost him nothing to bolster Pete's ego. "That's not true. I got the worst of it. I landed in the river." He extended his hand, shook without pressure when he noticed Pete's bloody knuckles. "Got to see Captain Hull."

He fled, forgetting to put distance between himself and the wagons, and nearly stumbled over Meggie's legs. She sat beneath the wagon, playing with the kittens.

"Will you marry the widow?" she whispered, her head bent over the ball of fur in her lap. Her fingers scratched behind the tiny ears and under the white chin. Hawken's left knee quivered. "She's a pretty thing, but to make a woman marry when she's in mourning, that's horrible."

"Pete and I will help her, so she doesn't have to marry

right away.'' Meggie raised her head, her mouth fell open and her eyes widened.

Hawken wondered what astonished her? That men could be kind to a woman, without expecting to bed her? Blast Meggie! He ran the length of the wagon train, but the captain yelled "Chain up!" before Hawken reached him.

"Captain, there's something—"

"Hawken, you get the widow hitched. Moran will lend a hand for now, and tonight we'll draw up a schedule.''

Hawken wandered aimlessly among the eighteen wagons, got his bearings when he saw the black-clad figure standing alone, except for two small children clinging to her skirts. Meggie, in a similar fix, would be out rounding up her teams, he thought. Blast Meggie!

Moran arrived with the oxen. Hawken grabbed one end of a yoke. Strenuous exercise would banish the image of auburn hair and slender fingers caressing kittens.

"Thank you. Thank you so much," the widow said in a voice barely audible above the shouts of the men.

"Who's to drive?" Hawken asked Moran.

"She can. She did it before, whenever her husband took it into his head to ride off on his mule." Moran's tone condemned Cooper. He left Hawken the job of hooking the chains. Mrs. Cooper lifted the two children into the wagon.

"Don't let them stand up," Hawken warned. "They might be thrown out if the oxen move of a sudden.''

"Yes," she said. Her damaged eyes met his, almost invisible above her swollen cheeks. "Thank you. I'm sorry, but I don't know your name.''

"Hawken.''

She blinked unsteadily, her matted lashes catching on the lower lids. "Thank you, Mr. Hawken." She extended her hand. "I'm sorry you must neglect your own work to care for me." As he grasped her fingers a voice circled in his head, meek and gentle. *Care for me.*

"My friends are setting out," he said. He dodged through the maze of wagons, running toward the familiar voice, wishing he might fall on his knees, beg it to stay, expand, envelop him. A meek woman. He had cared for a meek woman, had abandoned her in a maze of selfish terror. Leaving her with ravaged face and exhausted tears, like Mrs. Cooper.

The wagons moved around him, and in their wake came a breeze. He took off his hat to welcome it. Rain? Yes, streamers trailed from a cloud to the south. Why did he remember now? Why not before he had committed himself and his money to the post on Bear River?

Women. That's the difference. Respectable women. For three years he had associated with tavern girls and the women who dealt monte and faro in the gambling halls. Hardly the type to bring memories of his wife. What a fool he had been, hanging out with tarts! Sometime between now and Bear River, one day when he helped Mrs. Cooper, he would remember.

He would sell his goods to the first buyer and head back to Missouri. He would reach the frontier settlements by fall, and before the snow flew he would be in the bosom of his family, doting on his gentle wife, doing everything in his power to make up for the lost years.

The afternoon was half gone when Hawken recalled he had not talked to Captain Hull. Tonight, when everyone had settled in, he would manage a private conversation with the captain.

Chapter Seven

Meggie snagged the three kittens, shoved them into the nook where they spent their days and held her hands over their escape route. "You're nothing but a nuisance," she said. "I must talk to Tildy, and here I am, tending cats." The wagon jerked, the kittens mewed and pushed against the lattice of her fingers. They had grown into gangly adolescents. This morning they had clawed their way up the wagon cover. Before long they would be scaling the tailgate and eyeing the world outside. Meggie upended a washbasin over the nest, not a good solution because it confined Tabby, who had sense enough to stay in a moving wagon.

Meggie gathered her skirt, perched on the tailgate and, when the wagon slowed at a rough spot, jumped down.

"Tildy," she called outside Granny's wagon.

"I'm here." The door swung open, Meggie jumped on the steps and leaned inside.

"Have you seen Mr. Hawken all dressed up?" she asked, curling her toes in the moccasins to cling to the step.

"No. Not since dinner," Tildy said sharply.

"He's got new clothes on. Wool trousers and a shirt."

Meggie bit her lower lip, torn between wanting to know what was going on and bearing Tildy's teasing. "Is he planning to marry that widow woman?" she asked. She grinned, dismissing the affair as a farce.

"Matt and Captain Moran asked men to volunteer to help her. Matt feels we're safer traveling with the Oregonians." She extended a hand and Meggie stepped into the wagon.

"Sit down," Tildy said, shoving aside bundles of dry leaves. She twisted her hands together. "I'm sorry, Meggie," she whispered, "I lied when I said I hadn't seen Mr. Hawken since dinner. But it's terrible to say, Pete and Mr. Hawken had a fight. Down by the river. They beat on each other. They thought they were alone, but Granny and I went collecting willow bark."

"A fight? Why should they fight?" It must have happened before Hawken came by the wagon. Come to think of it, Pete had made himself scarce, and she had been so taken up with the kittens.... Had Hawken's face been marked? She'd been distracted by the new trousers and shirt and had hardly looked at his face.

"I hope Pete didn't hurt Mr. Hawken. He's already got the bruise from the buffalo hunter," Tildy said.

"No, I did that."

"You what?" Tildy nearly fell off the cot.

"He...he put his arms around me, so of course I slapped him," Meggie stammered. Tildy smiled her I-told-you-so smile.

"I suppose Mr. Hawken and Pete were fighting over who gets the widow," Meggie said. "It's horrible, not giving her a say in the matter. Poor thing, her eyes so swollen she can't tell a man from a muskrat."

"I don't know why they fought," Tildy said, "but just a few minutes ago your pa told Matt that Pete and Mr.

Hawken had had a disagreement, but they'd shaken hands. It's best the whole thing be hushed up, just a misunderstanding," she added in a whisper. "What I don't understand, neither one claims he won. Pete told Uncle Jim that Hawken won, but Hawken said Pete had the best of it, that Pete threw him in the river. But I saw the fight and Mr. Hawken laid Pete out with a blow to his stomach. Mr. Hawken fell in the river on his own."

"Mr. Hawken's both generous and clumsy," Meggie said, using sarcasm to disguise her bewilderment at this chaotic recital. "He got dressed up to impress the widow, so she'll marry him." She felt a strong urge to cry, and couldn't figure out why.

"If Pete and Mr. Hawken fought over the widow," Tildy mused, "wouldn't Mr. Hawken brag that he won?" She smiled suddenly, as if the solution had just revealed itself. "Does Pete know Mr. Hawken embraced you?"

"Yes," Meggie said. And Pete had likened her figure to a gatepost. A helpful brother he was!

"So maybe Pete was defending your honor."

"I can defend my own honor," Meggie said. "Pete should leave my affairs alone."

"Do you hear rain?" Tildy asked.

"What?" Meggie asked, startled by the unexpected question. Tildy studied the wagon cover, as if it were transparent and she could see the weather on the other side. One loud plop, a whisper of wind and a rustle, like a taffeta train on a carpeted floor. "There's one way to find out." She threw open the door and stuck her head out. Only a thin drizzle, but a black cloud obscured the southern sky. "I'd better go home before it pours."

Meggie jumped down without touching the steps. Her mother leaned from the wagon, handing Pa and Pete their long oilcloth coats. Farther down the line a man wrestled with a flapping cloak. Only his legs were visible, but she knew the legs, even in wool trousers.

"I wish I had a waterproof," Meggie said.

"You have no need to be out in the rain," her mother said. "Climb in before you're soaked to the skin. The road's smooth and we can get the mending done. Here, your father caught his trousers on the chain hook."

She stuck a finger through a large, triangular rip halfway up the leg, and shoved a selection of scraps toward Meggie as she climbed over the tailgate. Meggie selected the sturdiest fabric and laid a square of it beneath the hole. "This doesn't match," she said.

"There's no need for a match here on the Platte," Ma said. She laughed. "The only requirement is that our clothes stand between us and the elements. How my standards have fallen! Three months ago I would no more have let your father go into Pikeston wearing poorly patched trousers than I would have cursed in church."

"Things change on the frontier," Meggie said.

"So many strangers, with strange ways, and nothing can be said, for we depend on each other. I wonder what that poor widow—I believe she was properly reared, for she cobbled together a mourning costume—what must she think of us with our skirts hemmed to our boot tops?"

"They've hemmed their skirts, too," Meggie said.

"And Mr. Hawken in his buckskins, hair like an Indian—"

"Mr. Hawken changed into store clothes before he went to tend the widow."

"Perhaps Mr. Hawken saw the clouds building. Buckskins sag and stretch when they get damp."

The river, Meggie recalled. He changed because he fell

in the river. The pinched feeling about her heart relaxed. Her fingers clasped the needle with new confidence.

Hawken had not dressed up for the widow.

She found she could take small stitches, although the jolting of the wagons made them irregular. She turned the leg inside out to finish the patch.

"I found some blue calico in my workbag," Ma said. "Give it to Tildy for her patchwork."

Rain rattled on the wagon cover, louder and louder, until Meggie had to bend close to hear what her mother said. The wagon jolted, jerked forward, then stopped. Meggie crawled over the load and pushed aside the flaps. Pa was shouting, but the teams ignored him. Something hit Meggie in the face. She picked up a white stone the size of a pea.

"Hail!" she cried.

"Get your cloak," Pa yelled. "And a hat. Your ma, too. It'll take all of us to hold the teams."

The hail came like rocks from the sky, stinging her shoulders through the cloak and making hollow clunks on her head. For the first time she saw some advantage in long hair. If it were all piled on top—

"Turn this team to face away from the storm," Pete said in her ear. "I'll get the last wagon." He vanished in the white veil before she had a chance to look for bruises on his face. Meggie hunched her shoulders, grabbed one end of the yoke while Ma hung on the other, guiding the oxen in a broad U-turn.

"Fortunate that the road's so wide," Meggie said, knowing her mother could not possibly hear in the thunder of ice. Once the oxen had their backs to the gale, in the protection of the wagon, they hunched their shoulders and refused to move. Meggie crouched between the wheel team and the wagon, praying that the hail did not cut the canvas to shreds.

Another team and wagon drew up only inches from where she squatted, the driver clinging to an ox that bucked and bellowed in pain. Hail bounced off the canvas like India rubber balls, growing larger by the second, every impact more bruising. The ice no longer bounced on the ground, but buried itself in an inch-thick accumulation.

"Stop! Stop! Stop!" Meggie yelled at the top of her lungs, not daring to address the sky for fear she would be blinded. As if in obedience to her orders, the hail slackened and the size of the ice stones shrank. Within thirty seconds the roar had died to a mutter. She could hear splashes and drips as the ice oozed down the canvas in sluggish rivers.

The driver of the unruly team still clung to the yoke. He shoved back the hood of his cape. One of Hawken's drivers, the man called Les, Meggie saw. He stared at her, eyes bulging, dropped off the yoke, crawled to the other side of the wagon.

"Any damage?" voices asked on all sides. Meggie stood, her legs prickly as the blood rushed through cramped veins. The wagons faced the wrong direction, in no particular order, and the road had vanished under the blanket of white.

She waited by the teams for half an hour, the melting ice soaking through her moccasins, until Captain Hull reassembled the wagons in proper order. By the time they moved on, the wind had stiffened and carried a freezing mist into the faces of the drivers and oxen.

Meggie hung her muddied cloak over the tailgate before she climbed in the wagon. A clot of ice fell from the gathers of her sunbonnet, onto the trousers she had been mending. She pulled off her moccasins, crawled the length of the wagon, examining every inch of the cover for telltale points of light. Everything seemed secure.

Ma had taken shelter in some other wagon, leaving Meggie to her own devices. She went back to her mending, overheard men grumbling, half a conversation between her father and Captain Hull, then an order from Godfroy that sent the wagon off the road. An early stop.

Meggie held the umbrella over the supper fire while her mother fried bacon and made coffee. The sun glowed through a gap in the clouds, a promise of fair weather on the morrow. The drizzle stopped while they ate the hasty supper, and as the clouds withdrew the sky turned velvety dark and the first stars came out. No one seemed inclined to sit around the fire on the sodden ground. Meggie crawled into her wagon, and her knee landed on the roll of blue scraps. She might as well deliver them now, before they got lost in bedding and mending. On their next rest day she must do serious housekeeping in her wagon.

Meggie tiptoed past her parents' silent tent. If they were still awake, they'd hear the slurping her feet made with every step on the wet sand. Matt and Tildy's tent stood a dozen yards outside the wagon circle. The supper fire had burned to embers and there was no light in the wagon where Granny slept, so Meggie headed for the tent. She would talk to Tildy through the canvas, and leave the roll of scraps on the wagon tongue.

"Matt, anything! Anything you want!" Tildy's voice, but more breathless than Meggie had ever heard it. She skidded to a stop.

"Beauty, my beauty!" Matt murmured, a blurred excess of tenderness, far different from his precise voice of command.

They had not heard her, yet. Her feet sank into the

mud, and water seeped in around them. She lifted a foot and the splash sounded loud as thunder. Stay here, or walk away and risk betraying her presence? She hugged herself.

Two barely discernible slurps and a faint scrape. She dug her fingers into her upper arms. A man, the legs of his trousers rubbing together as he walked. A moan from the tent drowned out the tiny sound his boots made.

The buffalo hunters! fear cried.

Pooh! good sense said. If a buffalo hunter tried to ride into camp tonight she'd hear the horse.

"You are so beautiful. Let me do it," Tildy whispered. Do what? What could a woman do? And nearby a man waited... Meggie slammed her hand against her mouth to stem the cry rising in her throat. Her teeth closed around the calico.

"Oh, Matt! Oh, Matt!" Tildy's whispers rose enough to cover any sound her feet might make. Meggie turned around cautiously. The man stood six feet away, a dark bulk.

"My dearest beauty!"

"Deeper, love. Oh my love!"

The figure stepped toward her, Hawken, by the angle of his leg. His fingers grasped her elbow.

"Come away from here," he muttered right in her ear, so close the words felt warm. She let him pull her along, paying no attention to where her feet landed. He slowed and she took longer steps to escape him, but his hand tightened.

"Afraid?" he whispered.

She opened her mouth, found it still full of calico and shook her head violently to get rid of it. "Yes."

"Which, yes or no?" he asked, too obviously amused by the conflict of word and gesture.

"Yes," she snapped.

"Why should loving frighten you? Mrs. Hull enjoys her husband's attention."

"I heard you coming. I'm still nervy, I thought the buffalo hunter had come back."

A comforting arm slid around her waist. "No. No buffalo hunters. What brings you out in the damp?" She experimented leaning toward the arm. Even more comforting.

"I have scraps for Tildy."

"And I must speak to Captain Hull. We're both put off till morning. Perhaps a walk by the river will calm your nerves."

"I suppose." Something needed calming, for below her waist—below his arm—her body foamed like cream under a whisk.

"Has your brother spoken to you? About me?" he asked.

"My brother sulked all afternoon and hardly ate any supper. I hear you slugged him in the stomach, so that may explain his lack of appetite. Why did you two fight?"

"Because I behaved badly toward you, and I apologize."

Behaved badly? The foam surged higher. He must not consider an arm around her waist behaving badly. Where was the line between permissible and forbidden?

"I didn't mind that you put your arms around me," she whispered.

"It truly was an accident."

"I mean, I minded then, but now—" If she could figure a way to step in front of him, he might embrace her. Press his hips against hers and this time she would not panic. He stopped, but kept her at arm's length by grasping her shoulders. The river whispered against the bank, or perhaps it was the sound of the turmoil inside her.

"From now on we must stand clear of each other," he said. "Not that I think poorly of you, Miss MacIntyre, or don't find you tempting, but I'm recalling that I have a wife."

He's crazy. Meggie only half listened to his story of three years when he remembered nothing of his past, of the fragments of memory that came more and more frequently these days, because he was associating with respectable women and men.

"I must be very careful, so when I remember my wife, when I return home, I have less to be ashamed of."

"You have something to be ashamed of?" Meggie asked.

"Three years. And my wife's a gentle, meek creature, and I cared for her." His fingers tightened for a moment, then he stepped away and offered his arm with great formality.

"Nerves settled?" he asked.

"Yes. I'll go to my wagon now." A wife?

"I'm still your guardian," he said, placing a hand lightly on hers.

"The buffalo hunters won't backtrack this far," she said. He was married and hadn't remembered? Impossible.

"That's not what you thought a few minutes ago, Miss MacIntyre."

She clutched the roll of scraps, embarrassed that she had confessed her silly fears to this man. From now on she would beat fear down on her own. By talking, by remembering.

"The buffalo hunter meant to use me for a...he'd sell me to the other men in exchange for their hides."

He stumbled but recovered quickly. "I'll stay near you for a few more days," he said in a softer voice. They were near the wagons. "Until we cross the river, at least."

The widow did not greet Hawken with her usual smile. She teetered on the tongue of her wagon and stared at the river. "Is this the best place to cross?" she asked fearfully. "You've been here before. Is this truly the crossing?"

Men clustered on the shore in small groups, examining the mile of water, shoulders braced so they did not reveal the fear a man dare not openly admit.

"It's the best place," Hawken said. "Don't worry, you'll be in no danger, just sit with your little boys and pretend you're on an ocean voyage."

"Thank you," she said. Hawken pushed back his hat and waited for the curtain to waver. Two days ago the widow's hands had suggested other hands, small and white. Mrs. Cooper stepped off the wagon tongue and he glimpsed bare ankles above the slippers she wore in camp. Rather thick ankles, not so well shaped as Meggie's. He focused on Mrs. Cooper's hands to eradicate that stray thought of Meggie, and waited, hopeful, for a revelation of other female limbs. Meggie had large hands, fingers so long they nearly circled his arm.

My wife's ankles? Perhaps we weren't married. Only betrothed. That would explain his recollection of hands but not ankles. If they had been engaged, after three years had she given up and accepted another offer?

He'd not talk to anyone tonight, and the memory might sort itself out. Captain Hull waylaid him before he reached his camp.

"You've taken wagons across here?" Godfroy asked.

Hawken nodded. "Not emigrants. Traders' wagons."

"Sampson and I crossed with pack mules."

"No one in my party's been so far west," Captain Moran said.

"In other words—" Captain Hull grinned "—Hawken's in charge tomorrow." They all turned to him, expecting something. What?

"The sturdiest, healthiest horse—" Hawken began.

"Meggie's pony's in fine fettle," Sampson said. "She's not ridden much since the buffalo hunter came after her."

Hawken nodded. The thick-limbed pony would be a good mount for exploring the ford. "I'll ride across this evening and find the best route."

"If John Charles will let you," Pete said doubtfully. "He tolerates me on his back, sometimes, but he's so spoiled, Meggie's the only one who can for sure stay on."

"There's the widow's saddle mule," Moran suggested. "It's well rested."

"The mule," Hawken said instantly. Taking John Charles would involve negotiations with Meggie, and he would be tempted to analyze the trim of her ankles and the reach of her hands, contrasting them to stumpy Mrs. Cooper. And his unknown wife.

By the time Moran appeared with the mule the sun lay on the horizon. It was a handsome animal and lavishly equipped. Silver buttons secured the joints of the bridle and weighted the corners of the saddle skirt. Hawken urged the mule into the shallow water with trepidation, wishing he had a little less precious metal under his care.

A hundred yards out, a fast-running channel rose to the stirrups. He should have taken off his boots. He considered turning back, looked over his shoulder and found everyone lined up watching his progress.

"Let's don't fall down and embarrass ourselves," he said to the mule.

Three swift channels, the third one deep and wide. With all the zigzags, a two-mile crossing. Hawken congratulated himself on having something to occupy his mind besides involuntary thoughts of Meggie. Tonight he would lie awake worrying about the river and the wagons.

"What do you find?" Captain Hull asked before Hawken had left the water.

"Caulk the wagon beds, raise them as high as possible and put anything that might be damaged on top of the load. There's a sandbar two-thirds of the way across where we'll double team before crossing the deepest channel." He lifted his soaked feet. "Leave your boots in the wagon, for we'll be treading water most of the morning."

He handed the mule over to Captain Moran, pulled off his boots and headed for his bedroll.

"Mr. Hawken." Meggie spoke with a diffidence he had never heard before. "I know you don't want to talk to me, but I must know. The kittens. Should I make them a new nest, higher in the wagon?"

"Where do you live now?"

"In one of the storage cubbyholes, under the floor."

"Put them high as possible," he said. "Hang a basket from the bows."

"John Charles? Should I tie him behind the wagon or swim him across with the milk cows?"

"We'll need the pony," Hawken said harshly, unexpectedly facing the problem that had nagged at the back of his mind, unawares. "He's sturdy and can buck the current better than most of the horses. In the deepest place men will ride upstream, with ropes, to keep the wagons from turning over.''

Meggie nodded her understanding. "I'll be there," she said soberly.

"No, not you. Pete can ride John Charles, or—"

"I can swim better than Pete," she said proudly.

"No bareback," Hawken warned. "A strong saddle to hold the rider and the rope."

She bit her lip, said nothing, and Hawken took the moment of silence to walk away, pleased that the order had discouraged her.

Meggie pulled on her father's pants and topped them with her plainest bodice. She longed for a blanket coat, like the mountain men wore. Not useful today, she told herself. She would be in the river when the sun came up and what would she do with a coat then?

She didn't need to whistle for John Charles; he stood in the wagon circle. The men were busy blocking up the beds and paid no attention when she lifted out the saddle. Already wagons rolled away, disregarding their regular order of march. Hawken rode the black mule far out in the river, with five wagons right behind him.

"Margaret MacIntyre, what are you thinking of doing?" Granny glared at her.

"Mr. Hawken needs John Charles. You'll be glad I have a rope on your wagon when you reach the deep spot," she called over her shoulder. She splashed past a wagon from the Oregon train, then Godfroy's wagon, the canvas removed in case a wind should rise with the sun. Rachel sat high on a box, her eyes on her husband wading beside the teams.

"Hello," Meggie called.

To Meggie's delight, Rachel looked shocked. It must be the trousers. "Get in with me," Rachel called. "Father says the oxen will be swimming and the wagon afloat."

"Yes. I'll see you there!"

The wagons seemed to move in liquid gold. Hawken, too. Last evening, the first time she had ever seen him mounted, a faint memory had stirred. She had seen him on horseback before. But where?

"One of the finest pictures of a horseman I have ever seen." That was it! The words Captain Frémont used to describe Kit Carson. Hawken rode with the natural ease of the mountain men. Meggie pretended to watch the progress of the wagons, while, for the first time in her life, she frankly studied a man as a physical creature. Agile, his sureness of touch with the mule, the harmony of proportion.... He leaped out of the saddle, negligently exposing the spread of his legs. Heat rose in torrid waves and her face burned.

She slapped John Charles and yelled. The first wagon eased into the deep and she was not there to help. She had to pass through a crowd of milling oxen. The sandbar was not an island, but a bulge in the riverbed covered six inches deep by the golden sheen. Hawken leaned over, hitching an extra team. The new trousers stretched tight across his rear end. She transferred her gaze to the back of his head, because the froth threatened again.

"Tell me what to do," she said to the mop of brown hair. He straightened, spun around and stared as if he saw a ghost.

"My God! I thought your pa would have sense enough to keep you in the wagon!"

"He didn't see me. Only Granny. Tell me what to do."

He looked everyplace but at her, his hands working helplessly, as if they belonged to a someone else.

"You be the guide," he finally said, half-strangled.

"Oh, thank you." She almost grinned, but at the last second managed to frown.

"You stay on the far edge of the sandbar. The drivers head toward you, then have them swing to the right, where we'll line up the oxen. Never, under any circumstances, let a wagon stop before it gets on the bar." His broad gesture encompassed the mile of water between them and the south shore. It had taken on a mother-of-pearl quality. "The bottom's quicksand. If a wagon stops, the current digs the sand from under the wheels and it sinks."

"No one's to stop," she repeated, nodding her head.

"Don't move off the sandbar. If a wagon is having trouble, shout, get help, but don't go yourself." He dismissed her by turning to the wagon dipping in the waves.

"Up here," Meggie yelled to Godfroy. "Turn right," and her breath quickened when Will Hunter followed her directions without question. A wagon she did not know, then the Marshalls and the Burdettes, always neighbors on the trail as they had been in Indiana. The children grasped the naked bows and stared over the river in wonder. The sun poked over the horizon and brightened the surface with a million faceted jewels. The wagons and men and women turned into dark, two-dimensional shapes against the brilliance. Someone called her name and she had to squint against the dazzle.

"You went off without breakfast," Ma said. She leaned from the wagon, offering something. Meggie's hand closed around bread. She stuffed the biscuit into her mouth, then was sorry because it made her thirsty. She told herself to ignore the dryness in her throat, and not waste time contemplating the irony of thirst while surrounded by water. Later she would share the joke with Hawken. Except Hawken did not want to talk to her, and that thought made her feel sad.

Granny's wagon rolled onto the sandbar, carefully attended by Pete and Mr. Reid. A new crop of plants dangled, trailing an odor of herbage. Far away a wagon broke from single file. Three wagons stood at odd angles, and one of them did not move. She yelled in Hawken's direction, but he could not possibly hear over the rush of the river and the shouts of the men. Two more wagons swung out to pass the stranded one.

"Hawken," she yelled before John Charles had splashed halfway across the sandbar. "They're in a tangle." She waved broadly toward the opposite shore. Mr. Reid lifted a telescope to one eye, Hawken pulled himself onto the side of Granny's wagon to get a better view. Meggie admired the way he did it, muscles of arms and shoulders bearing all his weight, his bare toes dangling several inches above the water. He dropped with a splash. Meggie turned away and was discomforted to find her grandmother smiling at her.

"So that's the way it is!" Granny's lips said, although Meggie could not hear.

"It's the widow," Mr. Reid said.

"The oxen are going six ways to Sunday," Hawken snapped. "Meggie, get in with your grandmother. Pete, ride John Charles back and straighten out the mess. Unhitch someone if you must, but get that wagon moving."

Meggie thrust her feet deeper in the stirrups. "I'll go."

Hawken sloshed toward her, stood so close his wet shirt touched her leg. "You cannot do it," he said in a low voice. "Now, get in your grandmother's wagon on your own, or I'll drag you off John Charles and throw you."

Chapter Eight

The last wagon—Mrs. Cooper's—bucked the current. Hawken climbed into the saddle and felt the mule stagger under his weight.

"It would have been easier if I could make this damn pony back up, the way Meggie does," Pete shouted.

"Nothing left but to get us across," Hawken said.

"Will that mule make it?" Pete asked. "He's not as sturdy as he looks."

"A few minutes' rest," Hawken said, dismounting. Pete slid out of the saddle and braced himself against the current by leaning on the pony. Water up to his knees, Hawken noted, and rising every minute.

"We can both hang on to John Charles," Pete said. "He's got strength enough to carry two." The pony strained toward the shore, eyeing Meggie at the water's edge. She had borrowed a telescope and they and her pony had been under surveillance for the past hour. She wore a skirt.

"What did you say to Meggie to get her off John Charles?" Pete asked.

"I reasoned with her," Hawken said. Meggie would hate him from now on, which was a stroke of luck. Last night, giving advice about cats, he'd felt an overwhelming urge to care for her, to throw himself between Meggie and the world. And when he'd walked away, there'd come the hollow feeling in his chest.

Care for me. Care for me. He closed his eyes, eager to rise above the moment and find a new revelation. The echo faded. Sand moved beneath his feet.

"We were lucky," Pete said. "Only a couple wagons got water in them, I guess."

"Luckier than we knew. By evening this sandbar will have disappeared. Ready to head out?" Pete nodded. "You get in the saddle, I'll hang on to the upstream stirrup and lead the mule."

John Charles bounded off the sandbar. Hawken found himself spread-eagled between the eager pony and the mule, who refused to move. Pete jerked the reins from Hawken's hand and wound them about the saddle horn.

"Kick him," Pete yelled. Hawken kicked, but the force carried him under water before he had a chance to take a deep breath. Sandpaper tore across his face. A hand grasped his shirt and pulled him up. Hawken clung to Pete's leg, sputtering. John Charles swam in jerks, not smoothly as a horse should, and fear took what breath Hawken managed. He would lose Meggie's pony. He threw his weight toward the mule, tried to climb in the saddle, and only then noticed that the mule thrashed wildly.

"Cut him loose!" he shouted.

"The widow won't like—"

"Damn the widow. He's dragging on the pony." He could not face Meggie without John Charles safe and healthy. Pete's knife caught the rays of the sun, orange light a flame down the blade as he sawed through the sodden leather. John Charles rose higher and his swimming adjusted to the lighter load. Over Pete's legs Hawken saw the mule tumbling in the current, unable to right himself.

The river demands a toll, Hawken thought. A wagon, a human being, a mule. *We got off easy.* He would make abject apologies to Moran and Mrs. Cooper.

The pony's feet touched bottom fifty yards from shore and Hawken dropped off. No matter that he got his trousers wet, for every stitch he wore was soaked. He looked down to gauge the depth of the water and saw bare legs below his knees. No tatters of cloth. Simply gone. The river had sandpapered his trousers away.

He examined his shirt, ran his hands over hips and back to assure himself he was not completely naked, with Meggie peering at him through a glass. A fountain of glittering water, and Pete wallowed near his feet. Meggie splashed out to meet prancing John Charles, her skirts hitched high.

"Damn pony," Pete sputtered. "You should have let him go down and saved the mule."

"I couldn't face your sister if anything happened to John Charles."

"You think too damn much of my sister," Pete said. Hawken grabbed Pete's wrist and pulled him to his feet. Pete's eyes came even with his own, eyes without thanks for the hand up. "You stay away from Meggie."

"I plan to." An easy promise, because from now on Meggie would hate him. Hawken's feet slipped in the ruts of the wagons as he peered into the helter-skelter camp, hoping to see Monty and Les, a blazing fire and a bubbling coffeepot. He trudged past Meggie and John Charles, ignoring their affectionate reunion.

"Granny says you're to go directly to her wagon for

a hot drink," Meggie called. "She's made it for everyone who was in the river, to prevent taking cold."

She pulled herself straight and tall. No question about her anger. Perhaps he should list the reasons a woman would have been useless in righting Mrs. Cooper's wagon. But from the corner of his eye he saw Pete step onto dry ground. Thank heavens, here came Monty, with a cup of his strong coffee.

Hawken dropped heavily beside the fire and peered into the bubbling pots. "She bewitched the mule," Les said to a bowl of batter he held in the crook of his arm. Hawken tried to summon the energy to refute the cryptic remark. "Her horse made it across, but the mule didn't." Meggie the witch.

"Pete cut the mule loose. It would have dragged us *and* the pony down. The damned creature wouldn't swim to save its own life."

"Like I said, witchery." Les spooned the batter into the skillet, too enthusiastically, and grease spattered Hawken's bare calves. He scooted back. "She stopped the hailstorm," he muttered.

"Don't be ridiculous,"· Hawken said. His back hit the wagon wheel. He rolled under, into the shade.

"She did! I heard her. She yelled 'Stop!' to the devil, the Prince of the Powers of the Air, and the hail stopped."

Hawken shut his ears to Les's account of the devil's power, for he felt weary to the edge of collapse. And beneath the fatigue lurked dread that extended down, down, to a depth he could not fathom. It had started in the river, a certainty that some horrible event lay just beyond…beyond what? Fear of Meggie's anger? He thought back to her expression when she climbed into Granny's wagon. Had her blue eyes blazed with fury?

Eyes like the bluest of skies…she wore a bodice, nothing more, exposing long tan legs that ended in slender ankles…. He jerked awake, the legs above him thick and wide stanced.

"Captain Hull says we're to get in order," Monty explained. "You want something to eat, boss?"

Hawken ate flapjacks and bacon. The unease had vanished. Perhaps he'd just been hungry.

"Captain says we'll pull out early tomorrow, 'cause we must reach Ash Hollow, and there's a mighty steep hill," Monty said between bites.

"Yes." Chain the wheels and slide the wagons down. Last year he had nearly lost a wagon when the rope slipped from the bullwhacker's hands. Stupid, to depend upon the puny strength of men when the application of elementary mechanics… He'd better talk to Hull and the scouts.

The wagons stood in parallel lines, with those on the ends slanting inward to create a long, narrow enclosure, Oregon and California emigrants mixed together. Hawken walked the length and halfway back before he found Hull with Moran, Godfroy and Sampson.

"There's the man we're looking for," Moran said.

Now I catch it for losing the mule, Hawken thought. He would defend himself before Moran said a word. "The mule wouldn't swim," he said. "We had no choice."

Moran waved, dismissing the apology. "The widow's on her knees thanking the Lord that her kids aren't drowned. Her only regret is the silver on the tack."

"You've taken wagons down the hill at Ash Hollow," Godfroy said. "Any advice?"

"We chained the wheels and slid the wagons down

with two or three men dragging at the back. Damned hard on boot heels, though.''

''Cut some trees and tie them to the wheels,'' Captain Moran said. ''That's a more efficient brake.''

''There're no trees at the top,'' Hawken said. ''We'd have to haul them up the hill, over and over again. I was thinking, with three sizable trees we could make a windlass. It wasn't worthwhile last year, only five wagons, but with more than thirty—''

Hull was already on his feet. ''Pick the men you want to help you. Pete's got the tools—''

''Pete and you,'' Hawken said. The man with the tools and the soldier boy who'd had experience improvising on a campaign in Mexico.

''We'll leave in half an hour,'' Captain Hull said. ''Godfroy, loan Hawken a horse. We'll have the windlass up by the time the wagons reach the abyss tomorrow morning.''

''Abyss,'' Godfroy snorted. ''Not more than three hundred feet down.''

Hawken regarded his truncated pants. ''I'd better dig out new clothes. And give Monty and Les orders.'' He cut across the line of wagons, his mind busy with the tools he would need, and nearly collided with John Charles. A brush and a long brown hand reached across the pony's back. She saw him, stopped her work, her arm draped on the gray speckled withers, her rigid face emotionless.

''Thank you for saving John Charles,'' she said, the words so flat they sounded rehearsed. ''Pete said—''

''I didn't save him. He saved himself, and Pete and me after we let the mule go. We shouldn't have asked him to carry so much.''

"Thank you anyway. And did you get Granny's drink?"

"No. There's no time now, I'm heading out to build a windlass at Ash Hollow."

She returned to her grooming. He fled, pawed through the load for a new set of clothes, changed hastily, the stiff new fabric grating on the film of grit covering him from head to toe. He would bathe in clear water at the Ash Hollow spring.

"Wait!" Meggie ran toward him, awkward because she carried a full tin cup. "Granny says you must drink this so you won't take cold." She thrust the cup at Hawken, he grabbed it and stepped to the side to avoid her.

"Drink it and get Granny off our back," Pete said. "She made me swallow the stuff, too." Hawken took a sip. Sweetness vainly attempting to cover a bitter brew. He downed it in one long gulp, placed the cup in Meggie's outstretched palm. She spun about, her dislike radiating from the set of her mouth. Her short skirt twirled on her hips, revealing more than ankles. The plain, untrimmed bottoms of white muslin drawers.

"A long, dull ride ahead," Hawken muttered to himself as he set out toward Ash Hollow. "And hard work to do. Time to forget her drawers. Time to remember, I hope," he added after a moment's thought.

Matt Hull noted with disappointment that the first wagon to arrive came from the Oregon train. He had hoped to get breakfast, but felt shy about begging from a woman he did not know. The man joined Pete and Hawken, who were putting the finishing touches on the windlass, two forked tree trunks holding a horizontal log.

"Good God Almighty!" the man said, staring down the slope. "Isn't there a better way?"

A woman stepped beside him, blanched and grabbed her husband's arm. "The children and I'll walk," she said.

Sampson trudged up the hill, returning from his reconnaissance of the hollow. "A Sioux camp near the mouth of the canyon, but mostly women and children. The men must be off hunting. We'll camp at the spring."

"You stay with our women and children," Matt said. Thank heavens, there came Jim Mac's wagons, and Granny's trailing two hundred feet behind. Mrs. MacIntyre would have a limp flapjack or a cold biscuit to settle his rumbling stomach. Meggie rode near Granny's wagon. Her encounter with the buffalo hunter had been dreadful but had produced beneficial results. Without that fright she would probably, at this moment, be hobnobbing with the Sioux.

Mrs. MacIntyre had foreseen the long wait for dinner, and had baked pockets of biscuit dough filled with buffalo tenderloin. Matt popped one into his mouth and wiped his hands on his thighs.

"All the women and children will walk down," he said. "Meggie, lead John Charles. If there's any trouble, ride back here fast as possible. Sampson will go with you."

Meggie nodded, then detoured left to examine the windlass. It wasn't the engine that drew her, Matt was sure. He had sensed heat close to the boiling point whenever those two looked at each other. Too bad Hawken had his memory problem. A husband would settle Meggie. But Jim Mac probably wouldn't give his blessing to such a match. Married to Hawken, Meggie would stay behind in Bear River Valley. Unless Jim Mac convinced him California was the land of promise.

Hawken's head tilted and Meggie leaned down. They

were talking. Rather Hawken talked and Meggie listened.
Hawken pulled a pistol from his belt and handed it to
her. Ho-ho! The affair was serious when a man armed
his ladylove.

"If we're lucky," Matt whispered to Tildy, pointing
to the tête-à-tête, "Hawken will recall he doesn't have a
wife and he'll tag along to California."

Tildy shook her head. "Aunt Eliza and Uncle Jim
don't like it," she said. "Neither does Pete. No telling
what sort of man Hawken was. And he could be lying,
about not remembering. What a great way to hide the
fact that you're an outlaw."

"There's something of the gentleman about him,"
Matt said. "Educated." Tildy frowned.

The first wagon edged over the lip of the hill and splin-
ters of wood flew from the roller log. Meggie started
down the hill, walking behind the women and children.
She turned and waved, Matt thought the farewell directed
more to Hawken than anyone else. Hawken, however,
was occupied with the windlass and did not return the
wave.

The two of them should creep off tonight, into the
sheltered nooks of the grove. Jim Mac couldn't say no if
the deed had been done. A wave of nostalgia swept over
Matt. He thought of Godfroy's camp on the White River,
where he and Tildy had anticipated their wedding day by
several weeks. A good beginning, and everything im-
proving since then. From the bottom of the hill Tildy
turned and waved. Tonight he'd pitch the tent a long way
from the wagons.

It had not occurred to Meggie that she was homesick
for trees until she entered the grove and heard the leaves

rustling in the wind. Tildy must feel the same way, for she smiled at the green branches overhead.

"Tildy, do you like being married?" Meggie asked.

Tildy dipped her chin and massaged the back of her neck. "Of course I like being married. I wouldn't have married Matt if..." She blushed red across her cheekbones. Meggie put two and two together. Matt and Tildy had not waited until their wedding night.

"Why?" asked Tildy, a trifle cross. "Are you thinking about being married?"

"Maybe," Meggie said.

"I wouldn't if I were you, because you're thinking of Mr. Hawken, and your parents disapprove, and Pete—"

"I don't have anyone in mind," Meggie protested. "Mr. Hawken's not interested in me. Besides, your parents disapproved of Matt Hull."

"At least we knew who Matt Hull *was*," Tildy snapped. "And what he'd made of himself. Mr. Hawken's loafed in the Missouri River towns—" her tone hinted at nefarious deeds "—and been a teamster on the plains. He'll have no business at a trading post except during the summer. That doesn't seem like bettering himself."

There will be business in the winter, Meggie thought. Buffalo hunters. It took her half a minute to recall what she wanted to learn from Tildy. Lovemaking.

"I...a good wife makes her husband happy when they're alone together, and I don't know if I can."

"Respectable women don't experiment ahead of time," Tildy said sternly, but the red on her cheeks did not fade. "Meggie, when you're curious about something, you dive right in to learn. It wasn't a danger in Pikeston, where all you could do was read books, but now! I mean the buffalo hunter nearly landed you in a terrible fix. You were determined to see the Platte River before anyone else. Curiosity killed the cat.''

"Being with a man isn't fatal," Meggie said.

"Meggie, being with a man...puts you in a family way. A woman's got to be very, very certain and that means getting married, and Matt told me Mr. Hawken can't get married because he might already have a wife."

"I'm not talking about Mr. Hawken," Meggie said sullenly. "Why does everyone try to hitch me with him?" She imagined a child, a foreigner in her belly, but could hardly conceive of anything so drastic. Too bad the marvelous passion that made Matt and Tildy whisper loving names could change a woman's life so permanently.

Ma and Granny relaxed near the spring, their workbags open. Tildy sat down and set about darning a large sock. One of Matt's, undoubtedly. It hadn't occurred to Meggie to take her workbag out of the wagon.

One by one wagons rolled by. The odor of wood fires and the shadows of evening spread through the vale. She should wander on to camp, but a hill rose behind the spring that promised a view up the valley. If she rode only halfway up—to a bush sprinkled with pink flowers—she would remain within hailing distance of the men on the trail.

Five wagons rounded the bend, and behind them the men who had operated the windlass. Captain Hull, Pete, Godfroy, but not Hawken. After they passed she would be alone, and she'd not reached the flowering plant, which looked more and more like a rose.

Hawken walked around the bush, idly plucking a pink flower.

"You're not cured of riding off alone?" he asked after a long stare. He crumpled the rose and dropped it.

"There're no buffalo hunters here. And I wanted to check that everyone had come in before I left."

"There are Indians. Sampson saw a Sioux village, near the mouth of the canyon."

"Women and children, he said. And I was tired of the noise, everyone celebrating when their wagons came by."

"You like quiet and solitude, too?" he asked.

"I suppose. I never thought of getting off by myself as quiet and solitude. Just a time to think. Do you want me to go so you have quiet and solitude?"

"No. You have as much right to be here as I do."

Meggie slid to the ground and investigated the bush. Only a few straggling blooms, and the hips too small for profitable gathering. Far up the valley, shadows accentuated the ruts on the hillside. It looked far less terrifying from this angle.

"Are there more steep hills like this?" she asked, then remembered he had climbed the hill to be alone.

"Worse," he murmured. He had his back turned. She lifted her toe to the stirrup.

"How do you like Ash Hollow?" he asked. She lowered her foot.

"I love it, the trees, and birds fluttering through the branches. Mr. Hawken, I'm glad you're not interested in me, because I won't be a good wife."

The bright spark in his eyes might be temptation, or then again it might be an insult. A muscle twitched in her calf.

"Why should you think that?" he asked.

"I don't like to be ordered about, the way you did in the river. And when a woman gets married she says 'obey.' I forgot my workbag today and sat around doing nothing while everyone else knitted or mended. Women should not be idle."

"Do you often forget things?"

"Not most things. I can remember what I see and read. Captain Frémont says of the North Platte, it 'is of a variable breadth, from one to four, and sometimes six miles. Fifteen miles from the Chimney—'"

"You've memorized the whole book?" he asked.

"I don't think it's memorizing. The page floats in front of my eyes. I've explained it to my friends and they don't see books that way. But I can't remember my workbag."

"What a wonder you'd be in a store. You'd know what each customer owes on account, and what the kerchiefs and tin pans cost—"

"Perhaps I should start a trading post," she said gaily to counteract the nervous tics weakening her legs. "I'll buy yours when you tire of Bear River."

"There's to be no trading post," he said.

"No trading post!"

"I'll remember my wife before long. A few days ago, while I helped Mrs. Cooper, I recalled white hands."

"Your wife's hands?"

He shrugged. "I don't know. But hands."

"That's why you put your arms around me? You thought you'd remember quicker if you embraced a woman?" The words flowed from a reservoir of bitterness she had not suspected. "It makes no difference that I'm shaped like a gatepost, any woman will do—"

"No, Meggie. I admire you. The way you rode into the river to help, not many women—"

"But you ordered me off with Granny, and if I hadn't gone willingly you'd have tossed me into the wagon."

"An emergency. You're not strong enough to—"

"You should know how strong I am. I knocked you down."

"I stumbled over the dog," he muttered. He looked up and down the hillside, as if searching for the animal.

"Platte's in camp. He went by with your wagons while I waited at the spring." A man must find it embarrassing to have a woman knock him flat.

"I respect and admire you, and if I were free I'd speak to your father and court you. It's a great effort to be alone with you and not put my arms about you. If you step any closer, I might forget myself."

Meggie laughed. "You do a lot of forgetting, Mr. Hawken. Convenient forgetting. You're not giving up the trading post to go home to your wife. You've met the people who'll hang about your store, the buffalo hunters, and you've decided winters are more pleasant in Independence or St. Joe, with whiskey and women who call you 'lover' and breathe hard and beg to do the most despicable things—" She stopped because her surroundings blurred, and she couldn't recall words suitable for a woman.

"Your cousin likes it," he snapped. "So do other women. And you'll enjoy it, too. It's what you've wanted all along, with your brother waiting, his rifle cocked to march the poor guy to the preacher."

"If I want a man, why did I slug you when you tried?" she said, triumphantly puncturing his logic. She mounted John Charles on the wrong side to keep her distance. "You have gentlemanly instincts. I suppose your mother and father guided you, but you ignored their advice and yielded to temptation." The resonance of her words pleased her. Too bad a woman could not be a preacher. "You should examine your heart, Mr. Hawken, relearn the teachings of your childhood. It's not too late. 'I will declare mine iniquity; I will be sorry for my sin.' Psalm 38.'' Meggie wished she could gallop off as an exclamation point to her lecture, but the ground was too broken to chance it.

Chapter Nine

Meggie slowed John Charles to keep pace with Rachel's mare, who dared not go faster than a walk because of her recent injury. Even so they went faster than the oxen, and after reaching the head of the wagons, they backtracked to visit the boys driving the loose stock.

"We've finally reached the mountains," Rachel said, nodding toward the pale bluffs that bounded the valley. "Although Father says this is not truly the Rockies. We'll see the first peaks at Fort Laramie."

"When we stop for dinner, let's climb the Courthouse," Meggie said. The square rock dominated the southern horizon, looking for all the world like a public building topped by a dome. "From the top we'll see the mountains."

"Kit's having a hard time with the herd," Rachel said. "They wander off one side, then the other."

"We'll help," Meggie said, glad for something useful to do. "Head them off next time they stray."

Kit dashed into the sagebrush and prickly pear, shouting and waving his arms. Meggie guided John Charles to the opposite side of the road and turned the cattle when they tried to head in that direction.

"Thanks," Josh said, out of breath, waving his hat in the face of a thin cow who seemed determined to turn back.

"Where're the other boys?" Rachel asked.

"Climbing the Courthouse," Josh said, pointing with his whip. "As soon as they're back, Kit and I'll go."

"I want to go with you," Meggie said.

"I suppose you can come," Josh said, but his frown spoke louder than his words. He and Kit did not want a girl along.

"I'll put my boots on," Meggie said, holding out a foot to show Josh she wore moccasins. "Come up the Courthouse with us, Rachel. Tildy and Faith, too, and we'll have the highest sewing circle in history."

Rachel smiled indulgently, as if she were an adult asked to join a childish game. "We might not be back in time to cook dinner, and Will spotted buffalo ahead."

They caught up to Hawken's wagon, the tail end today. Meggie pretended to search for the easiest route up the Courthouse.

"Hello, Mr. Hawken," Rachel said. "I thought you'd be off climbing the rocks. The boys have gone, and Meggie's fetching her boots to go with Josh and Kit."

Meggie glared at Rachel. There was no earthly reason why she should inform Hawken of her movements.

"The Courthouse? What boys have gone?" Hawken asked, suddenly alert.

"Why, all the younger ones. They'll be back shortly."

"They'll not be back until nightfall," Hawken said. "The Courthouse is more than five miles from the trail, through gullies and prickly pear."

Meggie shook her head while she measured the distance with her eyes. Half a mile, three quarters at the most.

"Does Captain Hull know about this?" Hawken asked.

"I don't suppose," Rachel said meekly. "It didn't occur to the boys that there would be anything wrong—"

"Find Hull. Tell him I'm heading out right now to intercept them."

"It would be faster if you rode," Meggie said.

"I said rough country. A man can walk as fast as you dare ride. Faster even, and get where a horse can't."

He whistled, the yellow dog left the shady side of the wagons. Hawken walked into the prickly pear without so much as a tip of his hat.

"Let's go find Captain Hull," Meggie said, resigned. Hawken had simply used the most convenient excuse to get away from her.

"But I promised," Captain Moran was saying to Hull when she and Rachel rode up. Moran waved his arms.

"No one walks to the Courthouse, climbs it, and gets back to the wagons in the time we stop for dinner," Captain Hull said. "Godfroy says it's four or five miles to the base of the rock, and—"

"I doubt that." Captain Moran scrunched his face and studied the distance. "It can't be more than a mile."

"A mirage?" Meggie suggested. "Like in the sand hills along the Platte, where everything looks bigger or smaller, or like something entirely different."

"All the Tole boys but Kit and Josh's brothers have taken off to climb the rock," Rachel said.

"Mr. Hawken set out after them," Meggie added.

Captain Hull stared at the ground, gnawed on his lip and muttered something unintelligible under his breath. "What we'll do—" he lifted his head "—Meggie and Rachel, you come with me, so I'll have someone to send back if necessary. We'll ride in that direction."

"Mr. Hawken says it's rough country," Rachel said. "I don't think Josefa—"

Captain Hull nodded. "Her weak leg. You find your father and Sampson, tell them Meggie and I are riding after the boys. And warn everyone, they're not to set out for the Courthouse. You'd better speak to your people, Moran." Moran muttered something about a mile or two, but headed for the wagons under his command.

"We'll head for that ridge," Hull said. "It's more likely they'll hear us if we yell from a high spot."

He kicked his horse into a gallop, following the sandy track of a dry creek, then slowed as he cut up a hill. Before they had quite reached the top he put two fingers in his mouth and whistled. Three long, shrill blasts. He waited a full minute—Meggie could see his lips moving as he counted to sixty—then three times more.

"There's one of them," he exclaimed, pointing to a figure clambering out of a gully.

"No, that's Mr. Hawken," Meggie said. "See, his dog's ahead of him."

"Maybe the dog has picked up the boys' scent. I think so, he's got his nose to the ground." He stood in the stirrups and waved, Hawken waved and pointed. "He must see the boys over there."

The dog ran back and forth and Meggie found, if she strained her ears, she could hear it bark. Hawken lifted his hat high over his head.

"What's he trying to say?" Captain Hull asked. Did he think she and Hawken knew each other so well that she could interpret his gestures by instinct?

"Perhaps we'd better join him." Hawken ran a few yards toward them, skidded to a stop and swept his hat in a wide gesture from side to side. "Does that mean don't come?"

Hawken repeated the pantomime, reached the bottom of the hill, almost out of sight. He tried to run up the slope, slowed before he reached the top, obviously out of breath. He turned, waved his hat again and walked up the hill, backward. Platte leaped onto a block of stone capping the hill, thought better of it and jumped down. Gravel gave way beneath him, he lost control and was transformed into a ball hurtling straight toward Hawken.

"Run," Meggie screamed, just as the dog bowled into the back of Hawken's legs. For an instant she thought he had recovered himself, but in the next instant he tumbled over and over in a cloud of dust, legs and arms thrashing as he tried to catch himself.

"Hawken!" she screamed as he disappeared. "Hawken!" The dog managed an untidy stop. It rolled onto its feet and peered down, whined, then let loose a disconsolate howl. Captain Hull grabbed John Charles's bridle just as Meggie lifted a foot.

"He said we can't come directly across. That gully's deeper than it looks. We'll follow the dry creek bed. It has to meet another coming from the left."

"Hurry. He might be hurt." The dog ran back and forth, stopping now and then to howl. She wished Captain Hull would speed up. "Hurry, hurry," Meggie said under her breath. The crumbling walls gained height, and she could no longer hear the dog.

"If we tire the horses we do no one any good," Captain Hull said. "Your sweetheart's a strong man, not likely to be killed by rolling down a hill."

"He's not my sweetheart. He has a wife back east."

"If he remembers who and when and where," he said, grinning. "It's just as likely that Hawken's forgotten an aging virgin with a deep hope chest, and a father with a gun. The woman he ran away from."

"You think so?" He did not answer, for a fork in the gully confronted them.

"To the left," Meggie said, turning before he did. Fifty feet of sand, then a tumble of rocks higher than a house. But the wails of the dog were audible once more. She threw her reins to Hull. "I'll climb up."

Her moccasins slipped on the narrow footholds, a hand from below caught her and braced her foot. "Be careful. We don't want two people to carry out," he said.

He can't be dead. He can't be dead.

"Slow down, Meggie. You'll be no help worn-out."

Stop wasting your breath, she thought, but did not waste her own precious breath talking. Hull pulled himself up a boulder and reached a hand down. They stepped into a narrow defile, clogged with rocks. The dog shrieked fifteen feet over their heads, and twice Meggie saw a hint of golden muzzle. Somewhere in this labyrinth Hawken lay, hurt and unconscious.

"Where, Platte?" Meggie yelled. She clambered over a pile of rocks, her foot stuck in a crevice and she had to twist back and forth to get it out, leaving a moccasin behind. She heaved herself to the top of a boulder the size of a wagon. Hawken lay in the sand, crumpled on his side, his face covered with blood.

"Hawken, Hawken," she whispered. There were no footholds on the far side of the boulder. She threw herself onto the soft sand and almost landed on his legs. "Hawken, speak to me!" She leaned over his gory head, lifted him with an arm behind his shoulders, brushed back his sticky hair. Dear God, let it be just a cut on the scalp.

"Damn dog," he muttered. Meggie threw both arms about him and cradled him like a baby.

"Thank God! Thank God!" she whispered. She did not find the pounding of her heart abnormal, but the waves beating in gentle rhythm, bathing her in light, they were beyond her experience.

"You can find your way out of here?" Captain Hull asked as Meggie pulled on the tattered moccasin. The beads had been left behind in the rockfall.

"Of course I can find my way. And Platte certainly won't lead us astray. You go find the boys," Meggie said, pleased to give the captain an order.

"On the other side of the hill...the one with the big rock on top," Hawken said slowly. He looked like a man waking from a dream. With a strip from the bottom of her skirt tied about his head, he reminded Meggie of a picture in her *Illustrated Bible for Children.*

"Give me the reins," Hawken said.

"And have John Charles pitch you off? You hang on to the saddle horn and let me manage the horse." The picture assembled before her eyes. Job in rags, searching for wisdom. "'Wisdom cannot be gotten for gold, nor silver,'" she chanted, reading the words beneath the drawing, "'with precious onyx or sapphire. No mention shall be made of coral, or of pearls.'"

"What?"

"Nothing. With that rag on your head you remind me of a book I read a long time ago. 'The price of love is above rubies.' No, that's wrong, it's wisdom that's more precious than rubies." Why had she said love, when very plainly the word was "wisdom"?

Through the twists and turns of the dry stream, until they left the steep walls behind and the valley, road and river lay before her. No wagon in sight. She swung left before she reached the road, to shorten the distance Hawken must stay in the saddle.

"The wagons are about a mile ahead," Hawken said.

"There seems to be a great number, so perhaps I'm seeing double."

"Wouldn't surprise me one bit."

"Say that again, about the price of love being more than gold. It sounds familiar."

"It's wisdom, not love. From the Book of Job. The moral of the story was that we should study hard to gain wisdom."

Mr. Tole ran to meet them. "You look like hell," he said to Hawken. "The boys? Did you see the boys?"

"Captain Hull's after them," Meggie said stiffly. "Mr. Hawken saw them before he tumbled down a great cliff. He fell because he warned me and Captain Hull away from the abyss. Otherwise, it might be us lying dead in that rocky hole." Mr. Tole rubbed his square hands on his vest while he peered anxiously at the maze of hills and rocks.

Meggie half lifted Hawken into Granny's wagon and forced him down on the cot. She washed his face, Granny clipped Hawken's hair to expose the cut and Meggie held his hands while Tildy stitched his scalp together with white silk thread.

"I believe this calls for cowslip tea," Granny mused. "Maybe someone filled a can at the last stream. The river water's so muddy…"

"I'll ask at the wagons in front, and you ask at those behind," Tildy said, her eyes on Hawken's hands, knuckles white with the power of his grip.

"Her hands are smaller than yours," he said after Granny closed the door.

"Your wife's?"

"Yes. That's all I've managed to remember. Her hands. Tiny and white." Meggie frowned at her hands, darkened by the sun, rubbed raw by washing in gritty alkali water.

Captain Hull's wrong, she decided. No man would remember the tiny, white hands of an unwanted sweetheart. Hawken had a wife, a woman who loved him and grieved that he had disappeared. *Love is more precious than rubies.*

"I'll help you remember her," she whispered. "She loves you and longs to see you. Close your eyes and rest." Only when his fingers relaxed did she withdraw her hands. She pitied the woman left behind, ignorant of her husband's fate. "I'll help you remember your wife," she whispered. He nodded. The wagon stirred from weight on the steps. Granny.

"This will make you a bit sleepy," she said, offering the tin cup. "Meggie, come away. Let Mr. Hawken rest."

Faith waited for her with bread and meat. "Meggie, what happened to your skirt?" Meggie looked down. The front of her skirt ended just below her knee. Since she had not bothered with a petticoat that morning, her unadorned drawers stuck out for all to see.

"The only thing handy to bind up Mr. Hawken's head," she said briskly.

"Thank you for going after my brothers. They cause everyone so much trouble."

"They didn't know how far it was to the Courthouse," Meggie said, excusing the boys for Faith's sake. "I thought it a mile, at most, and wanted to go there myself."

"We can see the Chimney now. Mr. Godfroy says it's near the trail and although we can't climb to the top, we can reach the base of the spire." She pointed to a slim pinnacle of rock thrust against the sky. "We'll camp near it tonight. It does look like a chimney, doesn't it?"

"A funnel, upside down," Tildy offered.

"A knitting needle stuck in a skein of yarn," suggested Granny.

Meggie appreciated their imaginative efforts, but she knew quite well what the rock looked like. She took another bite of bread so she'd not be expected to voice an opinion on the Chimney.

She had promised to help Hawken remember his wife. It would not take much to tempt him past hugs and kisses, particularly when he was weak from a bang on the head. If he recalled pretty hands when he looked at the widow, he'd certainly remember everything with a woman under his blanket. And she'd learn what married women do. All women should find out ahead of time, she thought, justifying her decision. It was unfair to saddle a man with a wife who would rather not be in his bed.

Hawken's first impression upon waking was that he'd been shut up in a churn. When his eyes finally managed to focus—the wobbling hickory bows, the swaying wagon cover, the lurching bundles of herbs—the memory of the past few hours unrolled in his mind like a carpet being relaid. The frantic pitch down the hill, Meggie's urgent prayer, the pain of Tildy's needle puncturing his scalp.

He closed his eyes against vertigo. If he didn't get out of the wagon soon he'd be sick. He heaved upward, in vain, too weak to sit. Hurt bad. Had the dog broken his leg? He tried to recall what part of him landed first, but his memories of the fall consisted largely of noise and panic. Then the taste of blood and the dog going berserk someplace toward heaven.

He would concentrate on one limb at a time. Were his arms broken? He flexed the fingers of each hand. He moved his feet, he lifted his hips a trifle and concluded he had not broken his back or his legs. He explored his neck and head, and felt the bandage. He'd cracked his head.

He opened his eyes and held his hands close to his face. Only two hands. He wedged his elbows against the mattress and pushed, managing to lift head and shoulders. Two wide strips of sheeting tied him to the cot. He fell back on the pillow, laughing. The wagon lurched to one side, then the other, straining his bonds. He blessed Granny for thinking of the obvious.

What an awkward dolt he must appear to Meggie. She had knocked him flat. Of course that had been the dog's fault. He fought with Pete and ended up in the Platte River. Well, in a fight you can't take your eyes off your opponent to see where your feet go. Now he had rolled down a shabby little hill and cracked his head. If they gave a gold medal for clumsy he would win it, hands down. And Meggie would pin it on his chest, quoting from the Bible or Shakespeare. Her mischievous blue eyes would gleam, and the corners of her mouth twitch, trying not to grin, and the freckles across her nose would darken from gold to red. Her freckles were not terribly obvious, but when she leaned close and stroked his forehead, he saw little freckles, small rubies.

"Who can find a virtuous woman? For her price is far above rubies," a ponderous voice said, the echoes too sonorous for the interior of a wagon. Light streamed from high windows. Step back, a bit farther, one more, one more step into the past—

The wagon lurched, Reid yelled at the oxen, the fabric dipped between the bows, and Hawken held his breath, certain the whole thing would go over.

"Whoa." The word echoed in other voices behind and before.

"Are you awake?" Granny asked as the door creaked.

"You think a man can sleep rolling through a gully?"

Granny smiled. "You're better. Just a few buffalo trails before we circle for the night. I'll untie you, if you promise to lounge about all evening and be waited on like a rich man."

"I've never been a rich man, so it will be a new experience."

"How do you know?" Granny asked.

How did he know? "I figured if my family was rich, they'd have come looking for me."

"You're probably right. We're camped below the Chimney Rock." Granny's gnarled fingers worked at the knots, tightened by his weight straining against them. "Meggie and her friends have already set out for the top. Well, as far as they can go, for no one could climb to the top."

"Last year I carved my name as high as I could reach." Why had Granny said "Meggie and her friends"? Why not "Tildy and her friends"? Tildy was the granddaughter closest to her, the one who shared her wagon.

She assumes Meggie's most important to me.

"You can sit by the fire while I fix supper. Use your dog as a backrest. He's trailed the wagon all afternoon, sorrowful as a miser who's lost his money."

"He knocked me down. Probably feels guilty."

"Dogs aren't as useful as we make out," she said.

"But he found the boys. I wouldn't have known where to start looking, but he headed straight for them."

"I'll tell Mr. Tole. He'll feed the dog tonight so you needn't bother."

"Bother!" He reared up so suddenly Granny's arm shot out to restrain him. "It's my turn to unwitch the hidow. I mean, unhitch the widow's oxen."

"I'm going," Monty said just beyond the open door. "Les will see you to the wagons. He's making a broth for your supper."

"I forgot, you have good nurses," Granny said, stepping aside. At the bottom of the steps Hawken discovered he had an enormous headache. The banging of pots and pans, the squeak of the bail on the coffeepot, they'd never made so much noise before.

"You in shape to listen to reason?" Les asked.

"I suppose." The throbbing in his head concentrated on the left side.

"Since we joined these folks you been smacked, nearly killed fighting a buffalo hunter—"

"I wasn't 'nearly killed.'"

"—tossed in the river—"

"I fell in on my own."

"—had a mule drown under you—"

"Nobody's fault but the mule's."

"—and now rolled down a hill and your head cut open. I told you that gal was a witch. She's bewitched you and you don't even know it! You think everything's smooth as a glass plate, but in truth you're standing on a slippery slope." Les dipped clarified water from the top of the bucket. "A slippery, slippery slope! She tells that pony to buck men off, but today you rode like a lady in a carriage. Why? Because she whispered a charm and it behaved like a lamb. And she charmed you, too."

"Charmed? How?"

"Why, I heard her plain, saying strange things."

"She was quoting the Book of Job. It might have been in the original Hebrew for all I know."

"It was a charm in witch language. Now you tell me, what does that gal look like?"

"She's got reddish brown hair, short curls, and when she takes her hat off in the evening, they make a halo round her head. She's slender, has beautiful hands and trim ankles. Her eyes are blue." He looked at the sky. "Like the sky beyond the Chimney. Altogether, a very pretty girl."

"Altogether you been bewitched. That gal is homely, she's got freckles and all the curves of a wagon tongue."

Platte shifted and Hawken had no choice but to follow his backrest. Bewitched? Perhaps in his solitude he endowed Meggie with qualities she did not possess. Perhaps she *was* homely. But her eyes *were* like the sky. Except now the setting sun scattered dusty pink.

Several figures struggled up the cone of loose rock that formed the base of the Chimney. If he squinted he could pick out four who wore skirts, a few feet below their goal.

Granny stood over him with a tin cup. "You feeling sick to your stomach?" she asked. Hawken shook his head. "Then drink this. For the headache." He drank. She knew he had a headache. She knew Meggie was more important to him than any other woman. Maybe she could tell him what he needed to know. He patted the ground, inviting her to sit. "I've got supper to cook," she said.

"Mrs. Hull's up there," he said, pointing at the spire. "She won't be down for an hour." Granny sat.

"I hear you tell fortunes."

"A parlor game."

"Tell mine, but not the future. The past."

"I'd have to get my seeds," she said uncomfortably.

"I'm not going anywhere."

She returned with an embroidered bag. On the bottom of an upturned skillet she poured the contents, seeds, slowly, a line from one edge to the other.

"You're a strong man," she said. "A potent man." She whispered the three words, as though they might be a secret he wished to keep. A parlor game. Her revelations were nothing but the obvious. Or a man's wishful thinking.

"Something important will happen to you. Soon."

"It already has. I rolled off a precipice."

"No, what's ahead will change your life."

"I asked you to see the past, not the future."

She leaned over the skillet. "There is no past," she said in a low voice. "It starts right now. You want to bed my granddaughter. You might not think it, but she wants you. Don't do it until you see your way clear to marry her." She swept the seeds into the bag, got to her feet with her amazing agility and left him shaken. Granny knew the lust he denied. She would know if he breached her trust and approached Meggie.

"Monty. Les. Is there room to make me a bed in one of the wagons?" They dashed about, fulfilling his request with such haste that it occurred to him that he might be dying. But the bed reassured him. They had constructed it with no particular concern for a terminal man. The sharp corner of a parcel poked in his back and his feet fell into a crevice. He dozed, half woke at the sound of a female voice.

"I just wanted to tell Mr. Hawken, the Chimney is wonderful, and we saw his name there but couldn't reach it," Meggie said. "We could see for miles and miles, all the way to Scott's Bluff."

Beyond Scott's Bluff, Fort Laramie. Maybe he could sell his goods to the Laramie traders and head home.

"I'll tell Mr. Hawken in the morning," Les said, dismissing her politely.

Not Fort Laramie. He had promised to take Les and Monty within reach of Fort Hall, where they would meet trappers from the Hudson's Bay Company. Englishmen, who did not own slaves. Might as well stay on the road to Bear River.

Chapter Ten

Fort Laramie loomed ahead, sun bright on its plastered walls. "How long will we stop at the fort?" Meggie called at Sampson's back, two lengths ahead of her and John Charles. He slowed and let her catch up.

"They don't like emigrants grazing their stock on the pasture hereabouts," he said shortly. "We'll go on."

She managed one long glance through the gate. No magic inside, only a bulky press for baling hides and furs, and the walls of rough cabins. She'd walk back from their evening camp.

But Sampson plodded westward, seven or eight miles, before he halted in a meadow tucked between a crumbling bluff and the river. No opportunity to backtrack to Fort Laramie. But here came Captain Hull. Perhaps they'd lay over a day, ride back—

"Good," he said, examining the campsite. "Too far from Laramie for a trip to buy whiskey. Moran said they'd stop for a quick look, and we haven't seen their dust since."

Meggie freed John Charles to graze, wandered through rocks and boulders to the base of the cliff. Names and dates crowded the rock face, some weathered to illegibility, others still sharp.

Hawken…1846. And below a second date…1847.

Twice he had gouged the soft stone to record his passage. Tonight he would add a third year.

From her vantage she saw him, trailed by his drivers, heading toward the cliff. He still wore a strip of muslin about his head, under his hat. Too late she ducked behind a rock. Les had seen her and he poked Hawken, who stopped. As one the three men turned back to the wagon.

Meggie huffed. Since the evening of his accident, Hawken had studiously avoided her. One morning he kept his men busy in camp and lost his position in line. His wagons no longer followed her father's. How was she to help him recover his memory if he wouldn't talk to her? Had she offended him? But if he kept to himself she had no way of learning *what* she had done. She sniffed and shook away unexpected tears.

She wanted to shout at his back, "There are other men in the world!" Except it wasn't true. No man in the world had ever touched her as Hawken had, and now he ignored her. Weeks would pass before they left him behind at Bear River, and those weeks stretched visibly before her, all boring and miserable.

An object, unnaturally square, stood beside the trail. Meggie moved to the side of the road for a better view around Godfroy. An abandoned wagon? The wall of a small cabin? Perhaps a mirage? Remnant fear of the buffalo hunters stirred, and she moved to ride in the shadow of Godfroy's horse.

The corners sharpened, and a pattern resolved into painted words. A sign.

"What does it say?" Godfroy asked. She read out loud.

"'Notice. To the ferry 28 miles, the ferry good and safe.' Ferry? Why didn't you tell us?" she asked, turning to the scout. "Everyone's been biting their nails, worried about crossing the North Platte."

"I wasn't sure if they'd be around this year. In the mountains things come and go," he said. "Like the beaver," he added sadly.

"How much?" she asked, thinking of the declining coins in her father's purse. If he had to dig into the stash of gold, everyone would guess he had money hidden.

Godfroy shrugged. "What the traffic will bear. But we're the first this season, so maybe they'll bargain for flour and bacon."

"If Hawken would unpack a few bundles, we could pay with shirts and tin basins," Meggie said. He wouldn't, she was certain. One day he had worn trousers that ended at his knees rather than put on new ones.

"We have no claim on Hawken's goods," Godfroy said, and looked at her sharply, not an accusation. A question.

A wagon hove into view at the base of a rising column of dust. An Oregonian. They'd only caught up last night; Meggie searched for the driver to see how he fared after the debauch at Fort Laramie. Gossip said Captain Moran had become so intoxicated he had slept through the night against the fort's wall, and resisted all efforts to rouse him until his wife bullied him back to his duties.

The driver showed no ill effects, because it was Mrs. Cooper. Accompanied by a man whom Meggie knew without seeing his face. Hawken. His easy stride, the way he moved his hands when he spoke. He and the widow talked most earnestly. Meggie thrust her feet deeper in

her stirrups and pressed a hand at the base of her throat
to steady an erratic pulse.

Mrs. Cooper reminded Hawken of his wife. The widow
wore a wide hat and a thick veil, to protect her complex-
ion. She had small hands and feet, and was short and
plump, the way men liked women. Meggie slid out of
the saddle and hid behind John Charles. He would see
she did not care.

"Why can't we cross by ourselves? We managed on
the South Platte," Meggie said to Godfroy.

"The North Platte's a deep, turbulent river, particularly
this early in the year. We'd lose a day or two making
boats and floating the wagons across piece by piece."

Hawken left the widow and hiked forward. He took
his hat off and scratched under the dirty bandage. "Ferry
still operating," he said. "They were here last summer
but the water was low and we didn't use it. Mrs. Cooper's
worried about her wheels. The spokes are loose."

"Tell Captain Moran. The Oregon men leave too much
to you and Pete."

"Hoping one of us will marry her," Hawken said
wryly. Meggie felt a hard edge cutting into her palm,
looked down and discovered she was twisting the stirrup
leather. She dropped her hand. She'd thought Hawken
was attracted to the pretty young widow. He and Mrs.
Cooper had talked about wheels?

"Oregonians soaked themselves at Laramie rather than
the wheels," Godfroy said dryly. "Tonight maybe they'll
find the strength to take them off and put them in the
creek."

A dozen men from the Oregon wagons pressed forward, and Meggie retreated a few steps, to give them a
view of the sign. "Moran says we'll spend a day or two

here, to take advantage of the grass,'' one of the men said to Godfroy.

"I don't think Hull contemplates anything of the sort," Godfroy snapped. "There's nothing compelling you folks to keep up. The cattle are bearing up and we're only three days from Independence Rock. That's the place to rest."

"'The rock is inscribed with the names of travelers,'" Meggie quoted Frémont under her breath. She had not climbed the Courthouse, but she'd not be cheated of Independence Rock. Hawken had left his name on Register Cliff. Had he carved his name on the rock, too? She left the protection of John Charles and stepped between Hawken and the sign. His eyebrows flew up, so high they disappeared under his hat. He dodged behind Godfroy, through the gathering crowd.

He kept out of her sight through dinner, and in the darkness Meggie let the tears that had threatened at Register Cliff flow free. He was the first man who had ever paid heed to her, a man she had scrambled over rocks for, cradled his bloody head, and now she had lost him. She tried to remember what she had said, leading John Charles through the maze of rock. Hawken's head bound up in a strip of her skirt. Rubies and wisdom. The Book of Job.

That must be it! It was not proper for women to comment on religious matters. "Let your women keep silence in the churches, for it is not permitted unto them to speak. First Corinthians 14."

The hell with men then! She would not pretend to be deaf and dumb. She buried her face in the pillow to stifle her sobs.

A rifle shot shattered the predawn darkness. Hawken rolled over and tucked his head beneath the blanket, try-

ing to hold to his dream. As usual the substance fell into
nothingness. He rubbed his eyes, allowed himself a minute to settle his pounding heart, then shrugged out of his
blankets. For three years no dream had crossed the
boundary into consciousness.

He broke a thin film of ice in the bucket, splashed the
water on his face, shivered fully awake and noted his
dread had returned. Why only at river crossings?

Monty handed him cold coffee and flapjacks left from
supper. In their anxiety to get the crossing done with, no
one kindled a fire. The night watch drove the oxen into
camp, and Captain Hull circulated with encouraging
words but a sober face.

Hawken helped Les and Monty yoke the oxen in the
half-light. There would be no sunrise. Clouds settled on
the high places, forecasting a chilly day ahead. Women
resembled mobile haystacks, two or three shawls covering multiple petticoats. Children shivered in their blankets, leaned from the wagons to catch sight of the boat
that would whisk them over the North Platte.

They'll be disappointed, Hawken thought, unless the
ferrymen had spent the winter doing carpentry. Last year
the ferry had consisted of cottonwood logs hollowed into
rough canoes, and two planks spaced for wagon wheels.
A dozen men pushed the first wagon aboard. A boatman
shoved with a long pole, and the wagon swayed as the
ferry met the current. Hawken sucked in his breath.

"Hope it don't go over," said a voice at his elbow.

His eyes played tricks. He scoured with his knuckles,
blinked, wondered that they had loaded oxen on the ferry.
The cattle would swim, of course. At this moment the
boys drove the herd to the edge of the water. He looked
again. Oxen in panic, bellowing in fright, leaping over

one another, smashing a nonexistent railing... "This isn't true," he whispered. "Can't be—"

The bellow rose, like a finger running up a fiddle string. A scream. Run, run, run...the scream following and enveloping him. Dodge through the gray day, anywhere but the ferry, the shrieks of terror, the tumbling wagon, the vision harrowing his back into raw flesh. His foot caught and he sprawled in the gravel.

"Mary Helen," he tried to say, but the fall had shoved the air from his lungs. Don't remember. Don't see her, half in, half out of the wagon, struggling against the canvas, don't see the wheels spinning in the air, the wagon tipping...blot it like spilled ink! Forget.

He caught his breath, found a moment's respite in the renewed flow of air. Then teams leaping, the wagon on its side, tipping into the water, floating for an instant, Mary Helen terror stricken, arms flailing...the ferry on edge, like the paddle of a gigantic waterwheel, down, down so heavily that the whirling debris showed nothing to suggest that a wagon had ever been on the river.

"Mary Helen."

Forget what is too painful to remember. But the curtain had disappeared, the horror replayed, the frightened oxen, the tottering boat, the swaying wagon. This time he saw the canvas flatten for an instant as it hit the water, the small woman vanishing as the cruel, crushing ferry blotted out her future. His future.

"No! No! No!" He was on his hands and knees, beating the ground with his fists. He stopped when the pain reached his deadened brain, when he saw the blood on the rocks.

"No!"

Hands on his shoulders, hands from another world. A dream? A nightmare, he thought with relief. He would wake, Mary Helen's little hands fluttering at his chest, begging him not to frighten her.

"Hawken. Can I help you?"

No fluttering white hands, but long brown ones with broken nails.

"Hawken. What's the matter? Granny fears the blow to your head—"

He gathered his strength to escape her, then recalled she carried salvation. "Is my pistol still in your saddlebag?"

"Yes. But there's nothing to shoot." She knelt beside him, questioning eyes moving from him to the sage and greasewood. "You've remembered." It was not a question. Worse and worse. He loved Meggie and desired her, and she, drawn in by his emotions, could read his thoughts.

"Give me the pistol." John Charles stirred, six feet away, carrying the pocket holding his relief.

"No," Meggie said.

"I can't stand knowing what I know." He had to speak slowly so the words hung together, so he did not scream in concert with the long echo from the Missouri, stealing behind, snaring him on the North Platte. He clenched his teeth and swallowed, throat so dry it hurt. "I'll take my chance in the other world. This one I cannot bear."

"She's dead."

"Give me the pistol."

"No."

He scrambled to his feet, head whirling. Meggie anticipated him and stood, a guardian between him and death. He stepped toward her, a longer step than he intended, and her skirt brushed his legs. "Give me the pistol."

Her hands spread open on his chest, shoved, and his legs buckled. Green flowering heads of sage surrounded him, the branches snapped one by one, lowering him gradually, and he did not resist. Mary Helen dead, drowned, and he would follow her if he had to fight Meggie…drowned…the river. So easy, just wade into the deep, sink into it.

A final branch snapped and he lay cradled in the sage, yet for a moment he thought the water hissed about him, a rustle that would change into the death-dealing roar of the current when he went under. Another hiss, this time too loud and close.

Hawken struggled against the encircling branches, shattering them heedlessly, threw himself away, rolling free a foot from danger. The snake lifted from its coil, tongue and eyes searching.

"You're a coward," Meggie yelled. "If you really want to die stay with that snake. Let him strike your neck. You'd be dead in two heartbeats. You don't want to die. You're just afraid to remember."

Hawken looked to the ground so he did not see her, preternaturally tall, a slender pillar towering over him. But he could not avoid the song in his head, a chant. *Who is this that cometh out of the wilderness like pillars of smoke, perfumed with myrrh and frankincense?*

"God help me," he prayed.

He closed his eyes, snapped them open when the vision came clear. The ferryboat pitched, the oxen tumbled in a maze of horns and legs, the wagon wavered and tipped in heart-wrenching agony. Hawken lowered his head until his eyes were within an inch of the gravel.

"Go away," he gasped. She hesitated a few seconds, he heard the heavier steps of John Charles and knew he was alone. Sand lined his lips and his hands hurt. No hat, and the healing cut smarted from its scrape through the sage. Focus on the pain, keep the memory at bay. Then distraction. Platte bounding around him, whining and barking.

"Mose?" Hawken whispered the name. The dog stuck a cold nose on his cheek and whimpered. "Mose," Hawken said as clearly and sharply as he could. Ears pricked. "My God! Mose. How did you get out of that wreck? How did you live three years?" He flung his arms about the shaggy neck and the dog's rough tongue licked his tears away.

"Boss, you okay?" Monty leaned over him. "You just playing with old Platte? Here, boss, let me help you up. Les says you do a lot of falling down, and I gotta agree. Only two more wagons and it's our turn. And Captain Hull asks, would you meet with him and the scouts when you get over, since you took a wagon on this road last summer?"

Hawken did not care where he put his feet, for Mary Helen preempted his vision, struggling against the wagon cover that would carry her down. He leaned his weight against the wheel automatically, pushed the wagon onto the ferry, deaf and dumb, grappling with the reality of her death.

"Is your head bothering you, Mr. Hawken?" Granny eyed him narrowly, sympathetically. He touched the sore place and shook his head. "You should wear a hat, even though the sun's behind the clouds."

He looked around, foolishly, as if expecting the hat to be hanging in the sage. "I lost it."

"Come to my wagon. Let me look at your head."

"My wagons are heading—"

"Your men can take care of the wagons. Come with me."

He searched for a path around the vision of Mary

Helen in her hopeless struggle, but the only way—life—led straight through the monstrosity.

"I'm fine," he protested. The vision paled when he spoke. His brain could do only one thing at a time. "Nasty day for a river crossing," he said to Granny's back.

"The oxen won't be frightened by the sun reflecting off the water," she said.

"True. This one, the Green, and we're finished with bad crossings," he said. The simple act of talking forced the ghastly memory to the back of his mind.

"Sit down," Granny said. She peered at the top of his head and poked at the wound. "Healing better than I expected. Meggie says you ran off because you remembered your wife. That she died."

Hawken got his feet under him, but collapsed back on the cot when his head collided with a hickory bow. "I don't want to talk about it."

"She's dead, has been for three years?"

"Yes." He bit his tongue to keep it still. To describe the scene would make it more real.

"It helps to talk. I know, because I watched a horse kick and trample my husband to death."

"I want to forget."

"You've remembered everything?"

Hawken nodded.

"So the good times have come back, too, not just the bad. Concentrate on the good, and pretty soon—"

He shook his head. "There's nothing good. Mary Helen's dead, Fred is dead, and I might as well be."

"Do you remember your name? What you were before?"

"That's the worst part. Mary Helen's dead and I have no hope of ever seeing her again."

"Why? You have no faith in heaven?"

"I have great faith. My name's Thaddeus Milner. Reverend Thaddeus Milner. What I've done in the past three years closes heaven's gate to me."

Granny's hand reached for his. Hawken drew his hand back, abhorring her apt sympathy, her wise counsel, when all he wanted was oblivion. He threw himself out the open door. Just time enough to leap on the ferry. The cattle swam through water gray as the sky, and among the horned heads the wagon tipped over, the boat capsized, falling upon Mary Helen, grinding her fine bones to powder. Again and again, while an unvarying, one-toned shriek reverberated between his ears.

Chapter Eleven

The ferry jerked as it grounded on the mud. Hawken left others to roll the wagon off the boat and elbowed his way through the men who clustered about Captain Hull and the scouts. He'd talk and concentrate on what others said, so he could forget once again. Silence was an enemy. Men gave him sidling glances, then looked away. The news of his recovery had spread.

"What do you think, Hawken?" Sampson asked. "Lay over here or head out?" Sampson examined the gray sky, his eyes finally resting on the glowing spot that marked the sun. "Last year, on horseback, Godfroy and I did the distance between the rivers in one long ride."

"Go on," Hawken said. A lazy day in camp? Nothing but memories to occupy his mind? "We'll reach Willow Springs by evening. Tie the extra teams and the milk cows behind the wagons so they don't wander into the alkali pools. Another day and we're at Independence Rock."

To Hawken's regret his suggestion elicited no discussion. Why didn't one man, two, object? The gathering broke up, leaving him alone. His hands seemed to have no purpose. He grabbed his coat, scratched his neck. He

plunged them into his pockets. Find Monty and Les and
share their small talk, about wagons and oxen, fires and
dinner. He would even discuss Meggie's potential as a
witch. He passed men hitching their teams, knew his hails
of greeting jarred too loudly. He swung away from Jim
Mac's wagons to avoid any chance meeting, but came
face-to-face with Meggie and Granny dragging bulging
India rubber bags of water.

"Here, Mr. Hawken," Granny said, pointing to the
largest of the bags. "Would you carry this to my son's
wagon?" She took off on her own business, leaving him
with Meggie.

Fill the silence. "Thank you for bringing me to my
senses," he said.

"I didn't know there was a snake in that bush," she
whispered, shaken. "Please believe me, I wouldn't shove
any man on top of a rattler."

"Les says I have a lot of accidents around you."

Meggie climbed into the wagon and he hefted the bags,
keeping his eyes on her hands so he would not be reminded of small white ones battling heavy canvas. Yet
they came, wavering from the blur of memory to sharp
outline against the rubber bags.

"Are you riding ahead with Sampson?" he asked.

"No. I wouldn't know good water from poison, and I
won't risk John Charles."

Jim Mac barked at the oxen. Meggie jumped down and
grabbed John Charles's reins. Hawken fell in beside her,
wishing he could pull words from her mouth.

"Don't worry, John Charles would know bad water,"
he said. "It's oxen who drink the alkali." The wrong
thing to say. With that assurance she might mount the
pony and ride off, abandoning him. "The Red Bluffs are
spectacular on a sunny day. Too bad about the clouds."

He swept his hand at the cliff, hoping to spark at least a sentence of appreciation. Instead she stared without words, and furnished a space. The vision coalesced from shadow to a reality firmer than the red rocks.

"I don't know what to call you," Meggie said shyly.

"I'll stick with Hawken." No sense degrading the memory of Thad Milner. Back in Ohio only the memory survived, if any of his parishioners troubled to recall the young man who had served their church. The man who scraped a living from the coins in the collection plate, the green firewood dumped in his dooryard, and the hogs donated by the wealthiest farmer in the neighborhood. Two full-grown swine. He'd felt degraded, standing beside the man dressed in fine Sunday broadcloth. His obsequious thanks had only encouraged the man's sinful pride.

"You say she drowned?"

"The St. Joe ferry. For some reason they loaded the teams, and the boat capsized when the oxen rushed to one side. My wife, her brother, the ferrymen."

"How did you get off?"

"I wasn't aboard." Hawken gritted his teeth and slid back to the April day in St. Joe. He searched for details. Spring just appearing, the first leaves on the underbrush. "I'd gone to the ferry the day before and reserved the first crossing of the morning. We arrived at daybreak, but someone had left an empty wagon on the landing, with a note telling the men to deliver the wagon on the other side first thing. Fred—"

"Who's Fred?"

"My best friend. My brother-in-law. He worried that the men would leave the wagon in our way. At the last minute I jumped aboard to make sure they shoved it aside. The people who saw me go ahead drowned when the boat capsized.''

''No one swam from the wreck?''

Hawken closed his eyes and flinched as he intentionally called up the scene. The oxen in the water, the wagon on its side, the boat poised on edge for what seemed like aeons, then toppling. A sprinkling of people on the bluffs of the town, running to and fro like ants in a hill that's been stepped on. His own foolish dash to an overturned skiff near the landing, tipping it upright, shoving it into the river, and watching it fill up with water through a hole in the bottom.

Reports of the tragedy must have spread up and down the river, and newspapers in far states reprinted the story. He tried following that day in memory, and found only huge blanks. The days between the river crossing and Fort Leavenworth, as near as he could fit the pieces together, three or four weeks, with no recollections at all.

''I think the only creature to survive was my dog.''

''Your dog?''

Hawken shortened a step so Platte caught up. He scratched behind the golden ears. ''He was a stray in St. Joe. He must have jumped off the boat as it went over, then swam to the east shore and found somewhere to hole up for three years. How he knew to head west with you people I can't figure. He recognized me, but I didn't know him.''

Meggie walked a long distance without saying a word, while Hawken fought his ghosts.

''Animals are smart in things we don't understand,'' she finally said. ''Horses aren't tempted by alkali water?''

''Not usually.'' She would ride off, leave him—

''You remember where you come from?''

"A little town in Ohio, north of Cincinnati."

"You were a teamster?"

Hawken regretted the moment of weakness in Granny's wagon. But she knew the truth, and by now was repeating his words to the other women, and from there it would spread throughout the party.

"I was a clergyman."

"A preacher," Meggie gasped. "*You* a preacher?"

"Does it seem so outlandish?"

"I've never known a preacher who wore buckskins, who…who…I thought preachers were just naturally good men. That's the reason they're called, isn't it? Not that you're a bad man, but you don't seem properly…that way at all."

"I'm afraid I'm not," he agreed. "I sailed under false colors, and an accident freed my nature. I fell into evil as fast as the next man, faster and deeper than most, actually. I yielded to temptation without a second thought."

"It won't count against you," Meggie said. "You didn't know what you were doing. You can go back to preaching the gospel, and now you'll have greater sympathy for the sinner, having been there yourself." Her glance suggested she was the sinner needing guidance. "Beg God's pardon, and tell yourself the last three years never happened."

"The last three years happened," Hawken said. "There's no avoiding them. I felt no shame. I wallowed in—" He caught himself before he said "gambling," but that word—and worse—rested bitter on his tongue. The tavern wenches, and the gambling hall girls. If only he could recoil from them as readily as he shrank from the disaster. He should think only of Mary Helen, mourn Mary Helen.

"Will Willow Springs be a pleasant camp?" Meggie asked brightly. Her lips smiled, but the crease across her eyes told him she manufactured her good cheer. And her thoughtfulness added to the torment rending his heart.

"No, not pleasant. Oh, the spring's pretty enough, a few willows, but it's in a gully. The water has to be hauled in buckets for the cattle and horses, and there's next to no feed. Just a little grass at the seep."

"We've reached the hard part of the trip."

Hard part? Nothing ahead of him but the hard part. Each day as unyielding as flint, the road always bearing straight through the image of Mary Helen's death struggle. He'd been a fool, expecting recovery to solve all his problems. Now he faced a lifetime of calamity, disgrace if he returned to the county of his youth, contempt in Independence, the possibility of recognition in any western town. A shaft of sunlight pierced the clouds and rested on the red cliffs.

"I'll go ride in my wagon for a spell," he said. "My eyes hurt when the sun shines, and I've lost my hat."

He reconstructed the uncomfortable bed and tried to organize his muddled brain enough to consider his future. Honor required that he fulfill his promise to Monty and Les. He nearly laughed aloud. Honor? No honor left to him.

After Fort Hall, pick up the pieces of his life. How and where? Not in Ohio, with Reverend and Mrs. Frazer, the aunt and uncle who had raised Mary Helen and Fred, who had taken him in for two years after his parent's death.

They must think him dead with the others. News traveled fast on rivers.

"Best I stay dead," he muttered.

Not to Oregon. That's where he and Fred had been heading, two young men aware of their own righteousness in volunteering for the Oregon missions. Unaware of the arrogance of their righteousness. Too risky to go to Oregon. He'd meet someone who remembered Thad Milner.

A trader on the Bear River? A mountain man on the Bear River. No emigrant would detect the clergyman beneath greasy hair, beard and buckskins. He would adopt the mountain vocabulary and speech, thus eliminate Thad Milner. He should count his blessings; he had gone unrecognized for three years. He imagined the scene, one of his former parishioners passing the gambling hall in Independence, seeing his ex-pastor stagger out, red eyed, to face the rising sun, perhaps a wench on his arm.

He wished he could cry for Mary Helen, but his eyes scratched dry as the sagebrush land. Couldn't he rouse one symptom of sorrow? Nothing but a deep-seated nausea. And regret. Regret that he had ever recaptured the past, for the boat overturned again and again, a mirage spinning inside his head, killing Mary Helen time after time. He dragged himself to the tailgate. He had to talk.

"So what will you do, when you get to Fort Hall?" he asked Les.

Les shrugged. "See what we face when we get there," he said, offering no help in maintaining a conversation.

"Why do you think Miss MacIntyre's a witch?"

Les rolled his eyes to the sky. "So, you're finally believing. You weren't there when she ordered the devil to stop the hailstorm."

On and on, accounts of witch talk with cats and horses and chickens, the probability that the dog was her familiar, for "didn't he just drop from the sky and isn't it the dog that sent you tumbling?" Hawken made nonsensical replies, and kept the specter of death in a compartment building slowly at the back of his head, one brick at a

time. The mass of that wall would weigh on him until
he died.

"I'm glad Mr. Hawken was honest when he described
Willow Springs," Meggie said to her mother, as they
searched for a fire pit out of the wind. "Otherwise I'd
have been disappointed, for the name sounds so pretty."

The clouds had thickened since they'd left the river,
the wind strengthened, and now it lifted bits of rock.
Meggie fed sagebrush into the fire, until pellets of snow
sharp as knives joined the blowing sand. They abandoned
any pretense of cooking and served the bacon half-raw.

Darkness caught the men still watering the cattle. Meggie, feeling guilty that she might crawl into her wagon
and out of the storm, crouched below the lip of the gully,
offering help that no one accepted. Hawken straddled the
spring, lowering buckets into the water. A lantern's flame
reflected on the ice encasing his legs.

"Another bucket," he called. "This the last for you,
Jim Mac? Has John Charles been watered?" He laughed
and Meggie shivered with fear, hearing the overtone of
hysteria. The memory of his wife's death would drive
him mad. She wanted to hold him, as she had when he
cut his head, kiss him, comfort him. But nothing, she
knew, would erase the vision.

"Meggie." Her mother stood above, visible only because the weak light reflected on her snow-plastered
shawl. "You do no one any good getting chilled. Bring
your blankets to the tent. We'll sleep warmer all together."

"I'm not cold," she lied. "I'll be fine in the wagon."

Captain Hull finally took pity on her and told her to
build a fire in the lee of a wagon, so the men could thaw
themselves. She filled the coffeepot and set it to boil. The

ice slid off Hawken's legs in chunks when he finally stopped long enough to warm himself.

"We'll need double guards all night," Captain Hull said, "or the oxen will drift before the wind."

"Count me in. I won't sleep in any event," Hawken said.

Meggie crawled under her chilly blankets. "Here kitty, here kitty," she whispered, but Tabby and her children had long since disappeared beneath the floorboards. She should have a dog, like Hawken. A dog so faithful he waited for three years and set out with strangers to find his master. No cat would do that, she had to admit.

She imagined Hawken curled up with Platte, and that fantasy led to another, more personal vision. He no longer needed her help to recall his wife, but she was still ignorant of the secret of marriage. He'd stopped avoiding her, walked with her all afternoon, talking. Now was her opportunity, when he needed comfort.

"Meggie." Had she imagined someone said her name? Or had it been the hiss of snow and wind? She sat up, keeping the blankets about her shoulders, and leaned to the rear.

"Meggie, let Mose...Platte in. He'll keep you warm. Wait, I'll brush the snow off his back." She exposed one arm to lower the tailgate.

"What about you?"

"I'll be with the cattle."

Firelight illuminated a long, woolen cape, its hood so deep she could not see his face. He boosted the dog, who scrambled in with a rattle of toenails on wood.

"Curl up with him," Hawken said.

"What a wonderful cape," she said. "I've never seen a man—"

"The mountain men call it a capote." He turned around.

"Mr. Hawken. I'm terribly sorry about your wife. You loved her very much. I'm sorry I called you a coward because you...wanted to follow her."

"I've got to see to the oxen," he muttered, and vanished in a whirl of white.

She doubted she could sleep. She wished she could help outside, but she did not have a warm coat. If she had a coat and a huge cape—a capote—she would sit through the night, talking to him. He must feel as she had after the buffalo hunter came, the memory haunting, playing over and over in her mind, a constant, wheeling nightmare.

She pulled the cord tight, leaving only a small hole open to the wind and an occasional snowflake. With her head under the blankets, the wind's buffeting faded to a whisper. Hawken might hear it as the whispering of ghosts.

Restless, Meggie flung her arms over her head, felt the rough wool of the blanket. Her hand touched Tabby, arched, spine bristled and tail swollen, spitting and caterwauling. Platte whined and barked, and lunged futilely at the tiny hole in the wagon cover.

Tabby leaped over her, body spread and claws extended. Platte yelped and the canvas shattered. The cat balanced on the tailgate, satisfied, proud, sounding her triumph in subdued rumbles of hate. Meggie crawled toward the light, dragging blankets behind her. A white world spread to the horizon, and through that world Hawken came tearing, his feet scattering snow like feathers. The dog had taken refuge behind his legs. Tabby retreated and perched above the nook where her family cowered.

"I forgot about the cat," Hawken gasped.

"So did I." His capote was dark blue. He threw back the hood and she saw where Granny had clipped his hair, bristly now as new hairs commenced to grow. His face looked unnaturally thin, his bold chin jutting from hollow cheeks, gray and haggard from lack of sleep, his brown eyes listless. *He needs someone to take care of him.*

"I'll get up and make you some coffee," she said. She searched through the blankets for her boots. She had not bothered to undress.

"Don't get out in the snow. Monty and Les have a fire going and breakfast nearly ready."

His men take care of him, she thought. He has no need for a wife. No need for me. She pulled on her boots anyway. "I must see to John Charles. He can't find anything to eat in the snow."

His eyes had sunk in their orbits, so deep Meggie could trace the skull beneath the skin. Dark circles dipped into his cheeks and the quarter-inch beard. "This snow won't last," he said, his voice tight. "In twenty miles we'll be at Independence Rock, on the Sweetwater River, grass and a day to rest."

Happy laughter echoed through camp but did not alter his bleak face. Pushing the remnants of canvas aside, Meggie saw the boys frolicking in the pristine field, preparing for a snowball fight.

"It don't make snowballs," someone cried. "No more than a pint of dust."

Meggie took a handful of snow from the top of the wagon. It fell through her fingers, refusing to be anything more substantial than snowflakes. "How strange."

"Welcome to the West," Hawken said. "Why don't you join me at breakfast? Your family's still in their tent." His hands grasped her waist and lifted her down.

She snatched the shawl she had worn last night, the wool crumbled beneath her hand. Charred. It must have brushed the fire while she made coffee for the men. She touched her hair, matted from sleep. What must he think of her, in her wrinkled, dirty dress, her hair uncombed, the shawl burned? Mrs. Hawken had been a lovely woman, a fragile beauty with small white hands. Meggie wrapped the shawl so it covered her hands.

She was the only woman awake. Or at least out of bed. Monty nodded a greeting. Les gave her a glare of disapproval.

"Miss MacIntyre will be joining us for breakfast," Hawken announced, "as payment for the damage Platte did to her wagon. He jumped out without untying the puckering string."

"Dog's got good sense," Les muttered.

Monty handed her a stick wrapped with bacon. The men squatted on their heels to cook the meat, but she stood, for fear of dragging her skirt in the snow.

"We don't dirty a skillet," Hawken said.

"But you can't save the grease. It's burned up in the fire. Mother saves bacon fat to spread on biscuits."

"We don't usually bother with biscuits. Now, what are your plans for the day we'll spend at Independence Rock? Climb the rock and carve your name, or—"

"Mother and I'll do the laundry. We'll repack the wagons, because everything turns topsy-turvy when we travel late, and we'll get out the oven and bake bread and biscuits, and maybe a cake. And cook beans—they take so long they're hardly worth the effort when we're on the road every day. And of course I'll repair the wagon cover."

"I'll help with that," Hawken said. "It's my fault. But you must set aside time to climb the rock. Perhaps this evening. I'll escort you, to keep you safe from rattle-snakes.'' He laughed as if he had made a joke. ''Now, here comes your father to fetch you home.''

Sure enough, her father plowed through the snow, examining the sky in the way of all farmers.

''Nineteenth of June!'' he exclaimed. ''No one goes wrong calling this a strange country. Thanks for your help with the cattle. Pete says you stayed out all night.'' Her father spoke to Hawken, but his eyes slid in her direction.

''If Ma's up I'll go help with the fire,'' she said. She made a mocking curtsy that took in Hawken, Monty and Les. ''Thank you for breakfast.'' Hawken and Monty bowed, but Les turned his back, pretending the fire needed his attention.

''Meggie, what were you doing at Mr. Hawken's fire and what happened to the wagon cover?'' her mother said without a ''good morning.''

Meggie rambled through the story of the dog and the cat, of being awakened at first light by the fight, before anyone else. ''Mr. Hawken's afraid to be alone, I guess,'' she said as an end to her recital.

''Afraid?''

''I think he keeps seeing the accident that killed his wife. You know how terrible sights hang on. Granny says she's never free of Grandpa being kicked by the horse, and sometimes the buffalo hunter... Mr. Hawken talks and talks, asking questions so people answer. He was afraid to go to sleep last night, for fear he'd dream, I suppose.''

''Pete said—'' Ma began, but at that moment Pete rounded the wagon, shaking snow off the chains.

''Last night I couldn't get him to shut up. He's a fallen-away preacher. He got the money for his goods by setting up a monte bank in Independence. Monte's a rigged game that doesn't give a man an even chance. A way to fleece innocents. You stay away from Hawken.''

"How do you know about monte?" Meggie asked in a subdued whisper, while she tightened her muscles so she did not kick her brother. Poor Hawken, in a state of panic had confessed his sins and Pete would gossip them to everyone.

"How do you know about monte?" she repeated. Pete stammered and made a great show of untangling the chains. "Have you no pity for the man?" Meggie cried. "He watched the woman he loved—his only family in the whole world—be crushed and drowned, and the sight was so dreadful he couldn't bear to think of it. So his mind failed. You're a great one to lord over him, Pete MacIntyre. You who've never spent a day of your life on your own, always with me and Granny, or Ma and Pa. What would you do if you found yourself all alone?''

"I'd remember who I was," Pete growled. "And I wouldn't turn gambler.''

"Peter, how do you know about monte?" Ma asked, her hands on her hips. Pete bundled the chain in his arms and returned to the other side of the wagon.

Ma glared at his back. "Sons are difficult when they are of age," she said, returning to the fire. "But Peter's right, you shouldn't spend too much time in Mr. Hawken's company. You'll discourage more qualified young men.''

"There aren't men along who might court me," Meggie said. Her mother did not dispute this obvious truth. "He wants to talk. Yesterday I thought he'd explode, or run about mad as a hatter.''

"Why must it be you who comforts him?''

Why? Because whenever she looked at him, something

happened inside, frothy cream in her belly, and she knew she would let...but she couldn't tell her mother *that*.

"He saved my life. No one else went after the buffalo hunter. And he hung about me day after day when I was afraid the man's friends would come back. A silly thing to be scared of, now that I think about it, but it didn't seem silly at the time. Turn about's fair play. He stood by me. I stand by him."

Ma turned the bacon. "Get out the oven, Meggie. We won't leave early this morning, for the road's completely covered. I'll bake biscuits."

"Ma, please, Mr. Hawken was very kind to me."

Her mother sighed. "You may spend time with him during the day, but take care that the two of you don't by misadventure find yourselves alone. I know I can trust you, that you'll not *arrange* an assignation with Mr. Hawken."

"Yes, Ma." She searched for the reflector oven, and grudgingly admired the way her mother had forestalled her planned experiment. Instead of warning her not to sin, she had praised her virtue.

Chapter Twelve

The Sweetwater River, viewed from the top of Independence Rock, lazed on the countryside like a friendly snake. Hawken turned the image over in his mind, mildly surprised. Had he changed his mind about snakes? No answer surfaced, because he was dreadfully tired. Sometime soon his mind would lose the battle and he would fall asleep. And dream.

Long shadows exaggerated the irregularities in the stream, turning ripples into towering waves. Inexorably they became the waves of the springtime Missouri, the ferry boat setting out in the gray light.... He flinched from the image and swung to face the four young women instead of the river. *Stay alert,* he ordered. *You brought them here and their families hold you responsible for getting them down.* From this new angle he could see the carving just beyond his fingertips. *Hawken, July 3, 1847.* He was tempted to add his real name, even though he had told himself, over and over again for the past twenty-four hours, that Thad Milner must fade into obscurity. Inevitably an emigrant from Ohio would stand here and wonder at the name of a dead man.

In memory of Thad Milner? But that required the ad-

dition of Frederick Frazer and Mary Helen Frazer Milner.
A day's work, carving all those letters, and he could not
bear to be alone for so long. He'd made it through the
day with Meggie's help, listening to her chatter about her
home, and every party and dance ever held in Pikeston.
She told him strange stories, the kind that lurk behind
the respectable facades of all small towns. Of a Yankee
who came to marry Tildy, and how Matt Hull turned
lawyer to expose the bridegroom as a fake. Of Godfroy's
fathering Rachel by stealth, so she learned he *was* her
father only last fall.

Maybe everyone had dark memories they'd rather forget. Not a thought he greeted happily. It made more evident the extent of his cowardice.

The wind caught the women's skirts and all but Meggie gathered the fullness against their legs, fists tight on
their thighs. Miss Tole—Faith—was the tallest of the
four, the eldest, and the loveliest in terms of classical
beauty. Tildy—Mrs. Hull he should say—was almost as
tall as Faith, but more buxom. She had a pleasant face,
hair nearly as red as Meggie's. Mrs. Hunter—Rachel—
was several inches shorter than her friends. Lovely, in an
unusual way, with large dark eyes and a wide mouth.

Les is right, Hawken thought. Viewed dispassionately,
Meggie was no beauty. Her pert charm depended on wide
blue eyes and a pointy chin. Her unrestrained skirt flew
up, exposing drawers that came below her knees and met
stockings that rose…he checked himself before his imagination reconstructed the length of her stockings. Meggie
twirled around to bring her skirt under control.

"We want to know what we're seeing," Mrs. Hull
said. Hawken managed a spry leap to his feet, and stifled
a yawn as he pointed to the obvious landmarks. The trail
and the crossing of the Sweetwater, the Wind River

Mountains, whose snow-spotted peaks reared against the sky.

"Captain Frémont climbed the highest peak in '42," Meggie said. Her hero, who performed deeds of derring-do and faced adversity with composure. He shrank from her. Did she make the comparison? To his discredit.

"Devil's Gate's a few miles west." Hawken waved his hand at the gap in the western mountains. "The whole river rushes through a space no wider then a road. And beyond, one of the most pleasant pastures we'll find in this country."

"And we're the first on the grass," Meggie said. She turned to the meadow. "There come Mr. Godfroy and Mr. Hunter."

"I must go." Mrs. Hunter said. "Their packhorse is loaded. See the antlers! A big buck."

Hawken offered the women a helping hand where the rock had fractured, creating a high step. Meggie came last and she held his hand longer than necessary. "Thank you," she whispered.

"Thank *you*. You've been a great help today. How did you know I needed company?"

"I remembered how I felt after the buffalo hunter. How grateful I was to you for staying near me."

"Tomorrow we'll climb up again, and bring a hammer and chisel to carve your name." Her friends zigzagged down, several feet below. He stood aside so Meggie could catch up with them.

"Perhaps you'll want to be alone," she said. "You could make a little memorial for your wife. Since you have no grave to visit... Granny says the hardest thing to leave was Grandpa's grave. She'd go there and talk to him."

"No. How many times in my life will I visit Independence Rock? Besides, Mary Helen didn't want to come west. She was on the ferry because Fred and I got a bug in our ears about the mission to the Indians. I doubt her soul would be pleased by a memorial on the overland trail.''

"Strange. Some women hate the idea of moving and others look forward to the adventure,'' Meggie said. "Granny and I could hardly wait for winter to pass. Ma came willingly, because Pa had the ague every summer, but she would never have set out on her own. When Mr. Tole said he'd head west, I thought Faith would simply die! We were quilting my double-ax patchwork and she burst into tears and I feared she'd wet my quilt. Now men—'' her gesture encompassed the camp ''—they're all eager and brave to risk it.''

"Not all men. The difference is, a woman may want to head west, but if her husband is tied to home she'll never go, because she must obey him. But a man, he'll drag the poor woman along whether she's eager or not.''

"I never thought of it that way. I'm glad I didn't marry back in Indiana. My husband might have been a laggard.''

"You wouldn't let a laggard husband stop you," he said, and was shocked that laughter welled in his chest. Only this morning he had doubted that he would ever laugh again. "I believe you would tell a husband to cook his own grub and tend the children, if you had a chance for adventure.''

"California will be quite sufficient.''

"Beyond California lies the Pacific, the road to the Sandwich Islands, and China. You won't be tempted?''

"I've never been on a ship," she said doubtfully. "I'd have to leave John Charles behind, and I might get sea-sick.'' She pursed her lips in thought. Kissable lips that emphasized her pointed chin and face of love.

"I could make a short voyage to find out if I get sea-sick,'' she said, nodding. Hawken gave her two years in California before she embarked for the Orient.

"I think your driver's trying to get your attention,'' she said.

Monty waved his arms and shouted, even jumped a time or two. Hawken solemnly escorted Meggie to her family's wagons before he investigated the cause of Monty's panic. As he approached his wagons, the last of his strength ebbed away, leaving him with little energy to cope with an emergency.

Monty held out a bucket. Hawken approached it warily, recalling Les's proposal that they catch a rattlesnake, for the medicinal properties of the rattles. Milk, so fresh from the cow it foamed.

"I don't have eggs,'' Monty said in a conspiratorial whisper. "But Mr. Jim Mac's got chickens, and one might have laid an egg today. You're getting thick with that girl, and if you could talk them out of an egg I'll make a pudding to set your tongue singing.''

"How?'' Had Monty pried open the tins of dried apples? Or the treasured sticks of cinnamon?

Monty leaned very close. "Gooseberries. Les wandered upriver and found them. Picked 'em before anybody else saw.''

"I'll ask about an egg,'' Hawken said.

The entire MacIntyre clan gathered about one large fire. The reflector oven stood well back from the flames, and several pots steamed.

"Come, Mr. Hawken,'' Mrs. Jim Mac hailed, pointing to the coffeepot. "Meggie and Tildy are telling us about the rock. They say we must exert ourselves tomorrow.''

Meggie sat cross-legged near the fire, petting the kittens who frolicked about her knees. He kept his eyes on Mrs. MacIntyre, even as his treacherous brain thought of a brown hand resting on his arm.

"Independence Rock's one of the wonders of the world," he said, a noncommittal statement.

"Forty yards high and six hundred fifty yards long," Meggie said. "It's unthinkable not to climb it while we're here."

He could almost imagine he felt the weight of her hand. He looked down, saw it, but gnarled and aged. Granny's. "I'll not live long enough to pass this way again, so I *must* get to the top," she said. "I depend upon you and Pete for an escort. Both of you, for you might have to drag me up by main strength and awkwardness."

"I'll get you there," Pete said, and Hawken agreed rapidly, without thinking. For some reason Pete must not outdistance him in service to Granny.

"Tomorrow is the Sabbath," Mrs. Jim Mac said, leaving a question hanging in the air: Was it proper to spend the Lord's day larking on Independence Rock? "But then," she continued, answering her own dilemma, "I'll be washing and baking. The Oregon party will probably catch up, maybe early enough that Reverend Cowie can preach in the evening, so the day's not completely irreligious."

A discussion on what might be allowed on Sunday followed, and several minutes passed before Hawken could politely draw Granny aside and mention the possibility of an egg.

"Is that your price for serving as guide?" Granny asked, the mischief in her face reminding him of Meggie. She left him before he found an answer, delivered the

egg in a small basket, nested in dry grass like a jewel
sunk in tan velvet.

Monty went into ecstasies about the perfection of the
egg. "I do like eggs," he said as he mixed the pudding
and set it at the edge of the fire. "Maybe when we get
where we're going, I'll grow chickens, and have all the
eggs I want, and plenty to sell. I'll need a dog, though,
to keep the foxes and rats away." He eyed Platte.

"No," Hawken said. The slow twang of Tildy's banjo
encouraged sleep. "I'll stretch out under the wagon until
supper's ready." A melody sung by a soprano, the swish
of the tall grass as accompaniment.

He looked down on a camp meeting, as if he floated
in the air. Fred told him he would preach after the hymn.
But he had nothing to say, not one single note for lesson
or sermon, no matter how thoroughly he turned his pockets inside out. He snatched the Bible Fred held. A monte
deck. He laid out four cards, pleased to see the ten of
hearts, always his lucky suit. Monty placed his wager, a
pile of gooseberries on the jack of diamonds. Western
gooseberries, smooth and yellow.

"That pudding's cool enough eat, boss."

It was a magnificent pudding, richly thickened by the
egg and topped with a heap of berries. Monty gave in to
Platte's whines and allowed him to lick the pot. The dog
vanished to his shoulders.

Hawken ate without tasting. For the first time in three
years a dream had followed him into daylight. Absurd
events that made no sense. The camp meeting resembled
no place he had ever preached, although the singing, dis-
cordant and uneven, had been realistic enough. The grove
had been too cool and moist. Camp meetings were held
in August, when the leaves hung dusty green and the air
barely moved. After the hay had been cut and the crops

laid by, when farmers could spare a day away from home. And to find himself unprepared? Part of his fame had been the readiness of his tongue, always available with a message....

The dream foretold his future. From now on he had nothing to say. A great sinner does not stand before good men and women and pretend to instruct them.

"We still heading for Bear River Valley, boss?" Les asked.

"We'll stop in Bear River Valley," Hawken said, this moment certain. "You help me build a stockade and cabin, then go on to Fort Hall if you want. Or stick around and I'll find something for you to do. Not far now. Over South Pass, across the Green."

"That gal won't stop with us?" Les asked fearfully. He pointed his spoon toward the MacIntyre clan.

"No, Miss MacIntyre belongs with her family and friends. She doesn't like buffalo hunters and mountain men in their natural environment."

Les grinned. "Wasn't a right thing, what that buffalo hunter did, but I'm *glad* he did."

Meggie examined the shrinking pile of dung, willow and sage. Barely enough fuel to cook supper and breakfast tomorrow, and the boys on top of the rock. She could not finish the laundry and collect wood at the same time. She filled the tub at the river, the water so cold her hands ached as she wrung out her father's shirts.

"A man's coming," Granny said. "On horseback." A trill of fear slithered down Meggie's back, and for a moment overcame the pain in her hands. The odor of buffalo hunter drifted in memory. Granny thumped the wash basket on the ground and the homely gesture restored the present.

"I suppose it's the scout riding ahead of the Oregon party," Granny said. Meggie nodded and returned to the washtub. No time to waste, for the clothes must be hung to dry before the evening church service.

"He's not looking for a camp spot," Granny said, shading her eyes. "Riding straight to us. Wants to speak to Matt, I suppose."

"He'll have to wait," Meggie said, lifting her eyes momentarily to where chisel and hammer clanged. She swished her hands through the water; they came up empty. She stood erect, stretched to work the cricks out of neck and back. The man, whoever he was, babied the horse. No wonder, it limped. He slid out of the saddle and walked the last hundred yards, hobbling on legs stiff from hours in the saddle. Not a man at all, but a boy of fourteen or fifteen.

"Where's Captain Hull?" he yelled. Granny pointed to the rock. "We need help." His voice broke from tenor to soprano. "Godfroy or Sampson?"

"All the men climbed the rock after they finished the blacksmithing," Granny said.

"Half our cattle's gone," the boy said. "Damn storm." The curse almost balanced out a sob. Meggie threw the kerchiefs over the rope strung between the wagons, pretending she did not see the tear furrowing his cheek.

"Mr. Hawken's in camp," Granny said kindly. "Meggie, take him to Mr. Hawken."

Hawken had spent the day unpacking his wagons, spreading the contents of barrels and parcels to air in the sunshine. He leaned over a sack of flour and stirred to bring the damp to the top. At Meggie's warning hail he straightened and adjusted the knotted bandanna he wore in place of a hat. The boy, who had been limping behind her, staggered forward and started talking and waving his hands without a word of introduction.

"We need help," he said. "The cattle ran, and half—"

"Whoa!" Hawken waved him to silence. "Meggie, would you pour this fellow a cup of coffee? The pot's still on the fire. Now, who sent you?"

"Captain Moran."

"What's your name?"

"Sam. Sam Tustin."

"Sit down, Sam. Captain Moran told you to come ahead because your cattle scattered?" Sam nodded. "Start at the beginning. Where and when did this happen?"

"Other side of the river. Two nights ago."

"In the storm?" Sam grabbed the tin cup from Meggie. "Half the oxen gone, you say?" A slight nod only after he drained the cup.

"When did you leave camp?"

"This morning before sunup. They're ferrying some of the wagons across today, those with teams, but most of the men rode out early to hunt for the strays. Captain Moran says for you fellows to come back and help."

"We rode out the same storm," Hawken said bluntly. He returned to stirring the flour. "We set a guard—"

"Mr. Hawken didn't sleep all that night," Meggie said, determined that Hawken should get the credit he deserved.

"Must not have been so wild where you was camped," Sam muttered. "We couldn't bear to be out, the snow sailing on the wind like bullets."

"Yes," Hawken said flatly. "Meggie, could you or your grandmother get him something to eat? I'd feed him, but Monty and Les put everything away and climbed the rock."

"But what are you gonna do?" cried the boy.

"Wait for Captain Hull and the scouts to come down. You unsaddle your horse and eat something, crawl under a wagon and close your eyes."

"Captain Moran said if you men would ride back through the night—the moon's near full—there's a chance—"

"I don't make the decisions. Talk to Captain Hull."

"Come, I'll find you something to eat," Meggie said, to spare Hawken any more of Sam's pleading.

"Your menfolks just gotta ride back and help," Sam said before they had reached the wagon. "There's women and kids stranded—"

"Talk to Captain Hull and the scouts," she said. Meggie wished the men would come off the rock, and relieve her of Sam's pleading. She sighed in relief when she heard the scrape of hobnails on stone, but when she looked she saw not the men coming down, but Hawken and the yellow dog heading up. She felt a rush of gratitude, that Hawken understood her position and would hurry things along.

She lowered the tailgate, pulled out crackers, stewed apples and cold beans that had baked overnight in the ashes. Rummaging in the wagon attracted John Charles, who trotted up, expecting a tidbit.

"Go away," Meggie said. He nuzzled her hand, she smacked his nose.

"Nice pony," Sam said.

"Spoiled," Meggie said.

"Captain Moran didn't think we needed night guards, since we'd camped right there at the ferry." Meggie handed Sam a plate of food and a cup of hours-old coffee. Granny was folding clothes, and Meggie went to help to escape Sam's whines. Clothes dried quickly in the desert.

But so did lips and hands, until they cracked open into sores that did not heal. Had the laundry helped or hurt? She stared at her hands as if they were new to her. An open sore on the side of the right, cracks between all her fingers. Big, ugly hands, darkened by the sun. Not small and white.

Sam leaned against a wagon wheel, his head drooping. Meggie touched his leg with her toe.

"Unsaddle your horse and turn him out with the rest. He needs water and grass." Sam's head bobbed, but he pulled himself to his feet and managed to get to the horse without falling down.

On the rock men clustered about Hawken. Meggie wondered if she should point this out to Sam, and give him a chance to tell his side of the story. But he was sound asleep under her wagon. Meggie emptied the tub and hung it facing the sun, crawled into her wagon, fingering the tattered canvas. Patching it seemed impossible. She found her scissors and clipped away a few of the ragged ends.

"Meggie!" Captain Hull trotted through the grass. "Where's the boy?" She pointed under the wagon. "Come with me."

The men were gathering around the embers of Hawken's fire, while Monty encouraged the flames on a thick trunk of sage. Meggie shook her wet skirt over the heat.

"Did the boy say anything more to you after Hawken left?" Captain Hull demanded.

"Talked constantly, over and over again, that they need help finding their cattle."

"We'd exhaust our horses riding back to the river," Godfroy said, "then spend two days in the hills, probably finding no more than they have on their own. Four or five days wasted. Our oxen can't stay here that long, there's not grass enough. The women would have to push on up the Sweetwater. Any of you men willing to leave your families unprotected?''

"It's better that Moran send to Fort Laramie for help,'' Sampson said.

Meggie thought of the women camped by the river, waiting in despair and fear. "But our Christian duty,'' she said, hardly more than a whisper.

The men did not look at her, but at Hawken.

"What do you say to that?'' Sampson asked. They expect him to give moral advice, Meggie thought. They know he was a clergyman, so they'll turn questions of right and wrong over to him.

Hawken shifted uneasily. "I can't advise on such things,'' he muttered.

"God helps them that help themselves,'' Pete said harshly. "We froze in the snow, Hawken and me, and every other man here took his turn. The Oregonians didn't.''

"They didn't even try,'' Meggie exclaimed in sudden remembrance. "Captain Moran didn't think a guard necessary the night of the storm. Sam told me. They thought, because they camped close to the ferry—''

The men got to their feet, and Meggie understood that her words had settled the issue.

"We won't put our people in danger to save the slack-witted,'' Godfroy muttered.

"I'll write a note,'' Captain Hull said, "and Sam can carry it back to Moran. We're going on.''

"Tell 'em to leave some wagons behind,'' Sampson said. "Throw out the plows and cookstoves. They've overburdened their animals.''

Overburdened. Sam's horse. "I don't think Sam can ride back tomorrow unless we give him a horse,'' Meggie said. "His is lame, that bony brown one." She indicated the animal with a tilt of her head.

"The boy can trail along with us until Moran catches up," Godfroy said, shrugging. "I'll not exchange one of our good horses for that bag of bones. Moran should never have sent a lone boy that distance. What if he'd crossed the trail of Indians? Leave the note in a forked stick, at the spot where the trail hits the river."

"Hawken, could you give me a hand with this note?" Captain Hull asked. "To ease the phraseology a little. My writing tends too much to the legal." A shadow crossed Hawken's face. His deep nod of assent dislodged the knotted bandanna and it slid to the ground.

Captain Hull and Hawken established themselves on the steps of Granny's wagon, the planed board on which she cut herbs balanced on their knees. They muttered, scratched with a pencil on the wood before marking the paper.

"Glad we're women," Ma said. "We may carry a load of work, but nothing so unpleasant as men. How hateful, to refuse succor to fellow Christians."

Poor Hawken! He had once lectured others on Christian duty. Meggie fed more sticks into the fire. Willow burned fast, with little heat, and the fire demanded constant tending.

"Meggie," Captain Hull said. "Come here."

"Why should she be involved?" Ma asked, stepping between her and the men. Meggie looked from her mother to Captain Hull, uncertain.

"She remembers the books," Captain Hull said. Ma stepped aside; Meggie dropped the sticks but did not leave the fire. "What does Frémont say about the road ahead?" he asked.

Meggie closed her eyes until the page resolved in her

mind's eye. "'Five miles above Rock Independence we came to a place called the Devil's Gate, where the Sweetwater cuts through the point—'"

"The trail, not the sight-seeing parts," Captain Hull said, a bit harsh, revealing the strain he felt. Tonight Tildy would comfort him. She must not think of that, but about the sort of message Captain Hull would want to leave for those straggling behind. Something encouraging, no doubt.

"'There was no timber of any kind on the river, but good fires were made of driftwood.'" Captain Hull nodded, encouraging her to continue. "'Green valleys open in upon the river. We encamped at night, after a march of twenty-six miles; and numerous bright-colored flowers made the river bottom look gay as a garden.'"

"Good," Captain Hull said. "Hawken, write they'll find a lush valley with plenty of grazing."

"Parts of the Sweetwater road are sandy. Real hard pulling," Hawken said.

"They'll find that out. Tell them we'll rest a day if we happen upon exceptional grass, so they're sure to catch us. Otherwise, we'll spend a day or two at Bridger's."

"You're going by way of Bridger's?" Hawken asked, jerking up from his writing.

"Sampson's meeting his wife and children there. We agreed before we left, we'd go by way of Fort Bridger."

"The cutoff is eighty miles shorter."

"But sixty miles of that's got no water," Captain Hull replied. "And Godfroy says it's easier to cross the Green River on the Bridger route. Tell Moran if his party uses the cutoff, we'll meet someplace around Bear River."

A ghost of a smile altered Hawken's lips. He had smiled very little since the ferry over the North Platte.

Meggie decided to take advantage of his momentary good humor.

"We'll have time for a detour to Devil's Gate?"

"Anyone can go who's willing to walk an extra mile or two," Captain Hull said. "They'll catch up with us at noon, in the pastures beyond."

Hawken scratched at the board with the pencil, not words, Meggie saw, but doodles.

"Write that out, Hawken. I'll go cut a stick."

"Mr. Hawken," Ma said. "Since the Oregon party won't be coming, we'll have no service tonight. Could we prevail upon you? Pete says you're a clergyman."

Hawken's face drained of blood, leaving him the color of putty. The pencil hung in the air. "Once," he said. "Once I was, but no more. I have nothing to say of any use." He returned to his writing, his smile gone.

"I'm sorry I mentioned it," Ma whispered. "What a terrible thing, like waking from sleep when you've had one nightmare after another. Except that his nightmares are true. Who would think of such a thing. A preacher turning gambler!"

Chapter Thirteen

The dog woke Hawken, a low huff in his ear and a cold nose on his cheek. He sensed more than heard a rasp that seemed to be the ending of a more significant noise. A skunk chewing the harness? A wolf? Hawken rolled over inside his blankets and at the same time pulled his rifle in front of him. He kicked at the blankets, and the cold air hit his legs, reminding him he was naked. Damn Monty and his preoccupation with laundry! When he had learned their next day of rest would come after South Pass, he stayed up past moonrise, washing every stitch of clothing.

Hawken strained his ears, but heard only the normal sounds of night. The moon rode straight overhead, casting narrow shadows that revealed nothing out of the ordinary. Platte slithered from under the wagon, looked back, asking his master to follow. He whined.

An indistinct rustle, which might be someone turning over in their sleep. Or had the dog's whine startled a thief? Hawken waited, alert. A minute. Two. Another rustle and definite movement, a crouched form leading a horse beyond the circle of wagons. The sound that had awakened Platte must have been the lifting of a tongue. Hawken rolled from under the wagon.

"Go, Platte!" he whispered. The dog leaped and Hawken scrambled behind him. He had reached the middle of the circle when a shriek brought him up short. Where? Heads poked from tents and bedrolls. Women and children leaned from the wagons, the women trying to disguise their nightdresses with blankets and shawls. For an instant Hawken almost turned back to his wagons to conceal his nakedness, but logic said he must keep after the thief until another man joined the pursuit.

In the moment of hesitation he lost track of which gap had been opened. No sense wasting time searching; simply leap over the closest tongue. Hawken had one leg in the air when a moon-silvered horse loomed, front feet off the ground. He threw himself sideways to avoid the flying hooves and hit solidly against a wagon. Pain shot down his arm, white light flared in his eyes. He had time to wonder if he had reopened the cut on his head before John Charles soared over him, a silhouette of legs and neck that blotted out the moon.

The camp erupted. Light glanced like quicksilver from rifle barrels. Someone would get killed! Hawken untangled himself from the chains that had been draped over the tongue. He got his feet under him, stood, but sank back down on the tongue, his head spinning. He leaned over, praying he did not faint. The tailgate before him dropped with a thud, the noise like a hammer blow on his skull. A fuzzy angel crawled into the moonlight. No, not an angel—Meggie in a white shift that came halfway down her thighs.

Hawken made the curious discovery that a naked man holding a rifle in one hand cannot cover himself decently. He wanted to point the fact out to Meggie, but the path between thought and speech had narrowed to the vanishing point.

"John Charles?" she asked.

He mulled over an answer for what seemed like an eternity, before settling upon a single word. "Safe." He lifted a hand to show her where the pony stood in the wagon circle, still huffing from his exertions, remembered that hand's duty and jerked his head toward the horses. His face was very warm, a curious reaction on a chilly night.

"The boy tried to make off with John Charles?"

Hawken snatched a thought as it whirled by. "The boy?"

"Sam, the boy Captain Moran sent. He admired John Charles and he wasn't happy when Captain Hull told him he had to stay with us because his horse isn't fit. So I put prickly pear in his saddle blanket. When Sam pitched it on his back—"

"Whose?" The muscles of Hawken's back twitched at the picture of a naked man loaded with prickly pear.

"John Charles's back. When Sam flung it...you don't have anything on! Aren't you cold?"

Hawken decided, after extended thought, that he was hot.

"Here he is!" a woman shouted from the other side of camp. "Crawling about under the wagons." A figure floated into the moonlight, other shadows intercepted him, moving with such slow deliberation their shouts seemed wildly inappropriate.

"Tie him to a wagon wheel so we can go to sleep."

"Let me go!" Sam cried. "My folks'll be fretting themselves sick if I don't get back."

Unintelligible begging and pleading, and a slight struggle that spooked the horses once more.

"Get in bed," Captain Hull shouted. "Sam, tomorrow you head back on your bony horse carrying the note. But I'm adding a postscript. That we tried to keep you, so when your folks find your bleaching bones they'll not blame me."

"Hawken, get up here and tell me what's going on," Meggie whispered. She disappeared under the canvas. He sidled along the tongue, keeping his rear end clear of the splintery wood, leaned his rifle against the wagon.

"Throw me a blanket."

A clump of fabric emerged from the wagon and fell to the ground. Hawken wrapped it about his waist, climbed onto the tailgate and sat with his legs dangling.

"The dog woke me," he began. Her fingers tangled in his hair, twisted his head and drew it in the shadow. Her lips flexed with an easy mobility, caressing his mouth from corner to corner. His head hurt because her hand pressed on the cut. He curled himself into a ball and worked away from her, trying to tell her to let go.

He must stay under the canvas. Don't let anyone see his legs hanging out the back of Meggie's wagon. He opened his mouth to explain, and the kiss deepened. He felt woozier than before, his heartbeat resonated lower and lower.

"Meggie," he whispered. She knelt before him, took his hands and placed them on the curve of her hips, one at a time. Hips narrower than Mary Helen's. Slowly he gathered the shift in his fingers, lifting it from her legs. Smooth skin beneath his fingers. He bent to kiss her and found her lips immobile, her entire body stiff.

Their roles had changed. He had become the aggressor, and the knowledge that he was in control caused a new surge of heat. And a streak of fear when someone lifted a lantern, a ray of light…a beam of moonlight slanting through the flaps. She sat on her heels, the shift under her arms, her legs spread.

"Granny asked me not to," he whispered, the only words halfway relevant.

"I wanted to know," she said. "But now I'm not sure."

He searched for a stable handhold, so he did not topple from his dizziness, and accidentally brushed the rise of her breast. She scrambled backward, he spun away, regretting the warmth and closeness as he hurtled into the cool night air.

Platte uncurled from his watch place beneath the wagon. Not the first time Platte had stood guard while his master satisfied the demands of the flesh. Hawken crept to his blankets, pulled the dog against him to still his shivering. Platte—Mose then—had never tried to enter the wagon when he made love to Mary Helen, if the one-sided passion to which she acceded could be called love. He hated himself for the recollection. She had never refused him, but every yielding accused him of sins of the flesh. Two days before they arrived in St. Joe he had reached for her, and she rejected him, whispering that she was with child. Without elaboration, he understood he was to leave her alone.

The ferry shoved off from the eastern shore, the long oars battled the current, the cattle thrashed, the boat overbalanced, the oars sticking up like the antennae of a crushed insect. The wagon tipping, tipping, and Mary Helen...she must have cried out, but the scream that reached his ears could not have been hers, so far distant. She must have begged him to save her. Save the child.

Hawken wrapped his arms about Platte. For the first time the image came with a degree of detachment. An emotionless event, related in an inexpressible manner to the strange sexual encounter with Meggie.

Tears overflowed, and sobs seized him. "Mary Helen," he whispered, but Meggie preempted his thoughts. He wished he lay beside her, that she comforted him with her alto murmurings and caressed him with her rough hands. The flexing muscles, her searching flesh, the eager attentions of her lips and tongue.

If he had not been addled by the blow to his head dodging John Charles, he never would have been tempted into Meggie's wagon. He loved Mary Helen, would always love her.

The truth flitted like a moth, he brushed it away, but it flew in from another angle. The memory was abhorrent, but not as abhorrent as Mary Helen's last moment, and he could stand to think of that.

"I did not love her," he whispered. The mission board had been quite definite, men going to Oregon must be married. The only woman for whom he had felt the slightest affection was Mary Helen. And Fred had been so insistent that she come along.

Fred, the clever fellow, had proposed marriage by mail to a clergyman's daughter in St. Joe. When they met in the flesh they had, by mutual agreement, decided against the match. And out of convenient reach of the mission board, Fred had set out a bachelor.

Just as well. The clergyman's daughter would have been on the ferry.

He rolled over, his head free of the wagon's shadow so he could commune with the man in the moon. Les had warned him against sleeping in moonlight. It would strengthen the witchery and drive him to lunacy. And so it had. He was in love with another woman when he should be mourning his wife.

He pulled his nakedness full into the glare. He would give Mary Helen her due, for she had served him gently and meekly. She had been his wife. He would mourn her openly. A bit of crepe around his hat and a black band on his arm, at the very least. But his hat had been lost at the crossing of the North Platte. Black crepe? Where would he find that on the Sweetwater River?

Avoid Meggie MacIntyre, she who bewitched him. The moonlight was an antidote to her charm, and in the moonlight everything made sense.

Meggie sprawled on the brink of the chasm, her head jutting into thin air, and stared down into the fury of Devil's Gate. Thrilling! The entire river tore through a space no wider than their barnyard in Indiana, and the walls of the gorge rose to heights she could not estimate.

Tildy's fingers tightened around her ankles and strained, telling Meggie she had spent enough time gawking. She inched back, amused by the relief that flooded her friends' faces.

"How grand!" she enthused. "Let me hold on to you, Tildy."

"I wouldn't do that for a thousand dollars," Rachel said, already turning down the hill.

Meggie shivered. The gorge reminded her of her expectations of love. But the instant the moonbeam had fallen on Hawken, she had been unable to go on. The kiss, particularly the way Hawken used his tongue, had been thrilling. But the rest? She would never be the giggling partner Tildy was.

Below, the wagons strung out on a sweep of green, like beads flung casually on green velvet. Tiny figures walked among the animals, people without identity. Except for one figure striding to the river. Her heart lurched as it had last night, in the instant of revelation. So different from other men that she would know his footfalls in the dark, his touch, and his voice at a level below a whisper. Last night, she had anticipated bubbling in her abdomen, but instead had been frightened out of breath.

Tildy veered toward the river, where they scooped up cold water in doubled palms. A clump of tasseled grass towered over her, green shoots emerging from a tangle of last year's stalks. Meggie broke off a stem.

"This would make a straw hat," she said. A hat to replace the one Hawken lost at the ferry crossing. A hat to thank him for last night. It wasn't his fault that she couldn't stand being touched.

Rachel ran her hands down the stems, nodding. "Will could use a new hat."

They gathered a great bundle and Meggie spent the final minutes of their nooning splitting the stems to the proper thickness. She plaited a few inches and started the coil that would form the top of the crown.

Hawken and his men spread a length of calico on the grass. Perhaps snow had blown into his wagons and dampened the cloth. Somewhere he had acquired a scrap of black broadcloth and knotted it about his upper arm. A sign of mourning. A sign that he would not come into her wagon again? A totally unnecessary signal to her. She'd been so relieved when he jumped out, she'd knelt and given thanks until her knees cramped.

"A hat?" Granny asked.

"Mr. Hawken lost his hat when we crossed the river."

"He asked me for a bit of black cloth this morning," Granny said, "so I raided the scrap bag. We talked for quite a long time."

Meggie held her breath. Hawken had told Granny how

she had tempted him last night. Now would come the scolding, not so easily dismissed as short hair.

"I was surprised when he didn't go to Devil's Gate," Granny said, "but he's feeling uncertain. How should he mourn his wife? After all, in reality she's three years gone. I told him the spirit mourns on its own schedule and his time has come. He doesn't know if her body was ever found and if there's a grave."

Meggie resumed breathing without being noisy about it and concentrated on the plait. Hawken had not told Granny about last night.

"Chain up!" Captain Hull shouted. Meggie shoved the grass into a gunnysack and tied it to the end of her wagon.

"Get your pony," Pete said. "There're alkali pools and swamps along the trail, and Sampson wants you to lead a string of horses so they don't get mired. We'll go ten or twelve miles before we stop beyond the poison water."

"Mr. Sampson might have asked me himself," Meggie snapped. She lifted the saddle from the wagon, flung it over her shoulder and set out to find John Charles. He saw her and broke away from the herd, and to Meggie's chagrin met her not twenty feet from Hawken's wagons.

Meggie maneuvered John Charles so she could turn her back on Hawken, who was tying oilcloth wrappers around the calico. She bent to tighten the girth, but John Charles danced out of reach. Something white tumbling over the ground. One of Hawken's oilcloths, now caught in a clump of sage, the ends snapping in the breeze. Hawken snatched the oilcloth and tucked it under his belt.

"I'm sorry," he said gruffly. "Hold him while I fasten the girth."

"It's my fault. I should have tied him to my wagon to

saddle him, but Pete just now told me I'm to lead a string of horses, so I had to hurry with the saddle and bridle, for I hadn't planned on riding today, and everything was in the wagon.'' She stopped, hearing her aimless chatter.

"He should have asked you sooner," Hawken agreed, the words muffled because he leaned over. "Meggie?" Shy now.

"Yes."

"What happened last night, I never should...I must have been out of my mind. When I dodged John Charles I hit my head." The final words came in a whisper, as if he hesitated to offer such a lame excuse.

"You should have said you'd hurt yourself. Did Granny look at your head this morning?"

Their eyes met over John Charles. "I felt the spot and it wasn't bleeding." He touched the bandanna and she recalled the hat.

"I'm making you a hat. I found some grass by the river almost like wheat straw."

"You must not. Everyone will guess—"

"Guess what? Simply because I make a hat when you desperately need one signifies nothing," she lectured sternly. "It's like Granny giving medicine."

"I'll pay you."

"Fine. Walk with me this evening."

"Everyone will think—"

"They'll notice more if we *don't* speak to each other. Granny wondered why you didn't go to Devil's Gate."

He rubbed his fingers across his mouth and chin. "I couldn't go to Devil's Gate. I had airing to do, for fear my dry goods will mildew."

"I'll find the horses," she said, swinging into the saddle and only then realizing she had left off her leggings. Everyone could see her stockings and drawers.

"You get your leggings," Hawken said. "I'll find the horses you're to lead and bring them to your wagon."

"Thank you."

How very practical, she thought. A man who's seen you naked doesn't blink at drawers and stockings. It would be ever so much easier if all the men and women exposed themselves buck naked, just once. Then for the rest of the trip they needn't waste precious time preserving modesty, putting up tents and taking them down, no more contorted dressing in a wagon, hiking miles to find a place out of sight to relieve yourself.

Meggie gasped for breath in the wagon, hot as an oven from its long stand in the midday sun. If she and Hawken traveled alone she would have no need for leggings. They knew the look of each other, an intimate sort of friendship, rather like husband and wife. Riding through the Rockies, free as the birds. Wild geese flying. That reminded her of her patchwork, lost somewhere in the reorganized wagon, a symbol of the lack of discipline that made her unsuitable to be a wife. Besides, lovemaking would be dreadfully one-sided, him having fun and her gritting her teeth. If she and Hawken rode alone, he'd expect to be in her blankets every night.

Her leggings smelled of dirty leather, faintly reminiscent of buffalo hunter. If she stayed on the Bear River with Hawken they would not be alone. The threat from mountain outlaws would fence her in, more completely than the rules laid down by her mother and father. Given half a chance buffalo hunters would kidnap and rape her, and the hunter's threat sounded in her skull and she felt faint. Or perhaps it was the heat in the wagon. Circumstances, not Hawken, would imprison her in his cabin. Faith was right. On the frontier a woman became a slave.

"In Bear River Valley I'd have less freedom than I do

now,'' she whispered to herself. Bear River with Hawken and the buffalo hunters, or California in the midst of friends and kin who expected her to grow up and settle down.

The leggings dragged on her damp skin. It would be cooler to walk. She stuffed the leggings under her bedroll, looped up the sides of the wagon cover to let the wind blow through. Hawken met her leading five horses, the most worn of the herd.

''I'll walk,'' she announced. ''It's too hot to put on leggings. How long before we reach Bear River Valley?''

''At the rate Sampson and Godfroy have us moving, three weeks.''

Three weeks. He would stop, she would travel on, leaving him in the wilderness, and never see him again. She had found no pleasure last night, but she did like *him*. Three weeks to become acquainted as a special friend, fix him in her mind so that for the rest of her life she recalled that she'd almost had a lover.

''Do you want a mourning band on the hat?'' she asked.

''It would be best.''

She leaned around John Charles, smiled at him, working hard to combine compassion and her eagerness for his friendship. ''I think Granny might have a piece of black ribbon. Ribbon would look more respectful than a scrap from the bag. Tonight let me hem the edges of the band on your arm.'' She stopped talking because Hawken's eyes glazed, he stared straight ahead, a man haunted. Mentioning the mourning band had reminded him of his wife.

Or else, horrible thought, he still wanted to stay away from her.

Chapter Fourteen

Monty snarled when his foot slipped in the mud. "Damnation, everyone's sick of being wet," he said. Hawken didn't respond, for that meant exposing his face to the rain. Three days of slogging through mire, eating half-cooked food and waking to water running around the blankets had left everyone on edge.

Hawken tucked his head deeper between his shoulders so Monty and Les did not see his smile. He welcomed the storm. Digging wagons out of muddy ruts, blocking up wagon boxes to cross swollen streams, goading oxen forward when they tried to turn their backs to the wind, all this kept the specters at bay. And in the evenings he sank into exhausted, dreamless sleep.

Since Devil's Gate he'd managed to avoid Meggie, except yesterday when she presented him with his new hat. And he had cut her off so quickly, he hadn't learned the origin of the neat strip of black velvet ribbon around the crown.

He took off the hat and pulled the soaked hood of his capote forward. Other men sported newfangled India rubber suits, or oilcloth coats and pants, but none rivaled the usefulness of the mountain man's capote. The tight wool shed water, the deep hood protected his face and neck, and the fullness of the cloak gave a man room to move. Hawken turned the brim of the hat in his hands. Well made, holding its shape despite the deluge. Except for the velvet band, which had shrunk to a narrow, sodden strip. He should thank Meggie for the hat, for it kept the rain off his face. He adjusted it on his head and tucked the hood around his neck to block the rivulets threatening his coat and shirt.

Thunder rumbled sullenly at a great distance and, as if in response, the raindrops quickened. Water cascaded from the hat brim in a curtain that obstructed the road. Today they would surmount South Pass, the crest of the Rockies, and few of his traveling companions would notice until evening, when they asked Sampson the name of the place he had picked for their camp, and he said, "Pacific Spring." Perhaps Jim Mac would uncork the treasured bottle of brandy, perhaps the boys would give three cheers despite their dripping clothes and damp blankets. Perhaps one of the women would stew apples or unpack a reflector oven to attempt a loaf of real bread.

The wagons slowed, then stopped. Hawken walked on, to the bank of another dry gulch turned into a river by the extended rain. Tole's wagon thudded off the low bank, Mrs. Tole and Faith peering out, Mrs. Tole clinging to her little blond girl who cried "Giddyap" and seemed to be enjoying every minute of the adventure.

"We'll noon on the other side," Captain Hull said, his voice hollow within his oilcloth hood. "Jim Mac has some dry wood in the sling under his wagon, so we'll all cook over one fire. Tell your men."

John Charles splashed into the stream, topped by a conical bundle that made Hawken take a second look.

Meggie, but riding sidesaddle? Her eyes met his and he could not politely turn away.

"I stay dry with my legs tucked under me and my cape spread out, so I borrowed Rachel's saddle. Well, not exactly dry. Not so wet."

He touched the hat. "Same with the hat. With it on my head, I'm not exactly drenched. I thank you."

"You're welcome. But I can't ride all day cramped up, my legs get numb. There's Granny's wagon, and I promised—" She waved gaily, whatever she had promised was lost in the rattle of rain on straw.

Burdette's oxen dragged by, little John Burdette hunched in an oversized oilcloth coat. Hawken stopped to speak an encouraging word, but hurried on when he saw the boy's face, wet with tears, not rain. Many a grown man would give his eyeteeth for the privilege of weeping. Hawken hoisted himself onto the rear of his wagon just as it dropped into the stream. Monty and Les ignored the water that poured over the tops of their boots.

"You should take off your boots," Hawken said when they pulled out on the other side.

"Got a hole in the bottom, so it runs out as fast as it comes in," Les said. He held up a foot, displaying the gaping seam between upper and sole. More raids on the goods in the wagon, Hawken thought with dismay.

Monty shoved back the hood of his capote and grinned cheerfully. "Would you ask that gal to stop the rain? If she stopped the hail, don't see why she can't bring out the sun for an hour or two. At least while we cook some grub." Les glowered at being made fun of.

"The MacIntyres have a bit of dry wood," Hawken said. "Get our dinner together, come to Jim Mac's wagons and we'll take turns holding the umbrella over the fire."

Only two women had thought to bring an umbrella, Mrs. Eliza MacIntyre and Tildy Hull. Mrs. MacIntyre's sensible, black oiled silk was large enough to protect the fire and the head and shoulders of the cook. Mrs. Hull's parasol was far less practical, a dainty contraption of yellow silk with pink roses, but it did serve to protect the pots before they went over the flames. Right now she held it over her grandmother. Three days had turned the pretty thing into a gray rag.

The men stood in a tight circle, shoulder to shoulder, their heads bent so the rain dripped from their hats and formed a puddle at the toes of their boots.

"Shall I go see if there's grass down this hill?" Kit asked from deep inside a knitted hood.

"No sense unhitching," Hull said. "We'll roll the moment we've had a bite to eat. How do the wagons look, Pete?"

"Fine. The rain's a blessing, not a single loose tire."

"How far to the pass?"

"Can't say for sure," Godfroy said, "all the landmarks huddled in clouds, but probably no more than a few miles."

"I never thought it would be like this," Jim Mac said. "Like driving through a river fog."

"At least it's not snowing," Kit said cheerfully.

Revealing, how men reacted to adversity, Hawken thought. Sometimes the bravest gave way to melancholy, while those who had appeared to be introspective cowards rose to the occasion. Hawken broke off this philosophical rumination. He was one of the outwardly daring, who collapsed when things got bad. A three-year collapse put him among the lowest of the low. He resolved to ignore the present discomfort, a resolution he put into action immediately when Monty offered him dinner, the only thing remotely warm a cup of tepid coffee.

"Hawken, do you have mackinaw coats and capotes in those wagons?" Hull asked.

"Yes."

"The women's clothes aren't warm enough. Some have nothing more than shawls against the cold." Hawken counted the women in the party by tapping his fingers on the bottom of his tin plate. Ten, without Marshall's half-grown girl and Burdette's smaller ones. Granny walked by, a heap of multiple shawls, and knew he could not refuse.

"Capotes would be the best," Hawken said. "They shed rain, they're warm, and full enough a woman can wear any number of layers underneath. And there's no matter of fit."

"We'll settle up later," Hull said. Hawken waved away the offer. Setting a price and keeping books seemed crass, since he depended on these people in miserable circumstances.

By the time he had overturned his load and distributed eight of the cloaks, whips were cracking flatly in the sodden air. Muscles strained against the gravity that tugged hooves and wheels into the mud. The rain eased to a bothersome drizzle, and the clouds dropped even lower. Hawken trudged beside Les, staring ahead, warning his drivers of the worst ruts, where the mud accumulated in narrow slits and could mire a wagon for half an hour. He would not have noticed John Charles off the road in the mist, except that Les made the sign of the cross.

Meggie sat stock-still, erect in the saddle, paying no more attention to the passing wagons than she would a trail of ants. What did she see in the fog? He glanced back, pretending to check on Monty and the second wagon. The loose stock parted around Meggie, as water around a rock. Hawken gathered his damp capote and turned back. As he neared her he could see, on either side of the road, faint mounds barely distinguishable from the swirling fog. South Pass! He tried to run, but his soaked boots rubbed painfully on heels exposed by unmended stockings. Neither of the scouts had spoken, but she, who had never been in this spot, knew where they were. She shifted restlessly. Hadn't she said her legs cramped, riding sidesaddle? She did not look at him until he offered a hand to help her dismount. She clasped his fingers but did not move.

"'We were obliged to watch very closely to find the place at which we had reached the culminating point. This was between two low hills rising on either hand fifty or sixty feet.'" Frémont's report, Hawken knew without asking.

For an instant the fog thinned, exposing the hills as more than specters, and in that moment he sensed the solemn delight that radiated from her. The exhilaration of her gaze warmed him, leading him to look up to check for the sun. He absorbed gratification, pleasure, and she was its source.

Meggie's grin mocked her seriousness and broke the spell. She flexed her fingers against his gloved palm. Instead of releasing her, he grasped more firmly, and joyful warmth flooded through his arms, into his chest. They shared the thrill of discovery! He had, in his college days, accepted this as normal between men. The shared pleasure of a well-translated verse, the revelation of identical equations, arrived at independently. But with a woman? He'd never thought it possible. But here it came again, an intimacy so strong it blocked the flow of his blood.

Inappropriate, when he wore black bands. He slowly

disengaged his hand, knowing part of him remained behind. The days of rain had worked a transformation, and he now regarded her less a sexual creature, more a promise of intimate friendship.

"If we'd crossed on a clear day you'd see the Wind River Mountains," he said. She studied the landscape as if committing it to memory. Which she probably was. Perhaps she would rather be alone.

"The storm's clearing," she said. "Far to the west there's a band of sunshine. You can't see it, but from the back of John Charles...come up!"

Their wet gloves stuck together. They shook their arms to detach the stubborn connection, laughed even as he straddled John Charles behind her. Sure enough, the clouds thinned over the desert wastes of the Green River, and shafts of sunlight towered against the muted sky. He slid off hastily.

She remained a woman, he a man. She tempted him through woolen cloaks and layers of clothes, even more after what they had shared. What would it be like to make love to a woman in the midst of that intellectual merging? He muttered some excuse about catching up to his wagons. The pony's hooves squelched beside him. Platte came, his nose sweeping the ground, tracking his master. Hawken expected Meggie to remark on the dog, but she said nothing.

The silence built into palpable tension, a black fog in his loins, expanding until he ached.

Did desire swell within her? She moved easily with the gait of the pony. She smiled at him, nothing sensual, only a studied happiness evident in her glance. The smile broadened. They'd passed the continental summit and she was glad of the achievement; it had nothing to do with him. Celebrating in her strange way...why did he call her strange? The strangeness was in himself, that he felt a merging that combined intellectual and physical pleasure. Nothing at all like what he'd felt for Mary Helen, or the sporting women of Missouri.

The wagons materialized in the haze, a circlet in a patch of green. Only when he hailed Les and Monty did it occur to him that since he had turned back into the fog, the memories had fallen away. In that long hour of companionable, sensual silence, the image of the ferry had remained quiescent. Being with Meggie, sharing her joy was distraction enough.

The clouds lifted and thinned, revealing limitless drops on the sage, glittering in the setting sun. Hawken stared west, searching out the heights beyond the Green River. The boundary of Bear River Valley.

The women strung ropes and hung their blankets to catch the few moments of blessed warmth. Jim Mac dodged the chickens, who toddled free of their cage for the first time in three days. He held a bottle of brandy like a torch.

"What were you doing with my sister?" Pete hissed. "You said you'd leave her alone you damned gambler."

"She hung back, and I thought—"

"You should have come for me and I'd have fetched her. Why was she sitting out alone in the rain—?"

"She celebrated South Pass."

Pete hooted.

"She was the only one who noticed when we reached the top," Hawken said.

"She couldn't know. Neither Godfroy nor Sampson said anything."

"Frémont tells how to spot it. Between two whitish hills."

"I wish she'd never read that damned book," Pete

said. "She's been lecturing—hectoring, I should say—all winter and spring, and if she keeps on this way she'll never find a man willing to take her. Who wants to listen to a woman spout off? I've heard her correct a preacher's reading of a Bible verse. Mention any place west of the Mississippi and she spiels off pages from her dear captain. I suppose we should count ourselves lucky she never took to Shakespeare."

"Hard for a man to accommodate a woman smarter than he is," Hawken said. He tried not to smile, but one side of his mouth contorted.

"She's not smarter than I am," Pete huffed.

"She's smarter than I am." Much smarter. She remembered whole books, while he had struggled for weeks before he learned to keep thirty-two monte cards in his head. How many of each suit lay on the table and which remained in the pack? My God! What a monte dealer Meggie would make!

"Well, leave her alone," Pete said. "My sister won't marry a gambling man, I'll see to that."

"I'm sure you will," Hawken said. Monty rapped a tin cup against his elbow.

"Mr. Jim Mac says to come get your share of the celebration."

Gaiety returned with sunlight. Tildy strummed her banjo, the Tole boys, their shirts steaming, ran in erratic circles about their little sister, who contentedly dug her bare feet into the wet grass. Will, Rachel and Godfroy stood in intimate conversation, their faces toward the last of the sun, some happy exchange, for the men smiled and Rachel blushed and put her hand to her cheek.

Meggie was only feet and a rump protruding from her wagon, enough of her to recall the contours of hips on the sidesaddle, if he had been able to see beneath the spreading cloak. The spirit of their encounter possessed him once more, and recollections of the night at Independence Rock, and the small swelling of her breast, that a man's hand might contain.

Lucky, you damned fool. If Pete ever found out you were in her wagon, he'd kill you.

Just down the hill, the junction of trails at the Big Sandy.

Tomorrow he could pull right at that forking and leave the emigrants.

Leave Meggie, see her only briefly when the wagons passed through Bear River Valley. He and Monty and Les, alone, heading straight west, avoiding the long swing to Fort Bridger. Sixty miles without water, he remembered. The days of muddy trail had taken a toll on the oxen. Hawken shook his head.

"Sad?" Hull asked. "Why? We've conquered South Pass!"

"Not sad. Just saying no to the cutoff."

"We never meant to take the cutoff. Sampson's wife's at Bridger's."

Also lush, wide pastures, a fort where a man might find old acquaintances, deer and antelope on the hills, a few days of rest before he climbed the last range of mountains, to Bear River. The prospect of a detour by way of Fort Bridger brightened, like the evening sky, which reminded him of a thin film of water running over gold.

Which reminded him of freckles.

A rumbling in the distance. Sampson and Godfroy strained without seeing, their eyes narrowed. Hawken judged the Green River was running full.

"I never thought the hardest part of crossing a desert would be water," Jim Mac said.

"More graves at river crossings than anywhere else," Godfroy said.

Godfroy's wagon first, Rachel sitting on a heap of provisions and bedding, steadying herself by clutching the bows. The wagon rocked when it bounded into the water, but the wheels did not sink. At least the Green had a solid, gravel bottom. Fifty yards out Hunter swung the animals left and the wagon followed, the current piling against the rear, helping the teams in their final effort.

Rachel jumped out on the opposite bank, wringing water from the bottom of her skirt. Water had flowed into the box. Hawken made a mental inventory of what he had packed on the bottom.

"Yiii," Marshall screamed as the water rose to his chest. "My God! It's like iced julep!" Monty and Les laughed nervously.

Meggie and her mother piled flour, sugar and bacon on the provision box and lashed the chicken coop across the top of the bed. A basket of kittens swung from a bow, as it had while crossing the Platte, but the kittens had grown and from the snarls, it was obvious they were unhappy in their confinement. The tabby cat scrambled on top of the flour sacks, tense, her tail whipping, her eyes on the basket.

"Our turn, boss," Monty said. He cracked his whip and gritted his teeth. Hawken waited until the first wagon made its turn in midstream before ordering Les out. He tossed his boots over the tailgate, grabbed the rear of the wagon and lifted himself. He leaned in and heard the sound of water against the tin washbasins. He would have to unload as soon as possible and dry out.

Cackles announced the embarkation of the MacIntyres'

first wagon. Pete swam with the oxen and Meggie rode John Charles on the upstream side, a rope stretched to her saddle horn. The morning sun slanted under her hat, lighting her face. Not a flighty eighteen-year-old girl, but a woman undertaking a vital job.

"Get the wagon out of the way," Godfroy said the moment Hawken reached the shallows. "MacIntyre's right behind you." Hawken dropped off to help push the wagons up the slope. The hens slid against the bars of their cage, the kittens screamed as the basket swung in a wide arc.

"Thanks," Meggie yelled, unwinding the rope from her saddle horn.

"He's down!" Godfroy took a thoughtless step into the river, pointing to midstream. Jim Mac's second wagon paused, with only five oxen. In the midst of rainbow arcs Jim Mac clung to the front yoke, in and out of the water. The left-hand ox struggled to find footing, went down, came up again. The wagon, without forward momentum, edged broadside in the current, water damming against the box. Mrs. MacIntyre stood on top of the load, the last refuge.

Hawken heard Meggie's shout and the splash as John Charles went into the river. Did Meggie understand? John Charles had the strength to rescue the ox, while a man did not. *Don't go to your mother,* he muttered. *You save the ox, you save your mother.*

He ran upstream, so the current carried him to the wagon. Unless the teams moved quickly, the river would push the wagon over. He swam to the rear, resenting the flash of memory that came—the boat slowly overturning upon cattle and woman. He shook his head to clear his brain, but only succeeded in getting a swallow of water.

Men and a yoke of oxen waded from the opposite
shore.

"Can you swim?" he yelled to Mrs. MacIntyre. She
shook her head. Hawken hung onto the tailgate, felt the
sickening yaw of a wagon nearly awash and dropped off.

"I'll be here," he yelled. "You stand on the tailgate.
If the wagon starts to go, you jump right at me." She
nodded. Meggie's mother had blue eyes, so like her
daughter's he felt a moment's qualm. Tole thrashed beside him, holding up the end of a chain.

"Can't swim," he gasped.

"Catch her if she jumps," Hawken said. The chain
must be hooked to the running gear, not the bed. Nothing
to be done but go underwater with his eyes open. Loop
the chain around the axle…wish he could breathe a sigh
of relief when the metal slid fast on the first try. His hat?
He'd gone under with Meggie's hat.

He saw it the moment he broke the surface, caught in
an eddy a few feet downstream. He lunged, his toe caught
on a rock, sending him tumbling through glassy green.
No up nor down, only force and bursting lungs. Strange,
how easy it was to die. He hoped Mary Helen had felt
this great peace. He wished he could tell Meggie—

A rock between him and death, some energy tight on
his arm, and in the next instant blue overhead. He gulped
a breath, so painful he knew it was easier to drown.
Hands dragged him into shallows, heaved him up, miraculous grass beneath his fingers, like the day Meggie
had knocked him down. Platte shook, filling the air with
captured sunlight and the men sprang away.

"Hat," he tried to say. Meggie's hat was floating down
the Green, away from him. Someone slapped between his
shoulder blades. He crawled away from the punishment.

"My hat," he said, this time clearly, and only then

considered how stupid he must sound. Mrs. MacIntyre might be following the hat downriver, swept from a cap-sized wagon. "Wagon?" he asked.

"It's okay," Godfroy said. Thank heavens, someone sensible had arrived. "Meggie got a rope around the ox and Tole straightened the wagon with the chain you hooked on."

He expected Meggie next, offering him a lift on John Charles. But it was Monty grabbing his shoulders and Les his feet, hoisting him like a sack of grain.

"Put me down. I'll walk," Hawken said. "A bit of exercise helps the lungs get back in shape." They laid him out as they would a corpse, wrists crossed on his breast, the position so disgusting he rolled over and got on his hands and knees. The ground seemed unnaturally rigid after the vertigo of the river. Platte leaned, a brace against his legs giving him strength, and Hawken guessed the identity of the rock that had rescued him.

"You've got a good dog there," said Godfroy. "I'm glad we let him tag along when we left St. Joe."

"Here, Mr. Hawken," Kit said, shaking the dripping hat. "Found it down a ways."

Two wagons bucked the crystalline water, both accompanied by a man on horseback. A woman on horseback. Meggie doing her job. She had stayed where she was needed rather than rush in panic to his rescue. He should be proud of her, except he'd come out of the river anticipating the warmth of her brown hands curling around his face.

"Monty. Les. Back to work. Shoulders to the wheels to help the oxen up the bank."

Smoke wafted to his nostrils; someone had a fire going. Captain Hull must have designated this their nooning, even though it was not yet midmorning. "Catch up!"

came the call, contradicting him. Wet sand pushed up in deep imprints around hooves and wheels.

"Here," Granny said, holding out the inevitable tin cup. "A tea of shavegrass. I didn't have time to brew it strong, but it helps the lungs."

"Granny, a man who's gone down in the Green's better served by a swallow of brandy," Pete said.

"No," Granny said, shaking her head, "alcohol has its place, but I've never seen a chilled man better for drinking it." Hawken took the cup. Not bad tasting. Sweetened with some of her precious honey, tart with a spike of lemon. "You should change out of your wet things."

"They'll dry fast enough," Hawken said. Changing meant rifling the precious bundles once more.

"You come and ride with me," she said. "Or would you rather walk?"

"Walk," he said, remembering the agonizing jolts of Granny's wagon.

"So my family is beholden to you again," she said.

"Not to me. To Tole, who had the good sense to get a team into the river."

"You told Meggie what to do."

"I didn't speak to her," Hawken protested, automatically searching for Meggie at the mention of her name.

Granny laughed, and he dropped his head. He behaved like an eager lover. "She's in the wagon, changing out of her wet clothes. Yes, you did tell her what to do. Men and women with deep feelings don't need words. One glance, and she did what you knew was best."

He hadn't looked at Meggie in that instant, or had he? "Meggie's got sense enough to take a horse to rescue an ox," he said to the toes of his boots.

"James has thought poorly of you," Granny went on.

"Is it true, you gambled last winter to get a stake for your trading post?"

"Yes."

"You were a minister." No judgment in the statement.

"I forgot what I was, along with everything else."

"You'll go back to being a clergyman?"

"I'm building a trading post on the Bear River."

"Meggie's very fond of you," Granny said. "You'd be good for her. She sees the wisdom of your opinions and doesn't argue when you give an order. And you've lived wild enough, you can forgive the life she's led. Nothing immoral," she added hastily. "Just…wild."

"I'm staying on the Bear River," he said.

"She'll never forget you," Granny said. "Here come Eliza and Meggie now. You must not judge Meggie's looks from her costume on the trail. In a proper dress she's quite ladylike."

Hawken spent a quarter of an hour fending off Mrs. MacIntyre's grateful thanks. He found no way to reject her invitation to dine with them.

Chapter Fifteen

Jim Mac guided Hawken away from the dinner preparations. "We owe you many thanks, first saving Meggie from the buffalo hunter, and today going into the river for Eliza."

"It was Tole's quick thinking—"

"Eliza told me what you said, that she was to leap to you if the wagon went over. It must have brought back memories of your wife's death, I hope not too painful," he said with great formality.

"Nothing brings *back* those memories," Hawken said. "They're always there." Except for that mystical hour on South Pass.

"You're a brave man to go into the river," Jim Mac said. He cleared his throat. "I don't doubt your courage. But there is the matter of the money...the gambling in Independence." Hawken wondered why Jim Mac should be concerned with his moral health. "Some men cannot free themselves from cards and dice."

Jim Mac was smoothing the way for a request for Meggie's hand in marriage!

"I ran a monte bank in Independence, a successful business, enough money to buy trade goods," Hawken said bluntly. "I didn't mark cards or stack the deck, for by playing on suits, not individual cards, the odds in monte lie with the dealer."

"I wouldn't know," Jim Mac murmured. "Your goods will sell as fast in California as on Bear River."

"My wagons won't hold together much beyond Fort Hall," Hawken said. "I didn't waste money on gear strong enough to go all the way to California."

"So you're set on Bear River?" Hawken nodded. Jim Mac's expression turned wistful. Did he regret this chance to unload his wild daughter? "Well, I want you to know I'm not ungrateful, and that a man can be forgiven a mistake or two—hell, we've all done things we're not proud of—so long as he learns from his mistakes and avoids such things hereafter. In your state of mind much can be excused, I think...." His voice faded as his wife called. He touched Hawken's elbow, pointing him to dinner.

One of the panicked hens had laid an egg during the crossing of the Green. Hawken found it on his plate, softboiled, nested on a split biscuit.

"California," Pete said around his biscuit and bacon, "lacks manufactures. That's why I'm moving. Californians make nothing for themselves, and I'll be sure to have floods of customers for wagons and carriages."

"Sampson warned us against carrying things to sell, the trip being so difficult," Jim Mac said. "But, since you're already on the way—"

"My wagons aren't fit," Hawken said.

"Meggie told me—you know, from that book—there's timber at the curve of the Bear," Pete said. "Between me and Tole, who'll unpack his tools if we lay over a day, we'll get your wagons in fine shape."

Hawken came close to blurting out his misbehavior

with the girls in the gambling hall, but could not mention such things in front of the women.

"I suppose, since the Californians are Catholics, there's a need for Protestant ministers in the country," Mrs. MacIntyre said. "The question of religion made me doubtful about moving, but Mr. Sampson said his brother-in-law, who's a preacher, would join us. Reverend Ludlow. But he turned back before we met you, Mr. Hawken. Reverend Cowie, if the Oregonians ever catch up, is welcome, but he won't be with us through to the end."

Hawken chewed each mouthful twelve times. The egg was delicious. The MacIntyres had rehearsed every possible argument to tempt him to California.

"Thank you," he said, looking about for a way to get rid of his plate. "I have to see to my wagons. Water got in and I told Monty and Les to unpack the load."

How many days to Bear Valley? Day after tomorrow at Bridger's, if everything went as planned. A day of rest, then three days north. A week at most. Monty and Les had lined up the washbasins and kettles facing the sun, like a strange crop sprouting among the sage.

"What'd they give you?" Les asked.

"A soft-boiled egg."

"That's part of the witchery," Les said. "Eggs have a power, why else do folks make over them at Easter?"

"That's ridiculous," Hawken snapped.

"Them folks wants you to marry their ugly—"

"She's not ugly!"

"See," Les said triumphantly. "Told you. Told you. You's truly roped in and hog-tied now!"

Meggie resented the men trailing off to Bridger's and leaving the women behind to make supper. But from what she could see of the fort, it hardly seemed worth making a fuss. Nothing but a rough stockade of vertical poles, with a few tepees standing off to one side, and another Indian village a mile beyond. Sampson had ridden off to that village, which seemed to belong to his wife's band. Hawken had not gone to Bridger's, but emptied his wagons and checked his goods. His drivers must have felt as put upon as the women, for they frowned and pouted while going about their work.

"Meggie, fetch a bucket of water," Ma said. Pete should be here to fetch water. Studying the shortest distance to the creek, Meggie smiled. Right past Hawken.

"Good evening," she said. "I hope nothing's been spoiled by wetting in the Green." That justified a brief stop, to give him time for a comprehensive report.

Hawken stared at the setting sun, so she did, too. A band of clouds above and below. "We packed the tinware on the bottom and it dries fast. The hatchets, they'd been oiled." He shaded his eyes. "Perhaps Bridger's not at home," he said. Meggie blocked the glare of the sun, and could just make out figures walking through the gate of the fort. "Sometimes, if both Bridger and Vasquez go off, there's no buying and selling. They probably didn't expect emigrants to arrive this early."

Pete broke from the group and leaped over the tiny creek. *He's coming to tell me to get away from Hawken,* Meggie thought.

"Bridger's not here," he yelled. "But Vasquez is. Meggie, you go visit tomorrow. Mrs. Vasquez's a white woman and would like to gossip. There's not much in the store. You could probably sell your goods to Vasquez, Hawken."

Meggie sniffed and wrinkled her nose. The fort obviously had one commodity in stock. Strong drink.

"Bridger's expected soon?" Hawken asked.

Pete shook his head. "He's gone east, taking his family. Something about a massacre in Oregon, a minister and his wife and other people—"

"Whitman?" Hawken asked quickly.

"That's the name. And Bridger had sent his daughter to live with them and she's disappeared, so everyone supposes she's dead, too."

"We should have met Bridger if he's heading east," Hawken said, objecting with both words and gestures to everything Pete said. "Although, he knows every cutoff that's worth taking, so we might have missed him." He sat down cross-legged and took off his hat. Shadows darkened his eyes and collected in the dimples at the corners of his nose and mouth.

"I'll tell Ma and Granny about Mrs. Vasquez," Pete said, "so they'll be sure to set aside time to visit." The odor of whiskey trailed away behind him. Drunk enough that he didn't care that she sat with Hawken.

Hawken looked blankly across the meadow. He had forgotten her presence. "I'd best get the water," she said, retrieving the bucket. A strange man, given to sudden melancholy. Perhaps he had known the dead minister. Perhaps that's where he had been headed three years ago.

At camp, Pete danced a jig around the fire, getting in the way of the cooking. Pa held his stomach against the hiccups and her mother frowned in disgust.

"Look at Mr. Hawken," Ma was saying. "A real Christian gentleman, who tends to his business, doesn't go traipsing off, sticking his nose into what doesn't concern him. You say these frontier forts aren't suitable for women. I doubt men find them profitable, either."

"Mrs. Vasquez is a white woman," Pete repeated, nearly tripping over the bucket of water.

"Don't spill the water," Meggie said. "If you do, you go fetch this time."

"I believe…I believe," Pa said, speaking slowly to avoid slurring his words, "that Peter did not realize the strength of what Mr. Vasq—" he stuttered, then gave up on the name "—what's kept in that cask."

Ma snorted her disbelief. "Help me with the new sack of flour, Meggie." It took all their strength to hoist the sack onto the tailgate.

"I'm very impressed with Mr. Hawken," Ma said. "He shows a sensitivity rare in men. He didn't go running off to the whiskey the moment we got here."

"I think another tragedy's struck Mr. Hawken."

"How can that be?"

"Mr. Bridger's not here. He's gone east because there's been a massacre out in Oregon. Mr. Hawken knew the man who'd been killed before Pete even said his name. He turned as pale as this flour."

Her mother pursed her lips. "Mr. Hawken appreciated your company after his memory returned. Perhaps you should offer him companionship."

"We've got supper to fix," Meggie reminded, uncertain that Hawken desired her company.

"Peter and your father ate something at the fort, besides drinking too much. When they say they're hungry, I'll warm up the leftovers from dinner."

Meggie swung the bucket, warning Hawken of her approach with the squeak of the bail. If he ignored her, she could pretend she was headed for the creek.

"Not here," Monty said. He pointed to a seated figure outlined against the western sky. Meggie detoured so she ended up twenty feet from Hawken. She sank the bucket at the bottom of a foot-high waterfall. "Why, hello, Mr. Hawken," she said, as if she had just seen him.

"Hello. A beautiful evening," he said. She looked across the meadow and waited. "Meggie, could you sit with me for a minute?" She walked to within five feet of him. "Do you believe that everything happens for a reason?" he asked. She flattened the grass with her foot, checking for burrs and undesirable varmints before she sat down.

"I really can't say. I've seen some dreadful things."

"What dreadful things can you have seen?" he asked, a faint mockery that dismissed her eighteen years.

"I was little when the horse killed Grandpa, so I don't remember much about that. But last December the tent at the Christmas fair in Muncie caught fire with a crowd inside. Tildy, too. Her dresses, even her wedding dress, have long sleeves because the accident left scars on her right arm."

He nodded. "And no good came of it?"

"I didn't know the people who were hurt, so I can't say. But it spoiled Christmas and burned up the Christmas tree before I had a chance to see it."

"You heard Pete? There's been a massacre at Reverend Whitman's mission?"

"Yes."

"That's where I was bound three years ago. It was my idea to go west and join the missionaries. I was leading Mary Helen and Fred to their deaths, whether on the Missouri or in Oregon. I'd be dead, too, drowned or my skull cracked opened, except that at the last minute I crossed the river with an empty wagon."

"You've been saved for something?"

"Three or four years ago I might have said that. But now? Doesn't it seem an awfully complicated and cruel scheme to direct the footsteps of one man? God might have crippled all my oxen and I wouldn't have gone to

Oregon. I didn't have money to buy more. He didn't have to kill Mary Helen and Fred. And the ferryman.''

"Perhaps you're needed for something in Bear Valley. Offer help to the emigrants, so California and Oregon can be settled faster. If a man planted wheat and corn, emigrants could restock—"

"I'm the instrument of manna in the wilderness?" he said bitterly, not expecting an answer. "God should have directed a farmer to the task, not me. I can't repair a wagon beyond hasty patching, I've never milked a cow, didn't even think to bring one along. What does God need in Bear Valley? A sinful man to preach to the Indians? Or maybe a gambling hall, where I can skin the emigrants?"

"Your father? He must have taught you some trade."

"He kept a livery stable. I helped, but he died when I was twelve. A fever that took Mother, too."

Meggie's heart faltered. An orphan who watched his wife drown without being able to help. No wonder he had lost his memory. "What you're to do in Bear Valley will reveal itself," she said, hearing the words cold and empty of solace. She regretted she had no comfort to offer.

"I'll bury myself and my sin in Bear River Valley. Do you suppose you—and your friends and kin—could forget who I am? Never speak of it."

"Anything you ask," Meggie said. "My family has reason to be grateful to you. Could I ask a favor in return?"

"What?" he asked, suspicious.

"Between here and Bear River, could we visit? Just to talk," she added hastily. "I'd like to know you better. But I'll never speak of you, or say your name to a living soul." She crossed her heart to fortify the promise, then

tapped her skull. ''Everything I know of you will stay
here, for my own pleasure in remembering.''

He said nothing. Only looked surprised.

At first Meggie thought Tabby had hauled some creature into the wagon still alive and that she heard its dying
groans. She felt in the nest, moving her blankets as little
as possible because the night was very cold. Only the
three kittens, curled in a ball.

The groan turned to retching. ''If you *will* drink,''
Ma's voice said firmly, ''you should not curse the results.'' More sounds of sickness. Pa's bender at the trading post had come to an unhappy end.

''Is Mr. MacIntyre sick, too?'' Unmistakably Faith.
Meggie pulled her skirt over her nightdress and wrapped
a shawl around her head and shoulders. So awkward, to
cope with bodice buttons in the dark.

''Pa and Kit have stomachaches,'' Faith said, ''and I
wondered if Granny...I hate to wake her in the middle
of the night, but they're in dreadful pain.''

Meggie slid off the tailgate.

''Oh, God!'' her father said thickly. ''Cholera.''

''What's going on?'' Captain Hull's head poked out
from between the tent flaps.

''James is sick,'' Ma said. ''And Faith says her father
and brother have both taken ill.''

''It's not just me?'' Pete gasped from under the wagon.
He rolled out, one hand on his forehead and the other on
his stomach.

''You're not sick, Matt?'' Ma asked. Meggie read her
mother's anxiety and fear in that social blunder, calling
the captain by his boyhood name.

''Don't seem to be,'' Captain Hull said from the tent,

his voice muffled. He had backed out of sight, probably putting on his clothes.

"Captain Hull signed a temperance pledge," Meggie reminded her mother. "He didn't drink Bridger's whiskey."

Pete staggered away from the wagons, dropped to his knees and, from the heaving of his shoulders, Meggie knew he had joined the ranks of those losing their suppers.

"We can't be sure it was the whiskey," Faith said, her voice weak. "It could be cholera. Go wake Granny."

"We *can* be surer," Meggie said. "Mr. Hawken and his men didn't go to Bridger's either. If nobody else is sick, it's probably the whiskey."

"Go wake Mr. Hawken," her mother ordered.

Meggie trotted around the circle of wagons. In one tent—the Marshalls'—she heard a whispered conversation that ended in a moan. Three bedrolls lay near Hawken's wagons, one flat, and Meggie gulped in fear before she recalled that Les had guard duty. She did not like to wake both men, but could see no way of determining which bedroll covered Hawken. Unless she pulled back the blankets.

"Mr. Hawken," she called. No one stirred.

"Mr. Hawken. I'm sorry to wake you, but it's terribly important." A mass of kinky hair emerged from the heap on the right. Only then did it cross her mind that no man in the grip of a choleric fever would sleep so soundly. Hawken and his men were quite healthy.

"Go back to sleep," she whispered. "I found out what I need to know."

"What do you need to know?" came Hawken's resigned query.

"If you and your drivers are sick. Pa and Pete, Faith's

father and brother...Ma thought it might be cholera, but I said it was probably the whiskey.'' Hawken threw off his blankets.

''Anyone else?'' he asked as he twisted and pulled his boots from the shadows. He was completely dressed.

''I think maybe Mr. Marshall,'' Meggie began, just as a man erupted, gagging, from a nearby tent. ''Mr. Burdette.''

''Is your grandmother awake?''

''Faith's waking her.''

''Who, besides me, Monty and Les, didn't go to Bridger's?'' he asked. He jumped over a wagon tongue to cut across the circle, and stopped long enough to give her a hand. Meggie had to skip to keep up with his long strides. What men had been in camp?

''Mr. Hunter wasn't here, but he wasn't at Bridger's either, for he brought in two deer about dark. Captain Hull's temperance, so he didn't drink, even though he went to the fort.''

Hawken vaulted the tongue of Granny's wagon, and rather than simply offering his hand, his grasped her about the waist and lifted her over. Captain Hull was lighting a fire. Tildy staggered up with two buckets of water and Granny backed down the steps of her wagon, arms laden with packets and pots.

''Pa is sick,'' said Tildy the moment Meggie stepped into the firelight. ''And Josh.'' Uncle Ira and Cousin Josh leaned side by side against a wagon wheel.

''I believe I ate something that did not agree with me,'' a new voice said from the dark. Mr. Reid crouched by the tiny flames, shivered and held out his hands to warm them.

''Hawken, you sick?'' Captain Hull barked.

''No, and neither is Monty. I don't know about Les,

he's on guard with Godfroy. Meggie says Hunter didn't go to Bridger's.''

''Sampson's with his wife's people,'' Captain Hull mused. ''Meggie, go wake Hunter. We've got to find out how many healthy men we have.'' Meggie set out at a run, skidded to a stop when she came face-to-face with Will and Rachel.

''What's going on?'' Will asked. Meggie outlined the situation in the twelve paces that carried them to the fire. From the other direction came Mrs. Burdette and Mrs. Marshall, both alarmed, both uttering unintelligible sentences.

''Did Godfroy drink?'' Captain Hull asked. ''He might be sick as a dog out there.'' Rachel gave a little cry and Will grabbed her before she had a chance to run off.

''Godfroy doesn't normally drink whiskey,'' Hunter said. ''Rachel doesn't like it.''

Captain Hull looked from man to man. He bit his lips and Meggie felt sorry for him, the man in charge, who had to grapple with this strange emergency.

''Meggie, you go with Rachel and find Godfroy. Just walk away from the fire, close your eyes for a minute to get your night vision, and remember the creek—''

''I know,'' Meggie said. She took Rachel's hand, trembling and cold. ''Your father's fine,'' she whispered as they stepped out across the grass.

The narrow stream glowed like a black ribbon flecked with silver from reflected stars. It reminded Meggie of the mourning bands on Hawken's hat and sleeve. As her eyes adjusted she could make out the dark humps of cattle, and heard an occasional soft snort as they woke. Then the unmistakable choke of human sickness.

''Father, Father,'' Rachel shrieked, running toward the sound. Les reared up from the tall grass.

"How'd you know your pa was sick?" he asked. He stared at Meggie, mouth gaping. He sank out of sight, and for a minute Meggie thought he meant to crawl away from her, like a nocturnal animal. He reappeared, holding two grass stems, overlapped to form a cross. Meggie backed off. What got into this man? He acted like a madman whenever he saw her.

"I'll get John Charles," she said. "Stay right here, Rachel, and we'll carry your father to camp." She ran toward the dot of fire, forgetting the creek until she was upon it, making a last-minute leap that barely cleared the water. A thin sheet of ice crackled beneath her foot.

"All you sick men, back to your own beds," Granny said. "It does no good to have you exposed to night air. I'll come around with the medicine as it's ready."

"Help me let down a wagon tongue," Meggie begged Hawken, the only man who seemed at loose ends. "Godfroy *is* sick. I'll fetch him on John Charles."

"Take care he doesn't buck him off."

"He won't if I lead him and sweet-talk him. John Charles is only cranky without me around. I think he's afraid of horse thieves."

"I'll come with you," Hawken said.

She had no trouble locating Godfroy, for Les stood tall in the moonlight, still armed with the grass stems. Hawken helped Godfroy onto the pony and guided his hands to the mane. "Hang on. Les, can you take care of the cattle alone or should I send one of the boys?" Hawken asked.

"Can't see any problem. Unless I get sick, too."

"You won't. It's Bridger's whiskey. You and Monty should thank me for keeping you at work."

Meggie led John Charles, Hawken walked behind her,

a hand on Godfroy, with Rachel on the other side bracing her father between them.

"Father, Father," Rachel said, following each word with a snap of her tongue behind her teeth. "You shouldn't drink. You know how it frightens me—"

"I didn't drink. For your sake I leave it alone," Godfroy said.

Hawken's hand descended on her shoulder, the fingers curling slowly, insistently, sharing the horrible news by touch. "If you didn't drink, Godfroy, it's not the whiskey," Hawken said.

Godfroy slumped over John Charles's neck, tried to speak, but instead threw up. Hawken's fingers gripped the point of her shoulder like a vise. *He knows we're all going to die,* Meggie thought. The men had caught some dreadful disease at the fort and they would pass it to the rest of them.

She would die virginal. At Independence Rock she should never have let Hawken know she had second thoughts. Perhaps in what remained of tonight…

"Bring Godfroy's bedroll here," Granny said. "Faith and Louisa have Mr. Tole and Kit to tend. By the grace of God you Tildy, and Rachel and Meggie, picked sensible men who don't tipple." Meggie opened her mouth to correct her grandmother, then decided it was near enough the truth and let it pass.

"Tildy, you and Matt stay with me, to carry wood and water. Rachel, you and Will take medicine to everyone on the north side of the circle. Meggie, you and Hawken tend the folks to the south. First, all the men who're sick must try to swallow a spoonful or two of jasmine and elderberry tea. Then we'll apply warm poultices of chickweed, to still the spasms."

"Granny," Meggie breathed quietly, "it isn't the whiskey. Godfroy says he didn't drink."

Granny stirred a simmering pot. "Matt, you were at the fort. What went on besides the whiskey?"

He shook his head. "We looked around the stockade, went in the store, a cabin smaller than your parlor back home. Everyone crowded in—that's where Vasquez keeps the whiskey—and you know how I am about crowds. I went outside and haggled with two Indian women for moccasins."

"The tea's ready," Granny said. "Just a spoonful for now, and more later."

Hawken carried the pail, and Meggie took a spoon and cup. Mr. Burdette lay on the ground outside the family tent, Mrs. Burdette on her knees beside him and four terrified faces peering around the flaps. The two youngest girls sobbed. Hawken thrust an arm behind Burdette's back and lifted him high enough that he might drink from the spoon.

"One swallow now," Meggie said, forcing herself to be as calm as Granny. "Another later, and a hot pack of chickweed on your belly as soon as it's ready."

"He should be in his blankets," Hawken said.

"He tried, but he fell," Mrs. Burdette said. She wrung her hands at her waist, dropped them to her sides, putting on a brave front for the children.

With three of them lifting and dragging, they got Mr. Burdette in the tent and wrapped in blankets. Marshall was easier, for he'd had the good sense to stay in his bedroll, but he could not understand the need for medicine.

"Nothing to be done for cholera," he muttered. "Either live or die."

"If you can talk," Hawken said, "you can tell us what

happened at the fort. It's not the whiskey, for Godfroy didn't drink but he's sick as the rest of you. Was someone at the fort ill?''

"Cholera," said Marshall.

"Who had cholera?"

"No one that I saw. Vasquez tried to sell us all sorts of foolish truck, thimbles and pins and fishhooks. Then he lifted a little curtain and there was the cask. He's a real gentleman, not a squaw man," Marshall wheezed. "His wife's a true lady, treated us like guests." He pressed his hands to his stomach. "Help me outside."

Mrs. Marshall produced a tin basin and dismissed them from the tent with a single sharp word.

"We'll be back in a few minutes, with more medicine," Meggie said as the canvas dropped.

She stopped Hawken after a few yards. "Is it cholera?" she whispered.

"I've never heard of cholera this far west. More likely mountain fever."

"What causes mountain fever?"

"I don't know. Newcomers get it." He set the bucket on the ground and laid an arm across her shoulders. "Some people say it's the water, and others say the wild swings of temperature, hot in the day and cold at night. Or too much fresh meat, or too much salt meat. Who knows? Not everyone gets it." His arm slid lower, the other joined it in a loose embrace. With the spoon in one hand and the cup in the other she could not hug him in return.

"Frightened? Want to go back to the fire, with your friends?" He kissed her forehead and she sagged toward him.

"No. I'm fine." *Ask him now.*

"We'd better get back to Burdette," he whispered. He

did not release her all at once, but eased away. The feather touches of his retreating arms caressed her ribs, near her breasts. Then nothing.

Mrs. Burdette wriggled about in the wagon. "Hello," Meggie said as casually as possible. "How's your husband doing?"

"I'm fixing things so the children can move in here," she said, "away from the sickness." She backed into the open. "He's got to get well. What would I do, alone in the wilderness like that poor widow heading for Oregon?"

"No one's dying," Meggie said forcefully, praying that she spoke the truth.

"Mr. Hawken, I've heard you're a preacher."

"Was," Hawken said.

"I want you to pray with my husband. Explain to God how terrible it would be—"

"You pray. God listens to everyone."

"Please." Meggie gave Hawken a hard look and a punch in the ribs. He walked to the tent. Meggie paid little attention to the cadenced phrases, words she had heard hundreds of times in church. At the "amen" she stooped to enter, dipped the tin cup in the now-cold tea and managed to get two spoonfuls down Mr. Burdette before he held a hand before his mouth.

"The tea's cold," Hawken said after they had dosed Mr. Marshall a second time. "We'd better warm it up." To the east a fading of stars forecast the dawn. She had to get Hawken in her wagon in the next few minutes. "Everyone will feel better when it gets light," Hawken said. "I don't know why, but nothing seems quite as dreadful in the daylight."

"That must be why...at night we want to hold someone. Not be alone. Why married people—" Why couldn't she come right out and ask him? Too late. They entered the ring of light and Hawken put the pot on the fire.

"The chickweed's ready," Tildy said. "Granny made hot poultices from flannel. I'll wrap them in a blanket."

"They must be placed, hot as possible, on the stomach," Granny said.

"I'll take them to Burdette and Marshall," Hawken said. "It's not proper for Meggie to nurse strange men in undress."

"Mr. Burdette and Mr. Marshall aren't strangers," Meggie said. Seeing a strange man in undress—feeling him, rather—was precisely what she wanted to do. But she could not say so in public. She watched in frustration as Hawken gingerly lifted the bundle and walked away. The sky paled, terminating her dream.

"Is anyone else sick?" she asked.

"No, just the men who went to the fort, except for Matt," Tildy said.

"Mr. Hawken says it might be mountain fever. No one knows what causes that."

"Old-timers don't get mountain fever." Godfroy's voice came from beneath a buffalo robe.

"Then what could it be?" Meggie mused. "According to Marshall, neither Mr. or Mrs. Vasquez appeared to be ill. Mrs. Vasquez was welcoming and treated you like...guests!" She yelled the final word. "Guests? Did she offer you something to eat?"

"Someone went hunting in the mountains and brought in a grizzly a day or two ago. She did something with wild onions and the liver." Meggie did not stay to hear further details. She caught Hawken in front of Burdette's tent, silhouetted against the morning sky, and threw herself against him. "Hawken, maybe we're not going to die right yet. Mrs. Vasquez fed the men bear liver."

He grabbed her hand and held it all the way to the fire.

"Hull," Hawken yelled as the captain dumped an armload of sage. "Did you eat the bear liver Mrs. Vasquez prepared?"

"Bear liver? Mrs. Vasquez? Didn't meet her. I talked to the Indian woman." Hawken's fingers dug into Meggie's palm. She twisted her fingers and tapped her own message into his hand.

"Godfroy ate it," Meggie said.

The head poked from the buffalo robe. "It was delicious," he said, groaned and collapsed.

"Spoiled food," Hawken said. "It probably doesn't bother the men here, they're used to it, but to civilized stomachs it's rank poison."

Hawken's hand eased its pressure, and his fingers caressed the edges of hers, tempting and comforting at the same time. She answered by scratching her fingertips across his palm, and Hawken laughed, nervously, under his breath.

"The tea's warm. We'd better go dose our patients," she said. She walked sedately beside Hawken, but her feet longed to dance. She laughed as she spooned out the tea, and later coaxed broth into stomachs able to keep food down. At sunup she skipped to the stream for water, thrust the bucket against the film of ice. She froze at the familiar sound of stomach sickness coming from a willow thicket. Rachel sat on a bending trunk, her husband leaning over her, murmuring words of sympathy.

Meggie left the bucket behind. She ran, fear nipping at her heels, and pulled Granny away from the fire.

"It's not the bear liver," she whispered. "Rachel's sick, too."

"Rachel," Granny said in a low, calm voice, "is expecting a baby, and morning sickness takes most women.''

''A baby!''

Granny laid her finger across Meggie's lips. ''Now, keep the news to yourself. It's Rachel's, to tell or not, as she sees fit.''

''But will a baby wait? Until we get to California?''

''Until we arrive and months beyond. In the winter, sometime after the new year.''

''I won't say a word,'' Meggie promised. The breeze strengthened with the rising sun. She spread her arms to greet the newborn day. In truth, a new world, for there could be no retreat from a baby. The sewing circle would never be the same.

I should have seen the end coming. Already we're separated, the married and the unmarried.

She shivered in the morning chill, regarded her bare, goosefleshed arms, and saw she wore no bodice. She had spent half the night with Hawken clad in nothing but a thin shift and skirt.

Chapter Sixteen

Meggie trailed her finger down his cheek and laughed. Hawken lifted a languid hand and grabbed her wrist.

His fingers closed upon grass, the edges sharp on his palm, waking him from light sleep. A breeze ruffled through the grass, stirred his hair. He rolled onto his stomach. A new view, from the vantage point of a mouse.

The convalescents lay out of sight in the shade of a tarp stretched from Granny's wagon. He could not see the children at the creek, but he heard their laughter. Three sunbonnets and one broad-brimmed hat floated above the grass, rather like hats on wire racks in a milliner's window. Meggie, Tildy, Rachel and Faith, sewing. The breeze caught a small flower—white with a brilliant red center—and swung it between him and the bonnets. Red as a ruby.

Who can find a virtuous woman? For her price is far above rubies. From Proverbs, the Bible verses inevitably read at a woman's funeral, as well as the lesson for a bride at her wedding, always spoken by men hectoring women to be virtuous and respectable. Everything backward, Hawken concluded, for no woman lay beneath the awning. Whoever wrote Proverbs hadn't gone out in the world, paying attention. Probably an old grouch, one of those ancient, toothless grumblers who accuse the younger generation of corruption, and call women weak-minded and sinful. Hawken longed to seize the old goat by his grizzled beard, point his weak eyes toward the convalescent men, then the four virtuous young women at their work. Virtuous women were not rare as rubies. Mary Helen had been a virtuous woman.

He buried his face in the grass, trembling a little, digging his fingers into the sod to steady himself. The implications of his heedless thoughts bore down with the weight of stone. He doubted the truth of the Bible?

He twisted his face to the sky, checking that no thunderbolts threatened. Not all of the Bible, just the parts that demeaned women. Judging from experience, men were far more susceptible to sin. A virtuous man? Rare as a ruby. The situation in camp demonstrated a truth he could not avoid.

And since he was confronting uncomfortable truths, what of Mary Helen? Did he truly find Meggie a more entertaining companion? Yes, again. He raised himself on his elbows, just enough to slide his right hand beneath his chest and touch the mourning band on his left arm. He ran his fingers from shoulder to elbow. Nothing. He rolled on his side and pulled the arm from underneath him. No mourning band. He closed his eyes, trying to remember when he had last remarked on its presence. Yesterday, certainly.

"Quit wiggling and get some rest, boss," said Les from down around his feet. "You was up half the night."

"You were up all night," Hawken mumbled. "Lost the black band off my arm."

"It's over by Marshall's tent," Les said. "Down in the grass. I supposed you'd thrown it off because the spirit of your wife pinched your heart when you hugged that witch.''

By Marshall's tent. Where he had embraced Meggie, his hands spread on her back, her small breasts crushed against his chest. She had not put her arms around him, but her hips had met his. He had been loath to end the embrace, and maintained contact even as he backed away. And the black band slipped off with the pressure.

Just as well. The hypocrisy of it insulted everything holy. Wearing mourning for Mary Helen while he admired Meggie, churned for Meggie? Rank hypocrisy.

The fickle breeze changed, the white and red flower bent the other direction and the voices of the women drifted to his ears.

''The men are well enough,'' Granny was saying. ''If you girls want to visit the fort, no harm would come of it.''

''If we refuse Mrs. Vasquez's liver and onions,'' Tildy said wryly.

''If she has needles in the store...'' Rachel, hesitant, looking for a companion.

''Don't go alone, Rachel,'' Godfroy growled from the shade of the awning. Hawken pulled his legs under him and got on his hands and knees.

''You're gonna give in, I can tell,'' Les said, resigned.

''Might as well,'' Hawken said. Might as well yield to fate. Hardly two weeks since his first awful vision of Mary Helen. No one in Bear River Valley would care. But if he let Meggie ride on to California, out of his life he would care to his dying day.

''I'll escort the ladies if they wish to visit the fort,'' he said formally. ''I'd like to speak to Mr. Vasquez.''

I would rather only Meggie came. I'd pick the white

*flower with the red center, present it to her, and ask her
to be my wife.*

"I don't know anything beyond what Joe Meek told
me when he passed through, heading for St. Louis," Vasquez said. "Just that the Cayuses came down on the mission and killed everyone. Meek's daughter, both Whitmans dead for certain, carried off Bridger's girl—"

"Why?" Hawken asked.

"Who's to say? Meek's riding back to the states to ask
Congress to furnish protection for the Oregon settlers."

"Here at Fort Bridger, have you ever had a hint of
trouble, any suggestion—"

Vasquez smiled. "We're storekeepers. We trade with
the Indians. The women sell their beaded moccasins and
hunting shirts, and the men their furs. We don't disapprove if they have a dance, or if the young men steal a
few horses from the tribes over the mountains. But that's
a missionary's job, to disapprove."

Hawken nodded, delaying the next, necessary hard
question. "How were they killed?"

Vasquez shrugged. "Hacked to death, shot. Some of
the women carried off, so no one knows for sure."

Mary Helen had experienced a briefer death terror than
the women of the mission. "Thanks," he said, wishing
he had not asked. It pained him to think of Mary Helen
as one of the lucky ones, struggling against the enfolding
wagon cover.

"Lose a friend?" Vasquez asked.

"Yes." Hawken ducked under the door lintel, into the
dusty stockade. A flimsy enclosure, made of narrow
lodgepole pines hauled from the mountains, not likely to
stand against a determined attack. The wide gates hung
open and from the way they sagged, Hawken judged they

often hung open. He laid a hand on the substantial tree trunk that formed the gatepost, appraised its strength and considered ways the structure might be improved. He heard her voice and leaned through the opening.

Meggie had not lingered in the store, but stood just beyond the gate with a young Indian woman. Judging by the hand waving and head shaking, she bargained for a pair of beaded leggings. When she saw him, Meggie curled a finger in invitation.

"She won't take money. I think she wants bread or flour, and I can't promise that without Pa's permission."

As Meggie's husband, who was her betrothed until Reverend Cowie caught up, buying the leggings would be his responsibility. Hawken plucked at Meggie's sleeve and drew her to the bank of the stream that ran near the stockade. The Indian woman held the leggings high, turning them so the beads sparkled in the sunlight.

"Meggie, last night I admired your bravery...in the face of adversity."

"I wasn't brave," she scoffed. "I was scared to death. When there's nothing to do but go ahead, you go ahead."

"You were brave. And I...when we fetched Godfroy, you said John Charles doesn't like to be away from you. I think...I want to be with you always. Would you be my wife? Stay with me in Bear River Valley?"

He considered embracing her, then decided not to risk an obvious demonstration of affection before she answered. There was always a chance that her friends were this moment heading for the gate.

"I'm sorry, Hawken."

His heart dropped so far he surreptitiously searched the ground. "You don't have to answer this minute. Think it over," he said, desperate, knowing she would reject him.

"I've already thought it over. When we started on this trip, staying behind in the wilderness seemed a wonderful dream. The most romantic thing I ever heard. But then I met the buffalo hunters and I saw the forts. I wouldn't be free. I'd be a prisoner in your stockade, like Mrs. Vasquez, who's frantic to talk." Her eyes swung to the timbered walls of Fort Bridger. "If I ventured out, the buffalo hunters or the renegades might carry me off. The Indians might attack, like they did in Oregon, and we'd all be killed, you and me and our children. I'll have more freedom with Ma and Pa in California. Pa says we'll find a farm, bigger than the one in Indiana." She smiled with a new idea. "It's not *you* I say no to, you understand. I like you. Come to California with us. There we can court, get to know each other, like a man—"

"No." Was it an assurance of freedom she wanted? "My wife can do whatever damn thing pops into her mind," Hawken said, angry that she could think him straitlaced and narrow-minded. "But I won't go to California, where every man will know I was once Thaddeus Milner, an ordained minister, who lost his mind and took up running a monte bank." He should have confessed the gambling hall women before he asked her. A virtuous woman had a right to know all a man's evil before agreeing to be his wife.

"Go back to being a preacher," she said. "You prayed with Mr. Burdette last night and God didn't strike you dead. Your prayers worked, because everyone's getting well."

"No one was on the road to dying," he reminded her. "It was just small-hours-of-the-morning fright." He clasped one of her hands in both of his, hard, as if pressure there might change her mind. Rachel, Tildy and Faith filed through the gate. Hawken dropped the hand

and backed away, but from the looks on her friends' faces, he knew they had seen.

"We'll lay over another day, until everyone's steady on their pins," Sampson said. He squatted under the awning with the patients, at the same time keeping an eye on his wife and children, who systematically emptied his wagon. Hawken supposed all women, Gros Ventre or white, wanted to arrange their households in their own way. The three eldest kids crowed over every treasure. The youngest slept placidly in its cradle board, hanging on the shady side of the wagon. A boy, Sampson had announced proudly, of whose existence—even potential existence—he had learned only two days ago.

"We must consider the glorious Fourth," Burdette said with a weak pomposity. "We're laying by tomorrow, out of necessity, so where does that put us on the Fourth of July?" He counted on his finger. "Four days hence."

"We're losing a day to the liver and onions," Captain Hull said. "We can't spare time for a holiday on the Fourth, but we'll celebrate that evening. Who brought a copy of the Declaration of Independence?"

"Independence Day demands a holiday," Burdette protested, but Hull paid no attention.

"You're a lawyer. Don't you have one?" Sampson asked in astonishment.

"No. I brought a flag to hang in my law office, but no federal documents. Hunter? You've got some books along—"

"No Declaration," Hunter said.

From where Hawken stood he could see Pete's face, and he nearly laughed out loud at the anxiety playing across the pale features. Twice Pete gave Meggie a sidelong glance. How long before he overcame his pride and announced that his sister could say the whole Declaration without any book except the one in her mind? Sampson got to his feet, Pete sank back, looking relieved that the conversation had ended before he blurted out the truth.

"Got company," Sampson said, shading his eyes. Every man with strength enough stood and faced the road.

"I count ten wagons," Hull said after a few seconds.

"Nine and a cart," Hunter corrected him.

"The Oregonians," Hawken and Pete said in the same breath. Both had had sufficient experience with Mrs. Cooper's wagon to recognize it at a distance.

The emigrants had harnessed a hodgepodge of animals, milk cows hitched with oxen, horses at the wheel with oxen in the lead. A mule here and there. No scout rode in front; Captain Hull set out across the meadow when the wagons began to form a circle.

"That's not Moran," Hunter said when a figure separated from the train and headed out to intercept Hull.

"After the debacle at the river I'd expect them to elect a new captain," Sampson said.

The two men stood together. Hull pointed, it seemed, to a suitable pasture, for three men herded the animals in that direction. Setting a guard, even in daylight, a clear case of too little, too late.

"They're locking the barn door, now that the horses have wandered," Pete said.

"A bitter lesson," Sampson said. "Some greenhorns need the experience before they take us old-timers seriously. If they lose these animals, they're well and truly stranded. I haven't visited the fort. Does Vasquez have oxen for sale?"

"Six or eight teams, but he'll bargain hard," Godfroy

said. "Why should he sell this early in the summer, with hundreds of wagons yet to come?"

"If the Oregonians could hang on as far as Bear River, Hawken could drive his own hard bargain," Sampson said. "He's got eight fine teams."

"I'll need my oxen to build my fort," Hawken said quickly, to end speculation in that direction. "I'll be hauling timbers ten miles, at least."

"Those teams need a rest before they set out for Bear River," Hunter said, a hand shading his eyes. "They've been driven hard. Hull's bringing the man over here."

"This is Captain Purdy," Hull said. Purdy shook hands with everyone who was standing, and gave the men on the ground a curt nod. Hull must have filled him in on the harrowing night of illness.

"Reverend Cowie prayed day and night that we'd catch you. We need help bad." His eyes slid toward the herd that grazed in a distant meadow. The deviation of his glance was so slight that at first Hawken thought it his imagination. But a second, longer look, and a calculating expression, sent a chill down Hawken's spine. Some infinitesimal movement of Purdy's mouth might be interpreted as a threat.

"After our bad luck on t'other side of the river, the men elected me captain."

"From what Sam told us, it wasn't bad luck, but stupidity," Sampson said harshly.

"Doesn't pay to elect a city man captain," Purdy said. That implied he had experience. Perhaps he had tied his own oxen during the storm, and avoided any loss.

"We left behind seven wagons—" he pointed to the circle "—and cut one down to a cart."

"Vasquez has some oxen he's willing to part with," Sampson said easily.

Purdy nodded, but his eyes flickered again to the herd. He smiled at Sampson, a jerking, momentary sort of smile that a man uses when he hates someone but wants to seem agreeable. "Wonderful grass here. Over the next few days we'll come to some accommodation that gets us all back on the road," he said.

"We're leaving day after tomorrow," Sampson said. Purdy threw back his shoulders, increasing his height two inches. "That's one day longer than we should have lingered."

"But our animals gotta—"

"Day after tomorrow," Hull said. "If you want to travel with us, take a deputation to Vasquez this evening and start haggling over the oxen."

Purdy opened and closed his mouth like a landed fish. His eyes slid from face to face, and in the split second that they rested on Hawken, he saw expectation. The Oregonians planned to acquire his teams.

"We'll see," Purdy muttered as he turned and walked away.

"We can't hold back for them," Sampson said. "Too much risk of an early winter in the California mountains. 'One day,' Purdy will beg, 'just one day.' But one day late's as good as starve to death."

"Does anyone in your party have a copy of the Declaration of Independence?" Pete yelled at Purdy's back. Purdy turned slowly, fists on his hips.

"We left every book behind to lighten the loads," he snarled. "Reverend Cowie has a Bible and a volume of sermons. Everything else abandoned for the ferrymen to appropriate."

Pete slumped onto his blanket, glum.

"Don't worry," Burdette said softly so Purdy did not

hear. "I put back a jug. We can toast the anniversary of the nation."

Hawken carried both his capote and coat when he headed for his four hours of guard duty. The stars glittered coldly, reminding him of a camp of laughing men on the other side of a canyon, in sight, but with no way across to gaiety and warmth.

"You feel like being out here?" Hawken asked Kit.

Kit shrugged. "Napped this afternoon. I wasn't sick as Pa, 'cause I can take liver or leave it. Johnny Burdette's helping me." He pointed to a cluster of animals near the creek. "The Oregon people asked to put their animals near ours, so they have a night free of guarding. They've had a sleepless time of it, afraid the teams they have left might be driven off by Indians or stray to alkali springs."

Most of the oxen had settled down to chew their cud and rest. The canvas of the circles shone pale in the starlight, silent, the supper fires flickering out. At twilight two Oregon men had walked to the fort, one of them Purdy. He was wise to bargain for the oxen before Vasquez learned how desperate they were.

"One of their men's coming out to help," Kit said, puzzled. "Captain Hull told me we'd be on our own."

Hawken strained his eyes in the uncertain light, finally made out a dark figure wandering through the tall grass, circling rough places, stumbling now and then.

"Tell him to take a place between you and the wagons," Kit said before he trudged to his own post on the far side of the herd.

"Hawken?" said Captain Purdy. "Captain Hull said you'd be out here, on the night watch. My men asked that I speak to you." They meant to talk him out of his oxen. The muscles of his calves tightened until they ached. "What do we gotta give you to marry Mrs. Cooper and join with us?"

"Marry?" Hawken exclaimed, astonished.

"Leaving behind so many wagons, we had to dump quite a load. Even food. What we figure, you as the widow's husband, we can count on the supplies you're carrying and none of us will be doing double work, tending her wagon and animals besides our own. This evening the men voted, you marry her and let us have the pick of your supplies, and every man will contract to give you forty acres from the land he claims in Oregon. We don't have money to sway you, but forty acres from each man..." His voice died in his throat, admiring the generosity of the offer.

How many men of age in the party? They had counted twenty at the funeral, so canceling the boys, eighteen at the most. He did some quick multiplication.

"Seven hundred acres, more or less, in little pieces scattered all over Oregon," Hawken said, waving his hand to show his opinion of the arithmetic. Purdy cleared his throat, as if he meant to say something, then changed his mind. "No," Hawken said. "I'd have to lease the land back to the owners to have any profit."

"But you could sell it."

"What man would buy such a puny farm when he can claim a whole section? My great-grandchildren might be able to sell, after Oregon's filled up."

"Mrs. Cooper's family's high placed. They came to Oregon in the Great Migration in '43. You'd join her father and brothers on thousands of acres, and in the boatyard they've built. They handle most of the hauling on the river."

Allied with her family, a fine position, until some man from Ohio turned up, one who had known Thad Milner.

Or one who had lost his money gambling in Independence. In a flash of insight, Hawken saw his disgrace as his salvation.

"Mrs. Cooper's brothers and father won't welcome me when I land on the Willamette," he said, making his voice hard although he kept it low. "I know nothing of politics or shipbuilding or farming. I'm a gambler. How do you suppose I got the money for two wagons full of merchandise?"

"They need never know," Purdy said smoothly.

"I need my oxen to build my fort, and I intend to keep them. Go to Vasquez."

"Buying from him takes most of our ready cash."

"You should have thought of that before you set out. Perhaps some Indian will trade for Mrs. Cooper. I've heard young warriors sometimes offer fifteen or twenty ponies for a white woman. That rids you of the work of tending her, and buys you teams in one stroke."

"You're not any help," Purdy snarled.

"Why didn't you go back to Fort Laramie, like we suggested in the letter?"

"We'd crossed the river by the time we got Hull's letter. He writes like a damned lawyer."

"He is a lawyer," Hawken said. His share in the writing had not softened the phrases adequately. "You didn't post guards at the ferry. Didn't any man object to leaving the cattle unattended?"

"We thought Moran knew best, for he's from Missouri and asked advice from men who traveled the plains," Purdy said. Purdy had lost his oxen, Hawken decided. He would brag if he hadn't. "Although we knew from the beginning that Moran wasn't the best choice as captain. He was...is lazy and a gossip." Hawken stood very still, pretending he had not noticed the change of tense. Something more than straying oxen had happened at the river. "But Moran brought hired men along, enough to swing the election, and said if he wasn't captain, he wouldn't join us."

"And you needed his strength."

"Yes. Look, you come along and we'll make you captain."

His confession had not accomplished a thing. They'd marry Mrs. Cooper to the devil if he had oxen and food.

"How much does Vasquez want for his teams?" Hawken asked.

"Eighty dollars a yoke."

"Buy them. Money's of little use here, while oxen are more precious than rubies." Unlike virtuous women. "If Vasquez can't furnish enough, at Bear River I'll sell you two yoke on credit, forty dollars a yoke. You send the money back next spring with the first man riding east."

Hawken expected some expression of thanks. Purdy looked at the ground and stirred the grass with his toe. "Flour and sugar. Coffee, too," he said. "On credit."

"No."

"But we haven't enough to get through to Oregon."

"Parties coming behind, bound for Oregon might have extra. Stay here, hunt, and dry the meat. Certainly at Fort Hall—"

"Your people could help, split their provisions with us, practice charity," Purdy said, nothing of charity in his hard accusation.

"My friends have a greater and harder distance to travel than you. These men won't deprive their families. They're contemptuous of you, that you started out carrying foolish things like plows and dressing tables, while they left everything behind. They went to the expense of hiring two scouts who'd traveled the road before."

"It's a man's Christian duty—"

"So everyone starves?" Hawken cried. He snapped his mouth shut and took deep breaths through his nose until he calmed down. "Buy Vasquez's oxen, two teams from me, reduce your load to the bare minimum. Nurse one horse along, let no one ride him so he stays strong. Then when you're within two or three hundred miles of the settlements send a man ahead. The settlers will take up a collection and meet you with provisions."

"And we arrive in debt," Purdy said bitterly. "The women don't complain publicly, but they talk among themselves, say we never should have started and that they warned their menfolk it would come to this. The men are disillusioned, finding how much it costs to travel, how much harder the trail is than they expected. The night before the storm they quarreled when they found out the charges for the ferry."

"Stick around here until another Oregon party shows up. Or go to the Salt Lake settlement, and ask—"

"Mormons!" Purdy snarled as if Hawken had mentioned snakes. Hawken shrugged and looked at the stars. Purdy would marry Mrs. Cooper to a gambler, but have nothing to do with men whose beliefs differed from his own. He gave up racking his brain for suggestions.

"You won't marry Mrs. Cooper?" Purdy asked.

"No."

"You're all damn, lying, selfish bastards. I don't condone thievery," Purdy said, his words blurring, "but if you don't see reason I'm not sure I can control the men. They elected me captain, but I got no more real power over them than a babe of two years over these animals if they should take it in their heads to run."

Hawken heard the underlying threat more clearly than the words. The men would take what they needed. The discrepancy in numbers rose like a tower, twenty versus sixteen, seven of that number weakened by illness. Perhaps Sampson could enlist his wife's village. Except that the band had moved yesterday, eight or more miles distant.

On the positive side, Purdy's men were already fighting among themselves. But on the other hand, a battle for food and oxen would unite the quarreling factions. Anyone who stood in their way...he saw Meggie toppling off John Charles, a bullet through her breast. Not Meggie! Dear God, not Meggie! He had been the instrument of death for one woman. He could not stand idly by and doom another.

"I'll speak to Captain Hull," he said as casually as possible.

"Immediately."

"Tomorrow morning," Hawken said, the lie essential to the plot his mind constructed even as he spoke. He shrugged his capote over his head and, when he could see once more, found Purdy walking away. They would attack just before dawn, while the sick repaired their strength in deep sleep. The wagons must move out despite the weakness of the men. He stood very still until he was certain that Purdy continued across the meadow, then edged slowly in Kit's direction. He'd covered half the distance when Kit sank in the grass. From the rustling, Kit was crawling toward him.

"What's he got to say?" Kit whispered from near his feet. "Something you don't like or you would have come to me directly."

"I judge, from what Purdy says, they're planning to steal enough of our oxen to pull their wagons, and probably supplies as well. Purdy asked us to divide with them, but when I pointed out that we endangered ourselves by sharing, he threatened. How mingled are their cattle with ours?''

''Hardly at all, for they wanted the thickest grass, down by the creek, and Captain Hull ordered me to drive our animals higher, so as not to bed on damp ground. And he's kept the horses in the wagon circle.'' Hull, Hawken realized, had suspected Purdy's intentions.

''I'll rouse Hull and he can make the final decision, but I think he'll say we move out. If you can do it without too much noise, stir the teams. Push ours toward the wagons and theirs away from camp.''

''Send the boys,'' Kit said. ''There's only me and little John Burdette. And he's probably asleep.''

''Hull's the one to decide,'' Hawken cautioned. He must not take too much on himself. But the constellations swung in their midnight positions, and the Oregonians might not be so tired as they made out last evening.

Chapter Seventeen

Hawken approached Hull's tent on tiptoe, made cautious by his having nearly barged in on a night of love. Everything silent. He scratched on the canvas. "Captain."

"Yes." The voice came from behind him, immediate and strong. Hull scrambled from under a wagon. "Sampson and I decided to keep our guard," he whispered. "I saw too many guns being cleaned and loaded over there."

"What you figure?" Sampson asked, a bulk blotting out the stars.

Hawken quickly summarized his conversation with Purdy. The tent flap stirred, and Mrs. Hull stepped out, fully dressed.

"Mr. Hawken," she said. "Go wake Meggie. You know her wagon?" He wiggled his head so the capote hood fell more completely over his face, then realized no one would see his blush in the darkness. "Meggie and I'll rouse the camp, while you and Matt help with the cattle."

Hawken shouldered aside the vision of Meggie wounded and bleeding. As he lifted the patched canvas, another vision, equally troubling, replaced it. Meggie naked and receptive.

"Meggie."

She reached for him sleepily. "Hawken," she murmured.

"Wake up." He brushed aside the hand that fondled his throat. "There's danger." He whispered a hasty account of what had transpired, hoping she was awake enough to understand. The shifting of the wagon told him she was dressing, pulling on a skirt, buttoning her bodice. He would stand between her and danger, if she would let him.

She crawled to the opening. "Kiss me," she whispered. "For luck."

"Kissing doesn't bring luck," he protested. But he laid his closed lips on her ready ones, while shoving her hand off his shoulder. "Remember, tell everyone, quiet as a hunting cat, or we'll tip Purdy off."

He walked right between Sampson and the six steers he was driving. "The boys are getting all the tents down," Sampson said. "Hull's out with Kit and John Burdette. Hitch up as fast as the teams come in, starting with the wagons that face away from the Oregon camp. Get some grease on the axles, for God's sake, and don't fuss about who gets whose oxen. We'll sort things out at dawn. Any man or boy who's steady and to be trusted with a gun, they stand between the thieves and the herd."

Disheveled women snatched pots and pans left at the supper fires. Clotheslines disappeared in jerky movements. Mrs. Sampson, her baby already strapped to her back, tied her three ponies to a wagon.

Chaos, Hawken thought. But on second glance an organized chaos. The jingle of the chains seemed as loud as a fire bell in the night, certain to attract the attention of Purdy—who must still be awake. Wheels turned, the squeal of axles and hubs more deafening than Hawken thought possible.

"Wait, damn it!" He leaned over, embarrassed to find he had directed the curse at Mrs. Marshall. "Pardon me. Don't pull out until we've set up some protection." Without guards, the wagons could be cut off as they left the circle.

"We're here," said Meggie. She straddled John Charles, a rifle balanced before her. Rachel perched on her mare, the combination of sidesaddle, rifle and knife so incongruous that Hawken giggled, out of control. "We'll stand them off if they dash at the first wagons. The able men will protect the rear," Meggie said, so sternly he put his hand over his mouth.

"Go," Hawken said to Mrs. Marshall. He bent to the chains of the second wagon, glanced up once, made a quick check to see if anyone was looking at him, and blew a kiss at Meggie's back.

Another wagon, then another, and Hawken lost track somewhere between six and nine. "They're stirring over here," Hull said. The boys drove their horses a mile off. They'll need an hour or so to find them. Just hope Godfroy can stay in the saddle."

"Godfroy shouldn't be—"

"Someone must lead and make sure we stay on the trail. Godfroy will handle it until Sampson can take over. Wouldn't do for the women to drive into some morass where we'd be sitting ducks."

Sampson's wagon rolled by, Mrs. Sampson holding the goad in one hand and a pistol in another. The eldest boy, no more than six years old, leaned out the rear, miniature bow and arrow poised for combat.

Hawken wondered that he could see so many details.

In the east the late quarter moon had cleared the hills and added its faint glow. The chains rattled on the final wagon—Godfroy's—and the boys openly drove the loose stock behind the screen of wagons.

Three armed men headed out to join the women. Hawken felt his belt. Nothing but his knife. *Mush-brain,* he said to himself as he trotted forward to find his wagons. He should have armed himself first thing. Pledging to protect Meggie, but with what?

"Here, boss," Monty called. Moonlight glinted from pistols and knives stuck in his belt, and the rifle in his hand. A walking arsenal. "Les has the other rifle and a pig sticker."

"A what?"

"Tied a knife on the end of an ax handle." One less ax handle in the load.

A spot of light across the meadows. The spark of the inevitable explosion, Hawken thought fearfully. Where was Meggie? The dot of light did not expand or multiply, but bounded up and down. For a few seconds it vanished from sight, altogether, then rose, closer.

A lantern, being carried by someone running toward them. A man's shout, very faint, that rose to a shriek in his determination to be heard. Hawken studied the placement of the mounted guards, his heart straining against his ribs. Where was Meggie in relation to the attackers?

The light closer, and he could make out only one man. Why would Purdy send one? A decoy, to stop the wagons while the rest of the men massed for the attack. The circle of light veered to the right, toward Meggie and Rachel. Hawken grabbed the rifle Monty held out to him.

"Don't stop on any account, and tell everyone else to keep on going." Certainly Hull, with his military training, would recognize a diversion. The cold grip of the rifle sent a chill up his arm, into his brain, steadying him. He planned a route to intercept the light, a problem made more difficult when the light slowed, even stopped briefly. The man was tiring, a reminder to Hawken to pace himself, so he had breath enough to react in an emergency.

Meggie turned John Charles slightly, twisted in the saddle and raised her rifle. "I'm here," Hawken muttered as he jogged past her. The man could not both aim a rifle and hold the lantern. And a tired man could not shoot a pistol accurately with a single hand. The light arced to the ground. Hawken skidded to a stop when the shadow fell to its knees. Ready to take aim?

"Please...don't," came the cry. Hawken aligned his sights with the core of the shadow. The chest. Difficult to hold steady as he fought for breath.

"Please don't." Very distinct panting. "I told Purdy...he would only make matters worse." Reverend Cowie balanced the lantern carefully on a clump of grass so it illuminated his face. He folded his hands in an attitude of prayer. "I warned him, this is a greater sin than we have already committed."

"Lower your rifles." The voice was softly feminine, but definitely to be obeyed. Granny's hands patted the air, the gesture she would use to calm excited children. "You should know better than to threaten a clergyman," she said, a brief glance at Hawken. He would have taken it as a reprimand, except she laughed. Her fingers curled, an invitation to join her.

She picked up the lantern with one hand, grabbed Cowie's arm with the other, and tried to pull him to his feet. Hawken shifted the rifle so he could help her, at the same time scanning the meadow for threats. A streak of gray in the east overpowered the moonlight, as if dawn had come all in a rush. The wagons moving slowly, the mounted guards maintaining their positions, rifles poised. The Oregon circle was barely visible, dirty canvas blending with the gray landscape.

"Fort up," Sampson yelled. By the time Hawken and Granny had half dragged Cowie to the wagons, all the men were on guard, those who had been most ill sitting in their wagons.

"Are you the emissary?" Hull asked roughly.

Cowie shook his head. "I had to come, even though Purdy threatened to shoot me, but you see he didn't, for he's a coward. I beg you, don't go. Purdy sees force as the only solution, and ever since the river—" The man shuddered.

"What happened at the river?" Granny asked. No one seemed to notice that she, Rachel and Meggie had joined the parley, an occasion normally restricted to men. Hawken eased away from Meggie lest he pry the rifle from her fingers and embrace her.

"Murder," Cowie whispered. "After he sent the message to bring you back, Captain Moran accused his wife of neglecting her responsibilities, causing the cattle to stray. Why would a man say such things? She shouted at him, said the move to Oregon had been his idea, not hers, that they must turn back. He drew a pistol and shot her. Killed her. And in his madness set fire to his wagons and tried to throw the children in the flames. Fortunately, he was subdued before…we had to hang him, of course." A despairing whisper. "His hired men, four of the strongest, turned back."

"So that's why Captain Purdy visited us alone," Hawken said. Moran dead? Hawken felt as if he knew something that Hull should know. Something Moran had said—

"He visited you alone, so you'd not guess how few we'd become," Cowie said. "What must we do?"

"How many children?" Hull asked, a strange question, to Hawken's mind. Hull should be dictating the terms for peace, not worrying over orphans who were not his responsibility.

"Three. And all their supplies burned, so they're dependent and resented as a burden."

"We'll feed them," Granny and Hull said simultaneously. A glance of agreement—of commonality—passed between the old woman and Hull, startling Hawken so much he stared impolitely. Hull was not her grandson. No blood relative, only kin by marriage. An aura of dawn seemed to unite the two. A brief meeting of eyes— washed-out blue and dark—and their smiles spoke of bonds so deep they would survive disasters. Even death. For an instant Hawken felt a wild jealousy, envying the man who possessed such security.

"Go back to your camp, tell the men to join us for negotiations," Hull said gently, patting Cowie's shoulder. "That little hill will do for a treaty spot." He pointed toward the morning sky, and the dawn rippled down his sleeve. "Unarmed, of course."

"Stripped," Sampson said. "Not a stitch of clothes on any man who walks beyond your wagons."

Cowie nodded. "Two of our men are so sick they can't leave the wagons. They drank alkali water and I fear they're dying."

A loud rasp. A snake's warning! Hawken jumped, swallowed hard when Granny bent to blow out the candle. He'd been spooked by the noise caused by lifting the isinglass shutter. Granny handed the lantern to Cowie. "Wait until I gather some medicines. I'll come with you.

Matt, tell Tildy to get food on to feed three hungry children.''

Captain Hull kept his eyes on Cowie and Granny until they blended with the tattered wagons. ''How's everyone feeling?'' he asked. Heads bobbed; if any man felt the least weakness, he refused to acknowledge it.

''Kit's wore-out as an old rag,'' Tole volunteered. ''Of course, he's been up all night.''

''Who can take over the herd?'' Hull asked.

''Rachel and I will,'' Meggie said.

Hawken watched her ride away, making no bones about his interest. Let every man see his concern. His affection. Hull had explained the situation long ago, but Hawken had not understood, perhaps not really listened. The MacIntyre clan was like a sponge, engulfing those who married into it. Not a bad submergence, Hawken concluded. Not like drowning. If he could find the courage to go on to California, and face the inevitable exposure.

''Hawken?'' Hull asked in a puzzled voice. ''You with us?'' Hawken realized he was still staring at Meggie, only a distant rider. And there was something he must tell Hull. Something Purdy had said? No, Moran.

''Meggie's quite adept at guarding cattle,'' Hull said, amused. Hawken turned back to Hull and shrugged off the twitching of the captain's mustache. ''Meggie's got a pile of talents. Quite a mint, that woman.''

Mint. Cash. Purdy's statement flowed around thoughts of Meggie without eroding them. ''Purdy claims they'll exhaust all their ready cash if they buy teams from Vasquez,'' Hawken said. ''Ask him what happened to the money Moran hid in his wagon.''

''Money?''

"Back when Moran tried to talk me into marrying the widow, he mentioned that Cooper might have cached money in his wagons. And that suggests that Moran had money hid."

"He burned his wagons."

"But probably not the money, for it wouldn't make sense to carry banknotes west. Who'd honor them in Oregon? It's got to be either gold or silver, and some-one's taken it."

Hull hummed, a thoughtful sound. "If I mention it, it might split the thieves from the ones who didn't get a share. If they fight each other, they're not fighting us."

"That's what I'm thinking."

"The money belongs to Moran's kids by rights."

Hawken shrugged. "Ethically, I'd say they should use it to save everyone's life. The lives Moran put in danger."

"You think like a preacher," Hull said. "I think like a lawyer. That's fine, we temper each other's extremes."

The Oregonians slunk up the hill, bent over. "Let's get this done with," Purdy said, eyeing the sun. "A burn all over can kill a man."

"No need for it to take long," Hull said. "You fellows agree to purchase the oxen Vasquez has for sale. You cut your loads to the bone—"

"We've cut more than we should have already," a man said.

"You open your wagons to Sampson and Godfroy. They'll be the judge of that. In Bear River Valley you buy two yoke from Hawken, cash money—"

"Last night he said credit."

"Last night he didn't know Moran was dead and his wagons burned. Who's got his stash of coin?"

"Money!" several men exclaimed.

"Purdy, you said nothing about money." A man pulled himself erect, making no attempt to cover himself. Hawken stole a glance at the women, who watched from the wagons, then at Meggie on her pony. Too far away to see much.

"You went through the wreckage," the irate man said. "You said you found nothing worth—" Half the men stepped behind the accuser.

"He's making trouble," Purdy yelled. "Don't you see his trick?"

"I believe Moran had money," Cowie said, managing to sound suspicious and reverential at the same time. "He sold a wholesale hardware business in St. Louis."

Purdy danced in fury. "He's trying to split us up, turn us against each other." Two men grabbed his arms.

"Shall I tell Mrs. Purdy to turn out the wagon?" Hawken asked.

"No!" Purdy shrieked.

Reverend Cowie raised his hand. "Quiet!" His most pontifical tone. "The good woman who nursed our sick, the lady who at this moment feeds the Moran orphans, we'll let *her* go through Purdy's wagons." He pointed at his captain. "Tie him up until we learn the truth. Your belts will do for…" His gaze swept the men, an awkward dropping of his eyes, as if just now appreciating everyone's nakedness. He turned appealing eyes to Captain Hull. "If one or two of your men would escort Purdy to our camp, they can verify that nothing's removed from the wagons before the good lady…I'm sorry, I don't know her name."

"Granny MacIntyre," Hull said. "Hunter, Sampson, hang on to Purdy and tie him to a wheel of his wagon. I'll be over in a few minutes with Granny."

''Relieve Meggie and Rachel,'' Hawken reminded him in a low voice. ''They shouldn't be guarding cattle.''

Hull grinned at him. ''You relieve them, since you're the one who's worried and got such raw nerves you jump when a lantern's opened.'' He jerked a thumb at the curious boys hanging on the outskirts of the conclave. ''Get the boys back to work. And the wagons better move on to a watering place and the teams relieved of their yokes.''

''Captain Moran was crazy,'' Meggie said, leaning from the saddle, wishing she could get closer to Hawken's ear so she might speak to him in confidence. ''Why else would he accuse his wife of being responsible for the cattle?''

''Boys grow up believing that a man never makes a mistake,'' Hawken said. ''Their fathers pretend to be infallible gods. Most men, by the time they come of age, have figured it's a lie, but some don't. They resent every critical word, for they must always be right.''

''That's no reason to blame his wife.''

''He depended on the men's votes to keep his position as captain. If he accused them of carelessness he'd lose their support. So he laid the blame on someone who had no voice, his wife. After all, aren't women fickle and eternally wrong? Moran had probably worked the same trick a hundred times and it got to be a habit, blaming his wife when things got out of whack. And ninety-nine times she submitted meekly. But the hundredth? She's angry, her children are crying because they're cold and hungry, the blankets wet, and she's no idiot, she can see they're stranded on the North Platte. Her husband, this man who posed as infallible lord and master, he doesn't know what to do. She shocks him with the truth.''

Meggie pretended to shiver in horror. She had never heard a man say such things. Least of all a man who had once been a preacher.

"Maybe Faith is right. She's against marriage, you know, says to be a wife is to be a slave. I'll be a terrible wife, for I'd for sure blurt out exactly what a man doesn't want to hear."

"I'd listen to what you have to say."

"No, you wouldn't. When the buffalo hunters came around you'd order me into the stockade, no matter what I wanted."

"Possibly," he murmured.

"Admit it! Acting like a little Napoleon—" she laid her hand on her chest in mockery of the emperor and was rewarded when he smiled "—when you ordered me into Granny's wagon in the South Platte, that would become second nature, and I'd have no friends to complain to. No family to run to when you got unbearable. I'm going to California."

"What if I told you I loved you?"

"Men get over love. You've already gotten over your wife."

"I didn't love her exactly."

Meggie dropped her hand so suddenly John Charles took it as a signal to stop. "You didn't love her? You married her without loving her?" A red stain spread over his cheekbones, like a brush stroke. He nodded stalwartly and met her eye. "Then you're a worse man than I thought. Gambling I could forgive, and being a fallen-away preacher, but—"

"The mission board said we had to be married before we went to Oregon, so we wouldn't be tempted by the Native women. Mary Helen was the only woman I knew well enough to ask. Fred skipped out by telling the board he had a girl waiting in St. Joe, and then not going through with the wedding.''

"After he'd promised?''

"Well, the young woman wasn't too keen, after she met Fred. I might as well tell you everything bad about myself, and get it out of the way. You see, women of bad repute hang about taverns and gambling halls. One, winter before last, lived in the same room with me. Will you forgive that?''

"You didn't love her, either?''

"I enjoyed being with her and respected her judgment.''

"A woman who lives with a man without being married doesn't show very good judgment.''

"I suppose that's true,'' he said.

He appeared downcast and shy, but his fingers opened and closed, forming fists. *I don't trust him,* she thought. She slid out of the saddle to put John Charles between them. She would test him, she decided, to see how far he'll let a woman go before he got angry.

"Men are the fickle ones,'' she said. "In the Bible, Ezekiel says women tempt men away from God by wearing kerchiefs on their heads. Then Paul, in First Corinthians, says women must cover their hair. They both can't be right.'' How would he react to that? She walked tall to spy on him across John Charles.

"Ezekiel also says women corrupt men by sewing pillows on their armholes,'' he said lightly. "Now, what man in his right mind would be attracted to a woman with a pair of pillows jutting out on either side? Couldn't give her a quick hug. Have to make the doors awfully wide.''

Meggie laughed, and Hawken joined in briefly. Peek-

ing over John Charles's back, she saw Hawken's chin
wobble, his lips move, but no words came out.

Hawken twisted in his blankets, unable to sleep. Bear
River Valley lay just over the ridge, no more than seven
miles away. Was that the morning star, swimming on the
horizon? He shook Monty, whispered he would hike
ahead, clung to his boots as he waded the stream on the
far side of camp, and set out to climb the last mountain.
The rays of the sun touched the summit at the same time
as his boots, welcoming him. Beyond, the trail dipped at
an alarming angle. He dug in his heels, hoping that
Monty and Les remembered to chain the wheels securely,
or improvise some kind of brake. No possibility of building a windlass. The closest large trees lay ten miles back.
After he got a good look at the curve of the Bear where
he'd build his post, he would walk back and help get the
wagons down.

At the first opening into the valley he glimpsed the
river curling seductively in the twilight. His feet took on
a life of their own, running, sliding, eager to plant themselves and take root. The high spot in a curve of the river.
He imagined he could already hear the purling of the
water as it dropped through a low rapid. Jump, from one
declivity to another, leap across the ruts deepened by
melting snow. The roughness of the track kept his eyes
busy, and he was not far from the bottom when he managed a first, long, satisfying look into the valley.

Something was wrong. He scanned the undulating
meadow, gray-green in the mountain shadows. The sense
of disquiet brought shivers to the back of his thighs.
Brightness flooded the river as a crescent of sun cleared
the mountain. A shadow of unnatural regularity. Square,
and beyond it the conical shape of an Indian lodge.

Hawken sat down in the middle of the road. The sun cleared the mountains and reflected from the wall of a second cabin, and a third. Someone had beaten him to Bear River Valley. He pressed his knuckles to his eyes, then took another look. Cabins and Indian lodges. By the time he heaved himself to his feet and set out for the river, he could distinguish four structures and a dark patch of ground. As he neared the little settlement the dark patch resolved into a partially plowed field, the plow standing idle in the furrow.

Someone had noted his approach, for a man walked from the cabins to the road. He turned in Hawken's direction. The man limped. Hawken stopped fifty yards away, the moment he was sure about the wooden leg. Only one man he knew of in this country with a wooden leg. Peg-Leg Smith.

"Howdy, stranger," the man called.

Hawken loosened his knife in its sheath, made sure of the angle of the pistol in his belt before he took another cautious step.

"Emigrants acomin' I suppose," the man said, extending his hand. "Tom Smith, here."

Hawken edged toward him and shook his hand without standing too near. "Hawken." The single word seemed impolite, but Hawken was uncertain how to greet a legend. Particularly a legend of Smith's volatile reputation. Mountain tales said he'd amputated his own leg after being wounded by Indians, that he had made a living down south kidnapping Indian children and selling them as slaves into Mexico. And he was wanted in California for horse stealing.

"How many are ye?" Smith asked.

"Ten wagons for Oregon, seventeen—" Seventeen for where? Two were his and he had planned to stop right here. "Seventeen for California," he said as the simplest deception.

"Vegetables aren't quite ready, except for greens and radishes," Smith said.

"I'll...I'll go back and tell the captain not to stop for noon until...we get here," Hawken said, ashamed of the limp texture of his voice. He must backtrack to the summit as quickly as possible and warn Hull and the scouts. Thank heavens Meggie had forsaken her habit of riding ahead.

"You tell them," Smith yelled. He waved his hat. "Everybody welcome."

Hawken went up the hill nearly as fast as he had come down. Smith's presence proved Meggie right. The Rocky Mountains were no place for a woman, even with the end of the beaver trade and the greater frequency of overland travelers. But California? He'd no more than get settled, and some man would tell the world who he was. What he had done. And Meggie, as his wife, would be disgraced, as if she had made every misstep and committed every sin.

Hull and Sampson stood on the summit, eyeing the slope and scratching their heads. Hawken had breath enough for only two words. "Peg-Leg."

"Smith?" Sampson asked with a start, paying no attention to the hill. Hawken nodded, panting. "Where?"

"Bottom of the hill, where the trail meets the river, just where I...where I wanted my trading post."

"How many men he got with him?"

"I don't know. The only person I saw was Smith."

Sampson's face constricted. "Hull, can you and Hawken organize the wagons down this hill? I want to stick with my kids. Peg-Leg Smith's made off with too many

Indian babies for me to feel comfortable otherwise.'' He dashed away without waiting for an answer.

''We'd figured three or four men trailing behind each wagon, as a brake,'' Hull said. ''What do you suggest?''

''That's the way we did it. The biggest, heaviest men.''

''Not many heavy men left,'' Hull said, laying a finger on the new hole punched in his belt. ''Monty, Burdette...''

Hawken walked the length of the train, rounding up the men best shaped to serve as brakes. He met Meggie on the ridge, leading John Charles, the three Moran kids perched on his back. Wealthy children, since Granny had found the gold stashed in Purdy's wagon, but money could not ease the death scenes that occupied their dreams. Unless they forgot. He prayed they would forget. A blessing for children so young.

''Don't head down the hill until we have everyone together,'' he warned Meggie. ''There's a man at the river we can't trust.''

''Sampson told me,'' she said. ''An old trapper who kidnaps children and murders people with his wooden leg. I thought maybe John Charles could help lower the wagons. Since I can make him back up.''

''Murdered people with his leg?'' Hawken exclaimed.

''He beat some men to death in a fight in a tavern.''

''You stay here, at the top,'' Hawken said. ''Until I'm ready to head down.'' Meggie grinned, an I-told-you-so grin, and Hawken realized he had given her orders instead of considering her suggestion that John Charles would serve as a brake. She was right. Her life would be hell with him in Bear River Valley. Then he remembered he had no life in Bear River Valley, either.

Meggie lifted the children off John Charles, one by one, ruffling their hair and squeezing their shoulders with her long fingers. She would have children of her own someday, and what wonderful childhoods they would have, with a mother who galloped about on a pony and gathered herbs in wild woods, who could remember every page of every book she had ever read.

Chapter Eighteen

Matt gave Smith a friendly wave as he led the wagons half a mile beyond the trading post, leaving Godfroy to visit Peg-Leg and purchase fresh vegetables. But Godfroy did not return alone.

"I invited him to have dinner with me," Godfroy muttered as they rode in. "Not easy to put Peg-Leg off."

Sampson shoved his children into the wagon and stood between them and Smith. Rachel, who must serve Peg-Leg his dinner, made no effort to conceal her fright. Matt decided to stick around Godfroy's fire.

Peg-Leg accepted the offer of a seat on an overturned bucket. He unstrapped his wooden leg, stood it before him and propped his stump on it. The wooden leg had the dimensions of a cudgel, and Matt found himself examining each stain. Blood?

"We're both scouting new trails," Smith said to Godfroy. "Now that the beaver's gone."

"Why settle here?" Godfroy asked. "I thought you liked the warmer lands, down south." If Smith noted this oblique reference to slave trading and horse stealing, nothing showed in his face.

"Up here in the cool mountains my leg's safe from

termites,'' he said. He laughed at his own joke, looked around, smiling at his audience, as if sharing his mirth. But his intense eyes lingered on women and wagons, not the men. Matt chided himself for his suspicions. The man had been out of touch with civilization for months, and probably had not seen a white woman for a year. Naturally he would be curious.

"How's business?" Godfroy asked.

"You're the first ones through this year. How many behind?"

"At least fifty wagons outfitted for California in St. Joe, and a hundred for Oregon. Any news from California?"

"Place is settling down, I guess, but the war messed up the horse herds, what with soldiers dashing up and down the coast, taking what they needed without so much as a by-your-leave from the owners," Peg-Leg said. Godfroy worked his mouth to suppress a smile. "Usual rumors float by. The Californios have rebelled. The Indians on the Snake have cut off the trail. Someone found gold. But that's old news. You remember, in '42 a fellow pulled up a bunch of onions north of Pueblo de los Angeles and found a nugget in the roots. Started a rush that came to very little."

"Heard a snatch about it," Godfroy said, "but I'm not a miner so it didn't interest me."

"A mine keeps you in one place," Peg-Leg said. A little disgruntled, Matt thought. "Like nailing your boots to the floor. I'm finding a trading post and garden and wheat field's mighty similar. Your new trade looks interesting, Godfroy. If I head east in September, I could guide emigrants as far as Fort Hall come spring."

He accepted the plate Rachel offered, including turnip greens cooked with bacon. Matt's mouth watered.

"I suppose you'll camp here tonight," Smith said, "being it's the Fourth and all."

"No. We'll drive on and celebrate up the valley."

Smith's disappointment vanished behind a great spoonful of greens. Matt licked his lips and edged toward the fire where Tildy prepared his own dinner. He passed Hawken, who nursed a cup of coffee and paid no attention to the plate Monty offered. He looked like a man who'd had a rug pulled out from under him.

"Keep an eye on the old buzzard," Matt whispered to Hawken. "He's paying too much attention to the ladies." Hawken spun about, ignoring Rachel, who was most threatened, and staring with wide, worried eyes at Meggie.

Maybe, Matt thought, Peg-Leg's presence solved Hawken's dilemma. Smith preempted the best location in Bear River Valley, and dealt Hawken's trading post a fatal blow. Hawken could join the MacIntyres and marry Meggie.

"Why not come on with us to California?" Matt said.

"My wagons aren't fit."

"We've taken every capote you carried. By the way, Meggie kept a record and will make sure you're paid."

"Meggie?" Love had a man secure in its grip when he came down fast on a woman's name, and ignored hard cash.

"And the Oregon emigrants will buy what they can afford. Maybe you could sell the rest at Fort Hall."

"Then what?"

"Join the MacIntyres." Matt laughed. "It's a good family. Jim Mac can't object to your suit, not since you went in the river for his wife."

"I was in the right place at the right time," Hawken said. "In California that memory will dim and I'll be the son-in-law he took on by mistake. Jim Mac's a farmer, I'm not, and would be as useful as a sheep in a sawmill. I'm not like you, with a respectable profession. And it's inevitable that one day a man will recognize me.''

''What's past is past.''

''What's past can be recalled and blacken a man's reputation. It's one thing for you, an army officer, a lawyer, to be accepted by the MacIntyres. Me?''

''I've not always been an army officer and lawyer,'' Matt said. ''My father's a squatter on the flats of the White River, my mother's a whore. I couldn't read until I was sixteen years old, when I ran off to the army.''

Hawken put down the tin cup and his mouth worked as if to dislodge a stone he'd swallowed by accident.

''Do you hear any MacIntyre make snide references to what I was? All you've got to do is dig in and make something of yourself in California.''

''What?'' A cry of despair.

''You'll find out when we get there, within a day or two of pulling into Sutter's Fort. If you sell your goods at Fort Hall, you'll have a nest egg to start a business. But make up your mind this week, because we turn off at Raft River and Reverend Cowie heads for Oregon. There won't be a preacher to marry the two of you till we pass the Sierra.''

Matt mulled over the situation while he ate bacon, turnip greens and flapjacks. Married people, happily married people—he smiled at Tildy—had this habit of trying to get their friends married off, too. Perhaps that's why he wanted Hawken to hitch up with Meggie. But deep down he knew he had another motive. Meggie would calm once she had a husband. All the MacIntyres had a stake in steadying her.

''Captain Hull.'' Purdy tramped forward, his face set

in a grim pout. "Hawken promised to sell us two yoke of oxen on Bear River. But when we went to collect, he says we got to wait because he can't settle hereabouts. That's going back on his word."

"Purdy, you ever heard of an Act of God?"

"Of course. You take me for an idiot?"

"In law, contracts aren't valid if an Act of God intervenes. I think Peg-Leg Smith qualifies as an Act of God, don't you? You want to risk getting smacked on the head with that wooden leg? Now you compose yourself and enjoy your dinner, and consider Hawken's position. And shut up until he decides what he's going to do."

Purdy glared. "I always hated lawyers," he said.

"Until you need one yourself," Matt said. "I'm the only one along and if you move a finger toward Hawken's oxen, I won't represent you when the men weave the noose and lift the wagon tongues."

Hawken lowered a jug into a quiet pool. Bubbles burst on the surface as it gurgled full. Bubbles with no more substance than his punctured dream.

"So what are your plans?" Godfroy asked.

"Don't know."

"Give Soda Springs a look-see, maybe set up your post there. But to tell you the truth, I'd hate to be in the same valley as Peg-Leg."

"I gather the man stops at nothing."

"He gives mountain men a bad name," Godfroy said.

"Hurry up with the water," Burdette called, swinging his own jug back and forth temptingly.

The boys had tied Hull's flag to a wagon tongue and lifted it high, the youngest reverently holding the banner until it cleared the dust.

"Cut the whiskey by half," Hull warned. "We're not far enough from Peg-Leg to risk a camp full of drunks."

"Hail, Columbia, happy land!" Burdette cried, hoisting his cup.

"The shot heard around the world," Sampson said.

"Shot," Kit said, snapping his fingers. "Get the rifles, boys. We'll fire a proper salute."

"Before you're too far gone in whiskey," Hull said. "And check there are no balls in the loads."

One by one the boys took their places in line, rifles aimed across the river. They waited for Lewis MacIntyre, who dragged an old Kentucky rifle, longer than he was tall, hopping and skipping in his rush to join the squad. The gun exploded so close to Hawken's ear he staggered. Lewis sprawled on the ground, giving Hawken one awful moment when it seemed the boy's arm had been blown away. Lewis rolled over and Hawken saw both arms in place. And no blood spurting. A bevy of women rushed forward, but a masculine yell of distress drowned out their cries. Who'd been hit?

Burdette held up the jug. Rather what remained of the jug, for the bottom was no longer attached to the top. The rifle lay at Burdette's feet, amid shards of pottery. "Damn your salute!" he screamed. He lunged at Kit with the handle end of the jug, the very last drops of whiskey flying.

"What the hell? The guns weren't loaded," Kit said.

"It kicked." Hull lifted a leg to block Burdette before he lacerated Kit's face. "Lewis didn't have a firm grip and the rifle kicked up. An accident."

"Damn salute!" Burdette slammed what remained of the jug to the ground. "No whiskey, no holiday, no Declaration. What a swine-breathed Fourth of July!"

The five men who had cups of watered whiskey shared

them around and voiced halfhearted toasts until the last drop had been drained. Burdette sat on the ground, gathering the remnants of the shattered jug, as if putting it back together would recreate the whiskey.

Someone had to resuscitate the celebration. Hawken begged pardon of the women still hovering over Lewis, elbowed his way to Granny, who held a cold compress on the boy's arm. "Granny," he said quietly. "May I borrow the washtub on the side of your wagon?"

"Making home brew?" she asked.

"No, a recitation, and the speaker needs a platform." He upended the tub in the midst of the glum crowd, and returned to the women.

"You can say the Declaration, can't you?" he whispered in Meggie's ear. She nodded. He pulled on her arm, was happy he felt only a momentary resistance. He should have warned her, given her time to change her dress. She wore calico so faded the original green showed only in spots. The bottom of the skirt hung in tatters, from snagging on the tailgate and wading through sagebrush. She put her weight on his arm to make the long step onto the tub, and at the last moment squeezed his elbow.

"Thank you," she whispered. "I couldn't volunteer myself, you understand."

"Ladies and gentlemen," Hawken announced. "The Declaration of the Thirteen United States."

Reverend Cowie lifted a commanding hand. "I believe a woman speaking in public is hardly—"

"Can she say the Declaration? The whole thing?" Burdette asked.

"The whole thing," Hawken said.

"Take a vote," Captain Hull said wearily. Only two men lined up behind Cowie, even though he quoted First

Corinthians 14. When he saw he'd lost, Cowie walked
out of camp before the words of a female orator sullied
his ears. His supporters eased to the ground about the
time Meggie got to the laws of nature and of nature's
God. Hawken watched her, pleased that Cowie's objec-
tion had not undermined her confidence. As she worked
her way through the inspiring preamble and embarked
into the complaints against King George, her words became more distinct and her tone and gestures more ora-
torical. A lump rose in his throat, from pride, and his
admiration for her. More than he respected any man. He
loved her, too, but love of a woman inevitably had something of sex about it. At the moment, admiration seemed
more appropriate.

He would talk to Meggie, not Jim Mac. He'd consult
with her on what he might do in California. An intelligent
wife would be more than a wife. A guide. And a woman
like Meggie could bear the shame when his past became
open knowledge. First chance he had to meet with her
privately, they'd settle things.

He recalled the service where he had pledged himself
to Mary Helen. The lecture on rubies and virtuous women
directed at the bride, the uncle giving the bride to her
husband, as if transferring a sack of dry peas. Nothing
like that this time. Truth to tell, if he persuaded her, he
was giving himself to Meggie, trusting that she could
make something of a man formed of dribs and drabs of
two separate lives, three if he counted his boyhood, before his parents died. Meggie would make the next life
worthwhile, and it would be his last.

She ended with a flourish of "lives and fortunes and
sacred honor." Tildy swept her fingers across her banjo
in a triumphant cord. A fiddle scraped out the first notes

of "Zack Coon," and there was a general scrambling to find partners.

"Who's playing the fiddle?" he asked, Meggie leaning on his hand to step off her dais.

"One of the Oregon men who was sick at Bridger's."

"Choose your partner, form a ring," came the call.

"My partner," he said, clutching her sleeve.

"Who else?"

He regretted the necessity of swinging the corner maid, of hands all around, any part of the dance that took him away from Meggie. The dance would go on very late. Tomorrow he would speak to her. No, the next day, while they rested at Soda Springs. They could walk out together, like a couple courting in Indiana or Ohio, to a hidden spot where no one would notice a kiss and a hug.

His feet lifted with unusual ease, as if a great weight had gone. No more worry about the future, no shame over his shaken faith or disgraceful behavior in Independence. Meggie would find words to forgive everything, and he would start his new life.

"I feel the ground all crumbly," she said when the last fiddle note faded and he led her to her wagon. "Like I'm standing on piecrust and would fall right through if you didn't hold on to me." He took her hands in his, to avoid any embrace more complicated. No almost-midnight commitment. They had to discuss this in daylight, logically. But logic fled when she leaned against him. Inviting him in? Granny hadn't said wait until he married her, only until he saw his way clear. He spread his hands on her back, leaned down and caught her mouth open, just as she started to say something. A tumble of lips and tongues, suckling in frantic hunger. Every time the tips of their tongues met she stiffened and trembled, so he made sure they met often. He wanted to dive into her, everything at once. He inched his hands lower, past the curve of her hips, and closed the distance between them. He couldn't speak.

She shook herself free and took a step back, right into the corner of the tailgate.

"Hawken, I'm scared. Ever since the buffalo hunter." A shaken whisper, unlike Meggie. "I mean, when I'm married I'll have to grit my teeth and bear it, but I'd just as soon not…." Scared? Meggie? "Every time I think of that big thing, my knees feel like pudding."

"The buffalo hunter exposed himself?" he asked, as distressed as she, trying to recall the man before his gruesome death. So far as he remembered, he'd been fully clothed.

"When we met them on the trail. I rode out ahead, and he pulled off his—whatever you wear above leggings—and said he'd give me a buffalo robe if I let him."

He reached his hand to her, exhaled a long-held breath when she accepted the clasp. The bastard had come back, held her in his power and threatened her with multiple rapes. No wonder the thought of lovemaking beyond kisses scared her.

"There's no need for you to be frightened of me," he whispered.

"But you want what the buffalo hunter wanted."

"There's a difference. I'll…we'll wait until you're ready. I love you." There. The words had come out without thinking. No retreat possible now. His honor was involved. He was on his way to California.

She came gently, slowly into his arms. "You'll talk to Pa?"

"Plenty of time," he whispered, brushing his fingers through her hair. The curls hung far down her neck. This time he'd help her cut it and make a neater job of it.

"We've got things to settle first. Tomorrow you think hard, all the consequences of being my wife. And day after tomorrow, at Soda Springs, we'll walk out together and decide what can be between us. Before I speak to your father."

"There's not plenty of time," she protested. "Only a few days to Raft River, and Reverend Cowie goes to Oregon."

"A lot can happen in one day. Will you kiss me again?"

He kept the kiss shallow and unenergetic, then boosted her onto the tailgate.

"Remember," he said, "if you're my wife, my past will haunt you, too. Your reputation's tied to mine, and you'll be shunned for things you had no part of."

"We'll laugh at them," she said. "Hold our heads high and go about our business." He nearly pulled her off the tailgate and back into his arms, for her confidence fed his hope. "They can't touch us. You love me, and I love you."

"Day after tomorrow," he whispered. "I'll go now. Sleep well." If he stayed any longer he'd crawl in after her and ruin everything. The small, frightened voice bore heavily on his mind and heart. He had to tread very carefully. But a small price to pay for love.

Meggie lifted the heavy trousers from the soapy water. The tub wobbled on the uneven ground and threatened to overturn. She dropped the trousers and found a large rock to wedge under one side, but that made it wobble in the other direction. If she had someone to help her...but her mother and grandmother had gone back to camp, to fetch more dirty clothes.

Inconvenient, to carry the tubs, buckets and laundry a

half mile, but the ease of dipping warm water straight from the ground made up for the walking. And the cedar and pine trees served as clothes poles, where she could string lines safe from running children and curious horses.

The chug-chug of steam escaping from the hot spring set the rhythm of her arms. The same beat as the dance, when Hawken's fingers pressed her ribs and waist, emphasizing the message in his eyes. She had abandoned herself to him, trusting the support of his arms when they whirled. Without words they had reached an agreement, and what they'd said at the wagon seemed as binding as a betrothal.

But he'd been so wrapped in his own words, she wasn't certain he'd listened to her. He must understand, she'd never be a passionate wife like Tildy. And she'd had no chance to make him promise that she could keep on doing the things she loved. She half hoped he had more sins to confess, giving her a lever for bargaining. She'd forgive and he'd allow.

How she had managed to get through the Declaration of Independence she did not know. That a man would actually ask her to speak—unbelievable. That a man who had once been a preacher would stand up to an older clergyman—inconceivable. She had kept her eyes safely on the distant hills as the words rolled out, meaningless words because Hawken had occupied her thoughts. He broke a Biblical commandment by asking her to speak. Which had to mean he would be lenient when his wife did unconventional things.

The ring of hammer on iron echoed from the hillside. Braces to strengthen Hawken's wagons. He meant to travel on, to California. Two months from now she wouldn't live with Ma and Pa, Pete and Granny, but with Hawken, and be Mrs. Hawken.

What was his name? He had to have a name besides Hawken.

The sudden thump of a tub heralded the return of Ma and Granny. She had not heard their footsteps, muffled by the pine needles.

"If you have laundry, Mr. Hawken," Ma said, "do bring it along."

"Les is on duty today," he said. Meggie kept her attention on the petticoats in the rinse water. No longer white, but dull gray, with permanent streaks of green and black near the bottom, stains impossible to remove.

"I'd like your permission to walk out with Meggie," he said. Asking her mother, as a suitor would do back home. "Downriver, to Sheep Rock. When the laundry's done, of course."

"We're nearly finished," Ma lied too eagerly. "Meggie, leave those petticoats for me."

"I'll take care of them," Granny said. Meggie looked from her mother to her grandmother, their mouths serious but their eyes glowing. "Walk out with Mr. Hawken. You've been working since sunrise."

"So have you," Meggie said.

"But you're young and should have some fun on a day we don't travel," Mama said.

Meggie ran her wet hands down the back of her skirt, realized it was the most decrepit she owned, the one with rents so long she had figured to throw it away rather than mend it. She did a rapid mental inventory of her clothes. All her petticoats and skirts in the washtub, except for the blue calico, preserved for the day they walked into Sutter's Fort. She had nothing to change into.

"If you're sure," she said.

"Go! Go!" Granny flicked water at her, as she would at a bothersome hen. Hawken offered his arm, she took it and followed him up the slope, toward the road.

"It's the wrong time of day to see sheep on the rock," he said. "Morning or evening would be more likely."

"You didn't ask me to walk with you to view the sheep," Meggie said bluntly.

"But I had to offer some destination to your mother, to be proper." He plucked a twig from a pine tree and stuck it between his teeth.

"True," she said. He turned down the road, and tree-covered Sheep Rock came into view, two or three miles away.

"I wish we had a boat to cross the river and climb the rock," she said. "The view from the top must be magnificent, and I'd love to walk in the shade of those tall trees."

"You're homesick for trees?"

"This trip has decided me, I won't live in a place without trees. Mr. Godfroy says giant trees grow in California."

"We'll see them."

"What do you propose to do with your goods?"

"Sell what I can at Fort Hall. The Oregon people will buy part of the flour and cornmeal. Tole and I put the best of my wagons together into one that may hang together as far as California." He grabbed her hand and guided her into a grove of trees, the scent like walking into a cedar box.

"Meggie, I know I'm no great shakes as a husband, a man without a profession whose life is a great confusion and contradiction. I can't promise I'll make a success of myself, for I have no idea *what* I'll do."

"I know what I want," she said uneasily, "and I'm

not sure I can be married and have it. I want to live in a town, for I know now, that's the best place for a woman who dreams of freedom. And I'll say and do as I please—''

''That's what I want in a wife. It's what I love about you, your daring, and wild notions.''

''Your wife was not wild and adventurous—''

''I'm not the same man I was back in Ohio. I've done more, seen more. When my parents died, our minister and his wife—Fred and Mary Helen's aunt and uncle— took me in. There was money enough for me to join Fred at college.''

''You went to college?'' Meggie asked. She had never met a college man before! Not even the schoolmaster in Pikeston had gone to college. Hawken could teach her ever so much!

''Oberlin College. Fred had known since he was a boy that he'd enter the ministry. Reverend Frazer and his wife encouraged me to do the same, and since Fred had been my friend through school, and we'd become almost brothers, I tagged in his footsteps. Oregon was my idea. I should have confessed to everyone, myself included, that I wanted to go for the adventure, not the missionary part.''

''You had no affection for your wife?''

''I felt for her as a brother does a sister. I didn't understand that a man's affection for his wife would be different. Wider. Higher. Love and pride, the promise of companionship, what I feel for you.''

''Mr. Hawken.'' Her voice stuck at something less than a whisper. ''I'm not sure I'll make a suitable wife.''

''Because you're headstrong? That's what makes you perfect for me. I turn myself over to you. You'll help me decide what I should do. I need a strong wife, one who'll tell me the truth, not say, 'Whatever you think best, dear.' You won't abandon me in a limbo of lonely decisions. I've made a mess of my life so far, and need an advisor. I can't wait for you until California and you can't wait for me. You're a passionate woman.''

''I'm sorry,'' she whispered, trying to keep her voice steady while edging into a difficult subject.

''Sorry about what?''

Meggie stared at the ground. She had never spoken of sex, except in quiet times with Granny, and then Granny did most of the talking.

''Tildy and Matt,'' she began, ''when we overheard…Tildy enjoys what he does to her. I'll be a dreadful disappointment to you in bed.''

''No excitement from kissing—?''

''I liked the kissing part. And when you touched me. Here.'' She pulled his hand from her cheek to her breasts.

To her surprise his hands slid lower and lower, and he went with them until he knelt in the pine duff. He embraced her knees, bent them and drew her down onto his legs. ''Meggie, Meggie.'' His whisper disappeared in the softness of a kiss. His fingers thrust deep into her tangled hair. ''The buffalo hunter, again?'' he asked. She nodded, he drew her down, until he lay flat on his back and she sprawled on top of him. He shifted her head to bring their mouths together. A relaxed mode of kissing, she discovered. He spread his lips and she followed his example. The odor of cedar blended with his fragrance, a man's smell of sweat and animals and the blacksmith's fire. His mouth and breath tasted of the pine twig, with a hint of smoke.

His tongue filled her mouth, gently flexed to touch her teeth and explore the ribbing of her palate. He withdrew in easy stages, an invitation for her to follow and inves-

tigate him in the same fashion. She ran her tongue along
the joining of teeth and gum, not smooth but a series of
bumps, like the edge of a scalloped hem.

Laughter, very close, and she lifted her head in alarm.

"On the road," he whispered. "The boys have fancies
of killing a sheep. They'll not bother us here." He shifted
her to lie more evenly on him. "We'll do nothing that
frightens either of us."

She tucked her head between his neck and shoulder,
kissed the muscle that curved to his upper arm. His fingers investigated the lower edge of her bodice, trying to
gain admittance, but the waist was too tight. Now at the
neck, loosening the buttons, one by one, very slowly. Too
deliberately, for her breasts prickled in anticipation of
him, and the rough muslin of her shift rasped on very
tender nipples. She sat up and fell off his legs.

"I'll do it," she said, opening the buttons with sure
fingers. His hands worked at her shift, pulling it from the
tight band of her skirt. The cool air and cedar smell fell
upon her skin as his fingers traced the fullness of her
breasts with a feather touch. Then a hand on her back
drawing her down once more. He touched his tongue to
her nipple.

"I'm sorry," she whispered. "I'm not very big up
top."

"You're beautiful," he murmured. "Did you know
Amazons cut off their left breasts, so they weren't in the
way of shooting a bow? You're perfectly fashioned for
archery."

She giggled, until his tongue moved on the tender
point, striking sparks as flint brings fire from steel. His
lips closed, and at the first gentle pulling, flame danced
through her loins as if she galloped John Charles very
hard. But the clutch of nerves expanded, into a sensation

many times more intense than anything she had felt before. Circling and circling, until her flesh drew inward, seeking something that was not there, and she cried out in protest at the emptiness. She clutched at him, and touched the strained front of his trousers.

"Hawken, please! You said you'd listen when I had something to say."

He stroked her back, in the same rhythm as the reverberations within, ringing like a heaven full of bells. "What, my dearest?" His hand eased through the long tear in her skirt, between her thighs, then low on her stomach. His fingers touched her core, throwing her back into chaos, wilder than before, into an ache of loneliness.

"My dearest," he whispered. She sprawled on him, legs wide. His shaft pressed hard between her legs, her drawers the last fragile barrier to his penetration.

"Do you want...I'll take off my drawers if you can't wait."

"Later, when you're certain you want me to. Do I have your permission to speak to your father?"

"The whole family. Ma will go along with Pa, whatever he decides, but Pete and Granny should have their say. That's how we decided on California. Everyone had to agree."

"Tonight?" he asked eagerly. "There's still time."

"Tildy packed her wedding dress. Yellow silk. It's too big for me, but we can take tucks, like we did for Rachel when she married Will, so I suppose—"

"A wedding, and Pete will lead the shivaree. He'll probably separate us until sunrise, and we'll not have a private moment until he drops from exhaustion. But being married at Soda Springs does offer champagne of a sort for the celebration."

She rolled off him. "When I was a little girl I wanted

to get married as soon as I could, for a bride was always the center of attention on her wedding day, and I'm...well, rather fond of showing off. Rachel has a piece of gold cloth. Maybe she'll lend it to me to wear on my head.''

"To match your freckles," he said.

"Do you mind them?"

"The first time I saw you, I thought they looked like flecks of gold, half-hidden beneath a film of water."

"That's all the gold you'll get from me," she said. "But we'll save every bit of money you make at Fort Hall, and I have more than forty dollars, from selling my chickens when we left Indiana."

"Enough to get started in something," he said. "You're leaning on a fragile branch when you marry me. Do you want to reconsider?"

"Maybe Granny could help us. Some people say she has money."

"Granny?"

"Grandpa left the land to his sons, Pa and Uncle Ira. But his cash went to Granny. No one knows where it is. But I suspect she helped Matt Hull, to outfit for California."

"I'll be particularly nice to your grandmother," he said, nodding very solemnly as he took her arm.

"Not too nice," Meggie said. "She guesses when people spread the butter on too thick. Flattery, I mean."

"Yes, ma'am," he said, even more sober. A good beginning, Meggie thought. He took her advice.

"And you must have a name," she said. "I can't call you Hawken when we're in bed saying silly things."

Chapter Nineteen

Hawken did not bother to drop down the hill to the road, but took off for camp cross-country, through the trees. The odor of cedar enveloped them.

"Sometime, when we're settled, I'll buy a cedar chest," Meggie said. "Every time I open it, I'll remember today."

Hawken's arm tightened on her waist. "We'll plant a cedar tree outside our bedroom window. I wish we could dig up a small one here and carry it along with us, but it's just too far, and the weight—"

"A cone," she suggested. "We could plant the seeds."

She left his arms to search for a suitable cone, one still closed, and unchewed by squirrels.

"Whose mules?" he said.

She found him staring intently toward the narrow band of grass along the river. She stepped beside him. Several mules intermingled with the oxen and horses.

"Must be a packer who's caught up with us and is sharing the camp," Hawken answered himself. "We'll have a bigger crowd at our wedding than we expected."

"The bigger the better," she said. A man's voice,

somewhere nearby. Then a splash of water. "There's a bubbling spring at the base of the hill," she whispered. "Sampson says it's the best of all."

"One last embrace. Your mother and grandmother will separate us until the ceremony."

He kissed her long and deep, lifting her on tiptoe. A volatile mixture of lust and affection passed from loin to loin. He boosted her and she wrapped her legs about him, and found herself loathing the fabric that prevented the culmination of their love.

"Tonight, tonight, tonight," he whispered. "The delay will only make it better."

He helped her straighten her skirt and checked that all the buttons of her bodice were fastened before they walked around the hill. Mr. Reid and Granny bent over the spring, dipping a bucket into the water.

"Hello," Granny called. "We're making the wedding champagne."

Meggie came close to shouting at her grandmother, but only glared. Couldn't she have the pleasure of announcing her own wedding? "Just because Mr. Hawken and I went walking together is no reason to suppose that—"

"Not you. Mrs. Cooper. Twelve men rode in, traveling with horses and mules. One of the gentleman, a widower, hails from Mrs. Cooper's hometown. He has a twelve-year-old son who's weary of riding every day. So he'll marry Mrs. Cooper and join the Oregon party."

"Tonight?" Hawken asked.

"Right now. You'd better go help Tildy, Meggie. She's letting out the tucks we put in the dress for Rachel. Mrs. Cooper's larger."

"Come away," Meggie whispered to Hawken. "I will not share my wedding day," she said after they'd walked several yards from the spring. "I want my turn at the yellow dress. You can talk to Pa, but say we'll get married at Fort Hall.''

"The yellow dress,'' he said, his face asking if the dress was more important than he.

"I've got a blue calico, but it's the kind of dress you wear and wear until it's a rag. Tildy will keep the yellow silk for all her life, and I'll be able to visit her and see it and remember the promises I made when I wore it.''

"Just as well,'' he said with a heartiness she thought was put on, but she loved him for it. "It's best to wait until Fort Hall, because Les will raise a ruckus the moment he finds out we're getting married.''

"Why ever should he do that?''

"He thinks you're a witch. But he and Monty will leave me when we find Canadian trappers who can take them out of the country. Not tonight! Two long days of waiting.'' He leaned down so his lips came within an inch of hers. "No day of rest at Fort Hall, not until we're well on the California road. I don't want to wait.'' He moaned.

"Neither do I. But there's no help for it now if I expect a real wedding all my own.''

Hawken squeezed her hand and his eyes turned pleading. "When Reverend Cowie reads the service, look at me and say the words to yourself. I'll do the same. Between ourselves we'll be married.'' What a wonderful idea! Meggie squeezed his hand. Maybe tonight she'd tell him they didn't have to wait, because Tildy and Matt hadn't waited.

"I'd better go help with that wedding dress.''

Mrs. Cooper crouched in Granny's wagon, wrapped in a blanket, while Tildy and Rachel worked on opposite sides of the dress, pulling out the stitches, one at a time, so they did not damage the fabric.

"Meggie, you take out the hem," Tildy said. "The skirt's too short."

The tucks would have to be replaced in just a day or two, deeper tucks than they had made for Rachel. But the skirt length would be right. She felt like rising dough contained in a pan with a tight lid. She opened her mouth to blurt out that she and Hawken were in love and he wanted to marry her. But at that moment she saw Mrs. Cooper's face. Smiling. Meggie thought back and could not remember ever having seen her smile before. Mrs. Cooper needed her own special wedding day, too. Meggie shut her mouth.

The fizzy lemonade tickled Meggie's nose. It made up a little for the plain wedding cake. She might have no wedding cake at all, unless they stayed a day at Fort Hall. She searched for Hawken. He had stood with the men during the wedding ceremony, but had kept his eyes on her rather than the bridal couple, as he had promised, and once or twice she'd seen his lips move.

Meggie hadn't liked the part where Mrs. Cooper said obey, so she'd skipped that, just promised to love and cherish.

But where was Hawken? He didn't stand in line for lemonade and cake, and she didn't see him with Monty and Les. The fiddle and banjo twanged discordantly before they gradually slid into agreeable tune. Why didn't he come to partner her in the dance? They could at least hold hands, and his fingers would tighten on her back in the promenade, reminding her of what was in store a night or two from now.

A shadow linked with hers. "Come with me," he whispered.

They passed the outskirts of camp before it occurred

to her that she had obeyed his request without question. Well, she trusted him not to do anything despicable. Trust must be part of love, so orders issued by a husband—or a wife—were more complex than she had supposed. Away from camp, across the road, to a clump of three trees just above the river.

"Step inside," he said. She lifted her skirt clear of the deadwood on the ground, ducked her head beneath the overhanging branches. Her feet touched softness; a buffalo robe and blankets. "Our bower," he whispered, his fingers already at her bodice buttons.

We'll be missed at the dance, she thought, but could not tell him, for he showered her face with kisses, searched and found her lips. He pushed her down, not to hard ground, but a springy layer of boughs spread under the robe.

"I can't wait until Fort Hall," he said firmly.

Meggie unbuttoned his trouser flap by touch, while he shoved the bodice off her shoulders. Now he worked at the tapes binding skirt and petticoat about her waist.

"It would go faster if we undressed ourselves," she said. "I know which ties go to which."

"But undressing you is part of...the seduction," he said. "Part of rousing you so you're ready for me."

"You're ready?" she asked.

"Hard as a wild stallion," and he followed the words with a snarl, his breath hissed inward, his lips drew back. She had never seen a wild stallion with his harem, but she supposed it was not much different from a stallion turned out with a mare in heat, ready to mount the instant the gate swung shut. She fumbled at the tapes of her petticoat, pulled too hard at the button loop of her drawers and it came away in her hand. More mending to do.

He pushed the garments down, one by one, as she loosened them, lifted the blanket, and she slid under.

He dragged his shirt over his head, kicked off his boots, stood bent over, balancing on one foot to pull his trousers clear. He was huge. She looked away. He slid in beside her. She closed her eyes and tried to relax against the moment of his assault. He thrust his arm beneath her head—a hard pillow—and lay still. She could hear the river whisper against the bank as it made its sweeping turn south.

"Will you kiss me?" he asked. She opened her eyes. "It's all up to you. I'm naked, with a spitfire who wouldn't say obey, and I'll not risk getting slapped, kicked and beaten."

"How did you know I didn't say obey?"

"You glared at Mrs. Cooper." Good grief! Could he read her mind?

"I'll say something better than obey. I trust you."

He raised on his elbow and looked down at her. "You have done me a great honor. May I kiss the bride?"

"Yes."

His kisses came slow and easy, as if they had all night. But they did have all night, unless someone missed them at the dance and organized a search. She caressed his cheek. Smooth. He'd taken time to shave. He had a patch of curly hair on his chest, and when she turned on her side and lay very close, the hair rubbed on her breasts.

He kissed her ear, his tongue following the arch, then made an intimate investigation that took her breath away. Down her throat, hesitating temptingly close to her breasts, back to her lips. She thrust out her tongue and enjoyed the pleasurable shivers that came with the tangled kiss.

He spread his hand high on her back, so she did the

same, exploring the pattern of muscles enveloping his shoulder blades and spine. Down, down alternating ridges and valleys, the beginnings of a deeper valley. She ran her hand back to his shoulders too quickly.

His hand had followed her lead, down her spine, but instead of retreating, his fingers slid into her cleft, found the very end of her spine and pressed in accent to the beat of her heart. Or his heart, for they lay so entwined she was not certain which pulse belonged to which body.

An easing back from the brink, his hands framing her face and his lips busy with gentle kisses. His chest rose and fell as if he had been running, and the wiry curls caught on her nipples. And lower down, on her stomach, a wetness and the prod of his shaft.

He dropped his head and drew a nipple into his mouth with sudden force. She gasped at the suckling, at the trace of fire burning a path from his mouth to a spot between her legs. An eruption built within her, a feeling that required space. She must spread her legs, and that exposed her... She lifted one over his hip. He slid down, and his imperious need lay upon her thigh. The conqueror at the gates.

"Tell me if it's not all right," he whispered. She brushed his hair back from his forehead and kissed him. He was so kind, had given her so much, she must grit her teeth and offer him relief. She said nothing when his hand crept lower and lower, when his fingers manipulated the fire, spreading it in tentacles, inside and out, until at her center came empty loneliness crying for fulfillment.

Empty! She grasped him firmly.

"In," she gasped. His fingers searched and the wet tip filled part of the vacancy. His fingers again on the center of the fire, mastering a chaos that fell together to create a world. He weighed upon her, his wild force enlarging his dominion, roaring a celebration of his conquest. His miraculous shaft penetrated every niche, sent waves rolling with its force, until they rose like cliffs in a triumph of seizure and envelopment.

"Hawken!" she screamed. He visited both joy and destruction upon her. No room for fear as his power flowed through her. Then an easing, only sporadic convulsions, and he collapsed upon her, his passion spent. She was unsure what he expected next, so she lay very still. He moaned, his mouth roamed her face in half-connected kisses.

She was wet. She must be bleeding, her virginity torn by his stabbing power. Her hips still moved, involuntary jerks against him, and she fought the spasms that pumped her life away. He straightened his arms, rose off her, lifting the blanket and letting in the chill of evening shadows.

"I'll crush you," he said.

A last ray of the sun glittered on the highest branch over their heads. "If I'd known, I'd have brought my quilt," she said.

"Quilt? A wedding quilt?"

"Not really. I never got around to making a wedding quilt. Just one, with patches shaped like double-ax heads. Granny doesn't believe in using new goods for patchwork, so it's only scraps."

"Scraps are perfect. It's what you're working with when you get me." He rolled off her, his flaccid sex coming away. It was not bloody. He adjusted her body against his, her head tucked against his shoulder, the embrace that had started his lovemaking. "You climaxed, too," he said, surprising her with a sudden shyness.

"I don't know. You filled every bit of me, and I lost track of...where I was."

He gave her a brief squeeze.

"You caress me," he whispered, "surround me, tighter and tighter, draw me deeper and deeper—" He gripped her until she couldn't breathe, and wriggled his hips, warm and wet. "I love you," he whispered. "You are my wife."

"I've had no experience with love," she said, "but I can't imagine feeling this way about anyone else. I must love you."

"Some things you can't prove. You have to take them on faith. Love's one." He kissed her, shoved a hand between their chests to touch her breasts.

Meggie lazily examined his lips with her tongue. His tongue darted out, made brief contact, and the molding of loin on loin changed with the alteration of his shape. In the middle of the night he would make love to her for a long time, and they would come together in the dark, with the stars shining through the trees. The trees she loved—

Hawken started and lifted his head.

"What?" she whispered. He put his hand over her mouth. A twig snapped, not far from their heads.

"Meggie, I know you're around here someplace 'cause I saw you in the trees along the river. Get back to camp. Hawken and I have something to talk about."

Pete! She lay absolutely still, holding her breath.

"What do we have to talk about?" Hawken asked mildly. "We're over here, where the three trees make a little house." Pete's boots crunched faintly on needles and twigs.

"I'd invite you in, but there's only room enough for two," Hawken said. Meggie could not see Pete, but from the sound he had stopped only a few inches from her head.

"You bastard," Pete snarled. "You've seduced my sister. Don't deny it. I can smell it."

"He did not seduce me!" Meggie said. "I came with Hawken of my own free will. Besides, we're married."

"Since when?"

"Well, we would be, except when we got to camp Mrs. Cooper was using the wedding dress," Meggie said. "This morning we walked and promised each other."

"We repeated the vows during the ceremony," Hawken said. "We'll do it again in a day or two."

"You haven't asked Pa for permission. He and Ma wondered where Meggie'd gone to. Granny guessed and calmed them down by telling a long story of how Grandpa got under her petticoat before the wedding."

A rustling suggested that Pete was sitting down and making himself comfortable.

"I'll talk to your father tomorrow, and Meggie and I'll be married publicly the night we get to Fort Hall. I hope to sell what's left of my goods there."

"Why sell your things at Fort Hall? You'll get a higher price in California. I figure you're coming on to California," Pete said.

"I've got one wagon that may make it, and Meggie and I've got to have someplace for our gear."

"Pa says with almost half the provisions gone we're hauling three wagons for nothing. He's thinking of leaving one behind, and I don't like that idea, for I spent a lot of time and effort making perfect wagons. Pack what's most valuable of yours in it, sell your dumpy wagons along with the loads at Fort Hall." He shifted and a twig broke. "But, by damn, I won't give you the wagon unless you and Meggie get married."

"We're married," Meggie said. "Married as tightly as we'll ever be. And you could have said all this tomorrow morning, Pete MacIntyre, instead of bothering us."

"I suppose, but damn it, Meggie, a brother's got to protect his sister, and make sure she doesn't marry a no-good tramp. You giving up gambling, Hawken?"

"Haven't been in a game since March in Independence."

"Got your monte deck along?"

"Yes."

"Burn it. Or better, give it to me and I'll burn it."

"No," Meggie said. She wished Pete would go away, because Hawken's fingers brushed her nipples, his erection poked into her stomach, and she desperately wanted to say silly things and decide on a name for her to whisper.

"I'll keep the monte deck," she said. "Hawken will teach me how to play, and maybe, if there're soldiers where we settle, I'll open a gambling hall and deal monte."

Pete let out a yell, so loud Meggie feared it would draw everyone in camp. "Damn it, Hawken! She needs a man who can control...if you can't put a lid on her wild—"

"Pete, go away," Hawken said. "I swear on a stack of Bibles that I'll talk to your parents in the morning. Have Granny retell the story of how she and Grandpa made it in the haymow—"

"They did it down by the river," Pete grumbled.

"Hawken and I are following an old family tradition," Meggie said, laughing, and the laughter seemed to echo far away, with the fiddle and banjo.

"I think the bridal couple have tried to sneak away," Hawken said. "You're missing the shivaree."

"Damn the shivaree," Pete said. "Meggie, you'd better come with me. It doesn't look good for a woman—"

"Pete, how do you know what sex smells like?" she asked sweetly. A long silence, then Meggie heard the whisper of the duff under boots, and the footsteps grew fainter. She cuddled close to Hawken.

The river made the same sound as the blood pulsing through his arm. He must have heard it, too, for he said, "I'd like to live near a river. With trees."

She hummed her agreement. "With a window over our bed, so we can hear the water and smell the cedar." She had to get busy sewing, so they had embroidered pillow slips and hemmed sheets for a thousand happy nights. And the Wild Geese Flying, so they had more than one quilt. "You need a name I can say when we make love."

Silence, then a kiss that did not quite reach its mark. "I gave you yesterday to think this over, remember?"

"Yes, but what does that have to do—"

"I thought things over. Eventually the truth will rear up and smack me in the face. Why not anticipate it? Hawken's good enough for a trail name, but when we get settled, I'll go back to being Thaddeus Milner. And I'll write Reverend and Mrs. Frazer, let them know I survived and why I didn't send them word of the accident. Would you mind awfully?"

"Mrs. Thaddeus Milner." She tried the name on her tongue.

"Margaret MacIntyre Milner." The triple alliteration turned her rather prosaic name into something rather distinguished. "I love it. And Th...a...ad—" she let out the word on a long breath that made it three syllables "—works well in bed."

"I love you." He was laughing when he pulled her on top of him, and that made for an uneven perch. "Do you want to sleep for a while?"

"No. Tell me, how do you deal monte?"

* * * * *

Author Note

The overland trail scenes in this book, while fiction, are based upon actual events culled from numerous travel diaries. Ezra Meeker describes a catastrophic wreck of the St. Joseph ferry, upon which I based the accident that killed Hawken's wife. James Clyman tells us of a woman cooking beneath an umbrella, Margaret A. Frick wrote dramatically of camping at Willow Springs in a snow-storm, Mrs. Benjamin Ferris left a record of the mirages of the Platte sand hills, where "a half dozen crows will look like men." These and dozens of other journals, besides being entertaining reading, give us a taste of the excitement and hardships of the journey.

In the autumn of 1996 I drove the route of the California Trail from Sacramento to St. Joseph, Missouri, as closely as a low-slung car would allow. From this journey I gained greater respect for those who made the trip on horseback or by covered wagon. Many of my descriptions of landmarks on the trail derive from this personal experience.

For anyone who plans to visit the locale of *Hawken's Wife*, I recommend they consult as a guide *The Oregon Trail Revisited*, by Gregory M. Franzwa. And for the simple pleasure of reading along the way, Irene D. Paden's *The Wake of the Prairie Schooner,* an account of the Paden family's exploration of the trail in the 1930s and 1940s.

If you have comments or question, write me at P.O. Box 402, Bishop, CA 93514. I enjoy hearing from my readers.

Love,
Americana Style

JOE'S WIFE
by Cheryl St.John

Available in February 1999
(29051-9)

THE TENDER STRANGER
by Carolyn Davidson

Available in March 1999
(29056-X)

Available wherever
Harlequin books are sold.

HARLEQUIN®
Makes any time special ™

Tough, rugged and irresistible...

THE AUSTRALIANS

Stories of romance Australian-style, guaranteed to
fulfill that sense of adventure!

This March 1999 look for

Boots in the Bedroom!
by **Alison Kelly**

Parish Dunford lived in his cowboy boots—no one was going
to change his independent, masculine ways. Gina, Parish's
newest employee, had no intention of trying to do so—she pre-
ferred a soft bed to a sleeping bag on the prairie. Yet somehow she couldn't stop thinking of how those boots would look
in her bedroom—with Parish still in them....

*The Wonder from Down Under: where spirited women win
the hearts of Australia's most independent men!*

Available March 1999
at your favorite retail outlet.

HARLEQUIN®
Makes any time special ™

Look us up on-line at: http://www.romance.net   PHAUS9

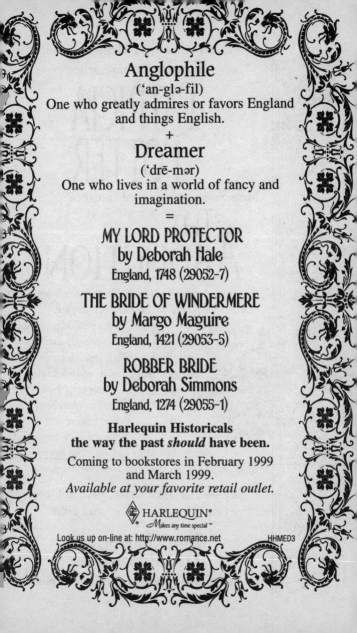

Don't miss your chance to read
award-winning author

PATRICIA POTTER

First Scottish historical romance

THE ABDUCTION

An eye for an eye. Clan leader Elsbeth Ker longed
for peace, but her stubborn English
neighbors would have none
of it—especially since the
mysterious Alexander had
returned to lead the
Carey clan. Now the
crofters had been
burned out, and the
outraged Kers demanded
revenge. But when Elsbeth faced her enemy,
what she saw in his steel gray eyes gave her pause....

Look for *THE ABDUCTION* this March 1999,
available at your favorite retail outlet!

HARLEQUIN®
Makes any time special ™

COMING NEXT MONTH FROM

HARLEQUIN HISTORICALS